WE SHIP IT

WE SHIP IT

LAUREN KAY

HARPER TEEN
An Imprint of HarperCollins Publishers

HarperTeen is an imprint of HarperCollins Publishers.

We Ship It
Copyright © 2023 by Lauren Kay
Illustrations by Catherine Lee
All rights reserved. Printed in the United States of America.
No part of this book may be used or reproduced in any manner whatsoever
without written permission except in the case of brief quotations embodied
in critical articles and reviews. For information address HarperCollins
Children's Books, a division of HarperCollins Publishers, 195 Broadway,
New York, NY 10007.
www.epicreads.com

Library of Congress Control Number: 2023930378
ISBN 978-0-06-323099-6
Typography by Catherine Lee

23 24 25 26 27 LBC 5 4 3 2 1
First Edition

For Mom, Dad & Jon

WE
SHIP
IT

ONE

TWO DAYS BC (BEFORE CRUISE)

I turned my computer screen so my parents could easily see the title slide of my just-completed PowerPoint presentation: a cruise ship behind a very large red X.

I had hastily thrown the whole lecture together in the three hours since my parents had oh so casually dropped the world's worst news on me.

They had booked a spring break cruise for our family.

It left in two days.

I cleared my throat. "A list of reasons why Olivia Schwartz should not be forced without her consent onto a weeklong spring break cruise."

My parents looked up at me with mildly bemused expressions as I clicked on the next slide, featuring a Brown University pennant and a photo of my tattered College Board prep book, which I had already completed three times.

"I could be studying to retake the SATs."

"Objection," my dad interrupted, raising a finger in the air. "You scored in the ninety-ninth percentile."

"Objection overruled," I said, rolling my eyes at his inability to ever turn off lawyer speak. "You know what's better than a score in the ninety-ninth percentile? A score in the *one hundredth* percentile."

"I don't think that's even possible, sweetie," my mom said.

"Regardless." I hit the remote, and the screen flashed to a photo of two sad-looking marooned baby sea lions.

"Do you recognize the massive damage the cruise industry is causing to our environment and marine life? And how by going on this cruise, we are offering our complicit support for that destruction with our wallets?"

"I don't think winning Temple Beth Shalom's Hanukkah raffle is going to mutilate any baby sea animals," my dad said with a wry smile.

Stupid Temple Beth Shalom and their stupid raffle.

"Okay, well, have you considered—" I clicked on the next slide: a photo of three teens lying on a beach, smoking what I believed to be a joint.

"Drugs? So many drugs. And alcohol. Are there even laws about this at sea?"

I saw my dad bite back a smile as my mom crossed her arms. "Yes, yes there are."

I should have seen that one coming. Questioning my two lawyer parents about, you know, the *law* was an amateur move on my part.

I clicked again, powering faster through the rest of the slides. "Boats. Water. What if I get thrown overboard? Death would be all but certain. And speaking of—the *Titanic*. History is known to repeat itself. Finally, fires. What do you even do if a boat catches fire—leap into the ocean? I don't think so. See point one—"

I could tell I was losing my parents' attention, so I jumped to the final slide, a blown-up version of my yearbook photo. It was the one day of the year I had wasted a precious fifteen minutes of sleep in order to get up and blow-dry my hair and dab on undereye concealer. I generally didn't care about that kind of stuff, but I knew how far high school photos could go. I didn't want my legacy to include seventeen-year-old me with bedhead and giant raccoon circles under my eyes. A photo like that could come back to haunt you in the future that you are so carefully crafting for yourself.

"In conclusion, I am a perfectly behaved, responsible child. Why would you want to risk—excuse the bad pun—rocking that boat?"

My dad stepped around the table and laid a hand on my shoulder. "You are a wonderful child, who is clearly in desperate need of a vacation," he said, giving my shoulder a squeeze.

"Says who?" I asked, crossing my arms in front of my chest.

"Says the ten-page PowerPoint presentation you just put together *for fun*. I think it's time you put aside technology for a few days and just . . . relax."

Ugh, *relax*—my least favorite word in the English language. With *travel* trailing right behind. I didn't get why people got so excited about relaxing and traveling. What about their own lives was so bad that they needed to escape? I was perfectly content with my meticulously organized, fully booked, and color-coded daily schedule, thank you very much.

A schedule that included the science research fair my best friend, Shruti, and I were entering in ten days. The one I'd scheduled into my calendar two *years* earlier.

"I just don't get why we have to go *now*. You know I have the research fair next week. The one that *Dr. Klober* is judging." Every year, Dr. Klober offered the winning team an extremely prestigious internship. I needed that internship. Without it, I didn't stand a chance at my dream program—Brown's eight-year combined undergraduate and med school program, which boasted a less than 5 percent acceptance rate. I felt butterflies whenever I pictured myself on the beautiful Providence campus, my boots leaving footprints in a fresh coat of snow as I sprinted from a lecture to a lab. All taught by top medical professors and researchers, of course.

"Sorry, hon, but we just realized the tickets we won expire this month. The cruise is all booked, and I think our family is overdue for a vacation."

I snorted. That couldn't be more of an understatement. My parents were infallible when it came to scheduling appointments and behavioral aides and preschool performances for my five-year-old twin brothers, Matt and Justin. But when it came to vacation? *Leisure* time? They were 100 percent genetically related to me. Which is why trips always got pushed to the last minute—and then never booked.

Except for this one. They had managed to book the last possible cruise date the voucher allowed—which left in forty-eight hours.

"But then I won't get to meet Dr. Klober, and I won't get that internship, which means I won't get into Brown and—"

"Whoa, whoa, slow down there, Ms. Worst-Case Scenario," my dad said, cutting me off. "What if you work on the research on the cruise and have Shruti present for your team?"

"But I still won't get to *meet* Dr. Klober, which is the entire reason I want to go." I had emailed her a few times, letting her know how interested I was in the internship and expressing how much I was looking forward to meeting her at the fair. It would look horrible and unprofessional of me to just not show up. Very much *not* ideal-future-intern behavior.

"What if I stay home and watch Mr. Snuggles Factory? You know how much separation anxiety he suffers from, which causes his eye infection to flare up and—"

"Olivia, you know Doug and Karen have watched Mr. Snuggles Factory many times before. He will be just fine for a week. He is a cat." My mom got up and picked up a folder from the counter. She opened it up and then pulled out a pamphlet, which she slid across the table to me. "Take a look at all the fun events the Regal Islands offers, on and off the ship."

I glanced down at the glossy paper, which was filled with clearly staged photos, an array of smiling, fake families. My mom was still staring at me, so to humor her, I flipped to the next page, which listed all the ports the cruise would be docking at, over the course of nine days. The first, second, fourth, and last days were spent at sea. The other days were spent at different islands—St. Kitts, Martinique, St. Lucia, Barbados . . .

But when I got to the final port, every blood vessel in my heart coiled up.

Antigua.

When I was younger, my parents didn't get home from work until nine or ten at night. My brother Logan—who was six years older than me—was left in charge, which meant that the majority of our meals came out of bright red cardboard packages.

But these meals were anything but boring. We would dress up in the fancy clothes reserved for our cousins' bar mitzvahs, and Logan would act as my waiter. Some days we did "dinner and a show," which involved a very quick meal followed by our two-person musicals—usually *Rent*, but occasionally *Annie* or *Les Mis*.

When I came home from third grade after a bad day—I was bullied a lot that year, for always shouting out the answers and for being a good six inches shorter than the rest of the class—Logan immediately knew something was wrong. At dinner, he arrived downstairs with an eye patch, a cardboard sword, and a bandanna wrapped around his fiery-red hair.

"Aye, matey," he greeted me, tapping me lightly with the end of his sword. "On tar-night's menu, we have mozz-ARRR-ella flatbread"—Celeste pizza—"and h-ARRRs d'oeuvres"—frozen hot dogs.

"Cap'n Plank" served our dinner on our parents' forbidden china plates. (I always made sure to wash them extra carefully when we were done; Logan never failed to break something when he was on dish duty.)

After I had cleared the plates, Logan smiled at me, his eyes gleaming. "When you take over the world as CEO of"—he swung his makeshift sword around, until it was pointing directly at our discarded pizza boxes—"Celeste pizza, you will . . ."

"Live in a castle with one wing just for cats and . . ."

"One wing for me. And at night . . ."

"We'll star in *Rent* at the theater we own. And during the days we'll . . ."

"Float in the sea. And explarrre shipwrecks!"

"You can do that," I said, wrinkling my nose, already feeling claustrophobic. "I'll watch you from the shore."

"We shall do it—strapped togetharrr!"

Knowing Logan, he would find some way to convince me. He was the courageous one, the spontaneous one, the one willing to try anything once. I was the cautious one, but when I was with him, I took risks.

"Where is our castle, though?" I asked. We had told so many different versions of this story, but by the time I was eight, I was a Planner. I didn't care how fantastical the plan was; it just needed to be concrete.

So Logan led me into our parents' office. He sat down in my dad's giant leather desk chair, closed his eyes, and spun the globe on the desk. Then he placed his finger on the revolving sphere, opened his eyes, and pronounced:

"Antarctica? Hell no!"

I laughed and Logan spun again, this time landing on Russia.

Finally, Logan gave up on letting fate decide and instead examined the globe until he found a group of islands. Then he put his finger on one of the tiny specks.

"We'll live in Antigua."

"Antigua," I repeated with a smile. I loved how easily the name rolled off my tongue, the comforting, neat way it started and ended with the same letter.

"It's a plan," I said, extending my hand to Logan.

Over the years, we'd added on more and more to the story, putting up photos of Antigua's white-sand beaches on our walls and begging our parents every Hanukkah for tickets.

But we never got to go to Antigua.

Logan died two days before my eleventh birthday.

I looked back up at my parents. At the tufts of soft gray hair on my dad's head that seemed to be inching farther and farther back each year. The permanent crease between my mom's eyebrows—one I already had a faint but noticeable matching imprint of. They looked tired—not just normal tired, but life tired.

"Fine. I'll go."

My parents exchanged a look. "That was a quick change of heart," my dad said.

I shrugged. "I assume I don't have any say in the matter, anyway." I hesitated, briefly considering whether I should bring up the real reason I had agreed to go so quickly. But I decided against it, wanting to avoid the awkward tension that filled the air whenever I brought up Logan, how my mom always found a way to change the subject.

My mom gave me a small smile. "I hope you'll be pleasantly surprised by the trip. They have so many great activities for teens."

I raised an eyebrow. "I highly doubt I will enjoy any activity that includes the descriptor 'for teens.'" I pictured rotating disco balls and awful, outdated "slow dancing" music, like the forced fun my high school attempted.

"There's even a track on the ship, so you can get your runs in," my mom said, still working hard to sell me on this monstrosity at sea.

"There's a track . . . *on* the ship?" I repeated. I knew my mom was just trying to be nice, but these new details were making me dread the upcoming ten days even more.

"Yes, and I believe it's the standard regulation, four hundred meters."

"That's . . . insane." Just how big *was* this thing? Bigger didn't mean better in my book. The one time I had volunteered to accompany my dad on a trip to IKEA, I had taken all of five steps into the endless maze of shelves before my breathing had gotten shallow and I'd had to leave.

"And I've heard wonderful things about their cruises from the members of our support group. Matt and Justin will even have their own aide."

"That's good." I might be in my own personal hell for the next week and a half, but at least my parents would have a little time to themselves for once. We hadn't been on a vacation in years—years before Matt and Justin were born, and they were already five. After they were born, my parents had given up their partner-track law firm jobs in New York and established a family practice out of our home so they could give the twins, who were both on the autism spectrum, 24/7 care.

"And oh," my mom said, clapping her hands together. "I almost forgot the best part. Cindy Lee and I were catching up on Facebook, and it turns out their family booked the same trip!"

"Jules is going to be there?" I hadn't seen Jules in years. We'd attended all the same summer camps as kids. The last time I had seen Jules was at Logan's funeral. She had texted me a few times after but had eventually stopped reaching out.

"Yes, isn't that nice? You'll have a friend to hang out with."

"I guess." Parents had a funny way of defining friends. As if someone you were friends with at four was automatically a friend for life.

Jules had always been fun to hang out with, but I doubted we had much in common anymore. And this wasn't exactly ideal timing for a friendship reunion. I might be physically going on the cruise, but I would be spending all my time camped out in my room, writing my research paper.

I closed my computer and tucked it under my arm. "Guess I'd better start packing."

I trudged back to my room and pulled out my cell.

Code blue, I texted Shruti.

At dinner, Shruti responded. A-minus on a math test code blue or bleeding from the esophagus code blue?

Yes, I responded.

My phone lit up a moment later with Shruti's name.

"This better be good," she said. "Or bad, I guess. Because I'm going to have to suffer through another one of my father's 'Cell phones are destroying this generation' lectures."

I exhaled dramatically as I dropped down onto my bed. Mr. Snuggles Factory let out a little sleep whimper at the sudden noise. "My parents are making me go on a cruise."

"Ha ha," Shruti said. "Very funny."

"I wish I were kidding."

"Wow," Shruti said after a brief pause. I could hear her dad shushing Terry—her Yorkshire terrier—who was yapping loudly, probably trying to gain entrance into Shruti's room. "I'm sorry. Like deeply. And for real. When does it leave?"

"In two days." I buried my face in Mr. Snuggles Factory's soft, white belly, missing him already. "Even though they *know* we have the research fair next week."

"It's like they're purposefully trying to obliterate your future career in medicine." Shruti was being sarcastic, but the reason we were so close was because we understood one another. We had different approaches to school—Shruti was a natural genius who crammed last minute and still miraculously got all As, while I worked on papers weeks in advance just to eke out the same grades. But our end goals were the same. Top GPAs. Densely packed, passion-driven résumés. Acceptance to our dream schools.

I had felt a little bad about asking Shruti to partner with me, since she didn't really care about the internship. But she had agreed, since she wanted to go into science research, and the winning paper would get published in a real medical journal.

I knew if Shruti did want the internship, she'd have no qualms about competing with me for it. Which was another reason I loved her so much—she prioritized end goals over silly emotional drama. The year before, Bridget Sherman, the valedictorian, had chosen not to apply early to Yale so it wouldn't hurt her best friend's chances. Her best friend still ended up getting rejected, and Bridget ended up at Princeton. But *still*. Just the idea that someone would jeopardize their dreams because of a hurt feeling was incomprehensible to me.

"Okay, deep breaths. There's gotta be a way around this." Shruti went quiet again, and even without being able to see her, I knew she was twirling her long black hair around her finger, her go-to move when she was deep in thought. "What if you video chatted in for the presentation? That would show you were extra committed *and* would help you stand out."

"Do you think they'd let me?" I didn't know why I hadn't thought of that before, but it wasn't a terrible idea. I wasn't sure exactly what the at-sea Wi-Fi situation was in this day and age, but I would figure out a plan.

"You never know unless you ask! And . . . you've got nothing to lose."

"I guess," I said, already sitting down at my desk and drafting the email. Shruti was right—this was my only option. Plus, this gave me another reason to email Dr. Klober and tell her *just* how interested I was in the internship.

A few minutes later, a new email appeared.

Presenting online is no problem. Enjoy your trip. —Dr. Klober

I tore apart my room that night as I packed. It was good I didn't generally bring friends home—other than Shruti—because even

I had to admit I had gone a little overboard in the decorating department.

Above my bed was a giant multimedia flowchart I had been adding to for the last five years. The bottom row was for high school—featuring an array of old report cards and certificates from volunteer trips. The row above that was "the shrine to Saint Brown," as Shruti called it—different Brown paraphernalia I had purchased on the annual trips my parents took me on, as well as a beautiful tapestry my parents had gotten me for Hanukkah the year before. The final row consisted of a series of framed photographs—Dr. Elizabeth Blackwell, Dr. Rebecca Lee Crumpler, Dr. Mary Edwards Walker—all famous female doctors whose life stories I had committed to memory.

It was a bit much, but it was helpful to wake up every morning surrounded by reminders of what I was working toward. Getting into Brown. Graduating with a medical degree at twenty-six. Finishing residency by twenty-nine. Becoming a real doctor by the time I was thirty. Not wasting any precious time toward achieving my dream.

I walked over to my printer and collected the hundred-plus pages of journal articles I had printed (along with duplicates, to be safe), which I would need for the paper. Luckily, Shruti was an amazing friend and had helped me come up with a new plan—I'd read through the articles and draft the paper while on the ship, and Shruti would be in charge of editing the drafts and doing the final, in-person presentation. I was doing the majority of the work because I a) wanted this more and b) didn't completely trust Shruti to take the lead, especially if a school grade wasn't attached.

I packed the articles alongside my laptop, highlighters, stapler, note cards, notebooks, and scientific calculator (you never know). Then I began throwing anything seemingly beach-appropriate into my suitcase. I didn't even know if I still had a bathing suit that fit, much less anything I could even ironically attempt to pull off as "beachwear." A little more than forty-eight hours' notice would have been nice.

As I ravaged through my sock-slash-random-knickknack drawer, discarding lone wool socks and cat figurines left and right, my fingers grazed a hard surface.

When I looked down to see what I had touched, my breath caught in my throat.

My journal.

The last gift Logan had ever given me.

I was blindsided by the sudden rush of memories that came flooding back. Spending the week after the funeral paralyzed, lying in bed. My dad knocking on my door and telling me Logan had left me a gift. My mind struggling to piece together the impossibility of those words, a gift from someone who no longer existed.

My dad had found the present while cleaning out Logan's room. Logan had wrapped it in the haphazard way he wrapped gifts—tons of packing tape and no folded corners anywhere.

I gingerly removed the journal from the drawer and ran my fingers over the beautiful embossed golden island on the cover. The island was surrounded by blue waves, and in Logan's slanted, left-handed writing, he had Sharpied in *Antigua*.

I slowly opened the journal to the first page and stared down at the message Logan had written. I could practically hear the high-pitched enthusiasm in his voice, the way his thoughts took off like a runaway train whenever he got excited. How everything he spoke, no matter how far-fetched, was pronounced as fact—and how I always believed him.

Olive—can't believe you're turning the big ELEVEN! These next 525,600 minutes are going to fly by so fast—and I just know this is going to be a great year for you. By the time this journal is filled, I'm sure you'll be the CEO of Celeste pizza, and we'll be living in our castle on the shores of Antigua. And explarrring shipwrecks fer treasurrre.

Love, Cap'n Plank (Logan)

After my dad had given me the journal, I had shoved it to the bottom of my sock drawer and hadn't taken it out since. It hurt too much to be reminded of Logan. Of all the promises and plans we had made that had vanished along with him. I couldn't imagine how disappointed he'd be if he could see me now.

I closed the journal, looking again at the cover. It was hard to ignore the significance of Antigua. Maybe Antigua would finally give me some answers. Maybe when I got there, I would feel closer to Logan. And maybe then I would start to understand what had happened to him.

Because who dies from a heart attack at seventeen?

TWO

When the taxi from the airport dropped us off at the dock, I had to throw a hand over my mouth to keep myself from bursting out laughing.

The Regal Islands SS *NY Sea* was the most garish eyesore I'd ever laid eyes on. I had read on the website that the ship was 1,200 feet long—a quarter mile, the length of five freaking city blocks. But reading that distance is different from seeing it in reality. Because the ship wasn't just 1,200 feet long, it was also freaking enormous in every other way—a gazillion stories tall, over 50,000 tons, and painted in bright, neon colors you couldn't look away from.

I glanced over at Justin, who had an adorable smile plastered on his face. He was pointing and repeating, "That's the ship, that's the ship, right?" Matt's face, meanwhile, was drawn in confusion. He tugged on my mom's sleeve. "But if we're in Puerto Rico, why is the ship called *NY Sea*?"

Great question, kid. We lived forty minutes from New York City, and back when my parents used to work there, they'd bring Logan and me along whenever we had off from school. Then we'd get to spend the day going to restaurants and seeing a Broadway show—always *Rent*, never anything but *Rent*. I was enamored with the city, its grittiness and bright lights and fast pace. Taxi drivers shouted obscenities, and people glared at you as you walked by, and I loved everything about it.

I looked back at the SS *NY Sea*, its sparkling clean white exterior and the neon-green Statue of Liberty painted on the side—with a grossly heretical bright red smile plastered on her face. This ship couldn't be further from NYC if it tried. The masses of people climbing on board were laughing and carefree—clearly not New Yorkers. Their sole purpose was to be entertained with cheesy, off-off-off-Broadway performances while they drank cheap wine and ate extremely fake and culturally appropriated dishes.

I gave the overly chipper Regal Islands employee my ticket. He handed me back an electronic "passport." "Enjoy your time at sea!"

As I took my last step on land and my first step on board, I kissed the air twice, said "Thank you God," and kissed the air twice again. It was a tic I had developed after Logan had died, that my body now did as a reflex, whenever something bad could happen—when I got on a plane or in a car or when I felt really anxious. I wasn't religious—I didn't even know if I believed in a god, and I always did the act so quietly, more or less just mouthing the actions, that even someone standing right next to me wouldn't notice. I had never told

17

anyone—not even my parents or my best friend, Shruti—that I did it.

I snapped back to attention as a mechanical voice shrilled, "Welcome aboard the SS *NY Sea*! Enjoy your Big Apple faux-tini!" A bartender robot was standing in front of me, its metallic arm holding out a martini glass, containing what appeared to be apple juice.

I wasn't sure how to politely turn down a robot, so I just kept walking, following the long line of people in front of me up an escalator. When we stepped off, I blinked twice as my dad let out a low whistle.

The two-story main promenade was decorated as the Coney Island boardwalk—wooden planks, hot dog stands—even a giant two-story Ferris wheel. But it had about the same effect as a pig wearing lipstick—you knew what it was *trying* to do, but the juxtaposition couldn't have been more glaring. Coney Island was Coney Island because of its history, because the old board-walk games hadn't been changed in years (minus the price tag), because of the cracks in the boardwalk and the chipped paint on the signs.

Meanwhile, everything in this ghoulish version of Coney Island shimmered and shined with its newness, its artificiality. The combined effect made my chest constrict, reminding me that I'd be trapped in this fake city for the next week plus.

The twins seemed just as terrified as I was. They held my hands tightly as we walked past carnival games and flashing neon signs.

I matched their strong grips, not wanting them to get lost among the seas of people.

It's only ten days, I reminded myself. No matter how bad it was, it would all be over in ten days.

Let the countdown begin.

We made our way over to the elevator banks and headed up to the ninth floor, where our combined staterooms were.

I began unpacking in my linen closet–sized room (although I was grateful my parents were bunking with the twins and had let me have my own room), debating the best organizational system for the few belongings I had brought.

As I was searching for a spot to stow my suitcase, a siren began blaring. My chest seized up—the boat hadn't even left yet, and there was already an emergency? I knew a 55,000-ton floating mall was a terrible idea.

"This is not an emergency," a voice boomed from the in-room speaker. I let out a breath, but my heart continued to race, oblivious to the lack of real danger. "Please make your way to the muster drill station labeled on your cruise passport. This is a mandatory drill, and the boat will not depart until all cruise passengers have checked in to their muster stations."

My family and I found our way to our station on the fifth floor, the Coney Laugh Lounge. We took seats toward the front and waited as the theater filled up with hundreds of people.

After twenty minutes, a blond man and woman took the stage—they looked like they could be siblings—and introduced themselves as our "muster captains," Michelle and Dan. They then began performing a horrifying song and dance that stated the rules of the ship and what to do in case of emergency.

I wondered if they had spent years studying musical theater, only to end up on a cruise ship rapping about life preservers. Yet another reason I was glad I had a safe plan. Med school graduates ended up as doctors, not as actors attempting to rhyme "water safety" with "don't be late-y."

After they had finished and everyone politely applauded, Michelle looked around the room. "So for this next part of our presentation, we will need a volunteer."

I sank down farther into my seat, in case they were as loosey-goosey with the definition of "volunteer" as my math teacher was.

But hands flew up all around me. It was clear that we were no longer within a 200-mile radius of NYC, where no one would ever willingly step forward for this type of public humiliation.

Michelle's face lit up at the enthusiasm, and she pointed toward the back of the crowd. "The boy in the gray hoodie— come on up!"

A boy with messy dark hair stood up. A much larger guy next to him began cheering and stomping his feet, as if his friend had just won the lottery and not a free ticket to embarrassment central.

"What's your name?" Dan asked, shoving the microphone in the boy's face.

"Sebastian," he answered. When most people spoke into a microphone for the first time, their voices were either muffled or far too loud. But not Sebastian. His voice was low and crystal clear. This was obviously not this boy's first time in front of a crowd.

"Sebastian, welcome on board the SS *NY Sea*! Where are you from?"

"Kansas City," he said, which was met with another series of woots from the large guy who had been sitting next to him.

"And who are you cruising with this week?"

"A few friends."

"Lovely! For this demonstration, I would love if you could model how to properly put on this life vest." Michelle handed him the bright orange vest, and he followed her instructions like a model student, nodding and smiling. He took his time and cheated out—turning his body toward the audience—so that he could be sure everyone in the room saw exactly how to buckle the vest and pull the safety straps.

"Now just blow some air into the oral inflation tube." As Michelle said those words, a loud cackling erupted from the back of the theater. I glanced behind me to find the group Sebastian was cruising with all laughing and nudging one another. I rolled my eyes.

When Sebastian was finished, he was met with a round of applause, as well as fervent foot stomping and cheering from his friends. The applause kept going, even after he'd found his way back to his seat. People were clearly smitten by his performance—not that he'd done anything actually impressive.

But I guess these were just the type of people I'd be surrounded by that week. Happy-go-lucky vacationers who were easily impressed. *So* not New York.

A smiling woman in a green Regal Islands polo walked up to us. "Hi, I'm Shari," she said, shaking hands with my parents, me, and then the twins. "I'll be the twins' aide this week." I eyed Shari up and down. Her hair was tied back in a crisp ponytail, and she had a small stud on the left side of her nose. She looked more like an overeager camp counselor than a real adult.

"How old are you?" I blurted out. My mom shot me a look, but I ignored her. After all, the twins' lives were going to be in this person's hands. I wanted to make sure she was at least legal.

"Twenty-one," Shari answered.

"You look young."

"Just ignore her," my dad said with a wry smile.

Shari laughed. "Don't worry; I'm used to it. So, can I take you on a tour of the ship?"

"We'd love that," my mom said. "There's so much to see; we don't even know where to begin."

"I know!" Shari's ponytail bounced as she spoke. "This is my seventh time on the SS *NY Sea*, and I still find myself getting lost!"

Not really selling yourself here, Shari. I wondered how soon would be too soon to request a new aide.

"That said, this ship is definitely *much* better organized than other cruise lines," Shari continued. "I also worked on"— she looked around, as if she were about to divulge top-secret information—"the cruise line with the animated mice," she loudly stage-whispered. "Where I was a godmother chipmunk in training. And let me tell you, the Regal Islands is *so* much better."

Shari paused briefly, as if she were waiting to be asked why.

22

"Oh, is it?" my mom finally asked. Shari was clearly a talker, but she had found the wrong audience. My parents and I were *not* oversharers. Far from it.

"It totally is! Because on that cruise line, you work six days in a row, but here you only work five. And also there, you have very limited eating hours and cuisines. But I think the best thing here is the individuality that Regal Islands allows. Like, I would *never* be allowed to wear my nose ring on that other cruise line."

"I see," my dad said. When Shari turned back around, my dad exchanged a small smile with me. I smiled back and shook my head, glad my dad at least shared my sense of humor.

We followed behind Shari as she took us to one of the large glass elevator banks at the back of the ship.

"Can I press the button?" Justin asked, just as a large group crowded in behind us.

"Sure, buddy," Shari answered. "Can you hit three?"

Shari started by showing us the laughably large three-story theater where the nightly "Broadway" performances of *Kinky Boots* would be held. The theater had thousands of seats and purple overhead lights, and apparently held some giant ship-wide karaoke contest that always "went down in history."

We then spent over an hour exploring the dizzying array of activities on the ship—the three-story main dining room; the main cafeteria (Penne Station); the kids' pool deck, which consisted of an entire water park and a 130-foot-tall (!) water-slide; the main pool deck (Pool Time Square); an entire floor dedicated to a wave pool for surfing; and too many additional restaurants and bars and coffee shops to keep count.

In that time, we had learned Shari's entire life story. That she was from Orlando, but her football allegiance lay with the Eagles because she went to Penn State. That she had studied musical theater and dance, which was why she originally worked on that *other* cruise line, but then she fell in love with cruise ships in general and thought maybe she wanted to go into special ed or something?

Shari was very serious about her job and was determined to show us each and every restaurant, bar, café, pizzeria, lounge, pool, spa, and knickknack on the ship—and she made sure to also include exactly why each place made the Regal Islands superior to the other cruise line. There were about a gazillion different eateries, but they all mostly looked the same, like the cafeteria at my grandparents' retirement community in Florida.

I zoned out as Shari spoke, only focusing on the few spaces that would actually be useful to me—the small business center filled with a few old PCs and a single printer. The café closest to my room, where I could stock up on Frosted Flakes and turkey sandwiches—safe, easy fuel to get me through my research sessions.

My parents now had their very-patient-client smiles pasted onto their faces. Matt looked like he wanted to cry. Justin, on the other hand, was overjoyed, thrilled at all the neon-colored attractions.

"We can probably skip any future bars or casinos," my mom told Shari, her patient facade finally cracking. "We're not really big drinkers."

That was the understatement of the century. The only time I ever saw my parents go near any type of alcohol was on Jewish holidays. And even then, it was just a few sips of Manischewitz. Logan had snuck me a glass once at Passover when I was eight; he had mixed it with water and served it as "juice." I had nearly blown our cover and spit it out after the first sip—it was sickly sweet and gross.

"Okay," Shari said with a false smile. She was clearly disappointed; I wondered if she made a commission on any additional purchases we made that week.

She began leading us into a restaurant with dark wooden paneling and a Jenga-style assortment of steak knives that towered almost to the ceiling. "Welcome to the Empire Steak Building!" Shari said, clapping her hands together. *Ah.* The knives were meant to replicate the actual building. Cute.

"Is this included in the standard food-and-beverage package?" my dad asked. My dad was very adamant about not getting suckered with upcharges. I once heard him using his lawyer voice on the phone for two *hours* with Verizon, just so he could save seven dollars. Which was why he had firmly declined the unlimited-drink package and the ship's Wi-Fi. "It's not about the money," my dad said, repeating the line I'd heard countless times before. "It's the *principle* of the matter. I don't want to raise wasteful children."

"Unfortunately, it's not included," Shari said. "But believe me, it is worth it for a special night out! This is actually where I went to celebrate my three-month anniversary with the Regal Islands. Which I also referred to as the celebration of three months of freedom from that other cruise line, ha ha!"

"I think we can skip this, then," my dad said. "I don't want to get the boys' hopes up if we might not eat there."

Justin was now doing his impatient wiggle. "Maybe we could just focus on the top few, no-additional-cost attractions you recommend?" my mom asked as she smoothed back Justin's hair.

"Sure," Shari said. She then rushed us through each and every "must-see"—the jazz club, the comedy club where our muster drill had been held, Rockefeller ice rink (which had a fully decked out Christmas tree . . . in the middle of March), Central Park (nothing like the real thing), the Brooklyn Bridge promenade (ditto)—which instead of offering a view of the Manhattan skyline, was crowded with vintage cars for sale, a Katz's Deli, and a "genuine NYC" hot dog stand (also ditto). The only thing that seemed genuine to NYC was the actual Starbucks sandwiched in among the row of airport-style clothing and perfume stores.

"And make sure you don't miss out on the famous Coney Island Mermaid Parade!" Shari trilled. "It may be even better than the real thing!" I highly doubted that.

"And this," Shari said, gesturing to the three lanes of red we stepped onto after exiting the elevator, "is the ship's running track. Yet another feature that no other cruise line can compete with." Finally—something I would actually be using. The track, as promised, was exactly 400 meters. The lanes were narrow, but at least there were three of them. The view of the ocean was blocked by rows and rows of lifeboats, but I didn't mind. At least that meant it would probably remain pretty empty.

Shari then showed us the rest of the deck, which consisted of a spa (which we would not be using, as it was a surefire upcharge), a fitness center, basketball courts, Ping-Pong tables, a mini golf course, and two giant rock walls that seemed destined for major injuries and lawsuits.

"Let's head back to the elevator banks. We'll be finishing at what will be Justin and Matt's home base—the Little Flippers Lounge!"

I found myself exhaling an audible sigh of relief but did my best to cover it up with a fake cough. This had seriously been the longest tour of my life.

When the elevator doors opened, Shari's hand flew up to her mouth, and she locked eyes with me. "I almost forgot!" she said, coming to a screeching halt and opening the door in front of her. "Welcome to the teen club!"

"Awesome," I said, doing the world's worst job at feigning enthusiasm.

"Do you want to take a peek inside?" she asked.

"That's okay!" I said, eyeing the time on the display. We had been on the tour for a full ninety minutes. "It looks really . . . cool, though."

"Oh, it is! So many great friendships—and romances," she said with a wink, "have started there."

I couldn't even begin to imagine the type of people who would fall in love on a mustard-yellow couch as disco lights danced overhead, but I managed another polite nod, knowing we were finally nearing the end of this impossibly long tour.

Shari held her card in front of the door. A moment later, a green light flashed and the door clicked open.

I eyed the play area. It looked similar to the day care the twins had attended, all squishy blocks and rainbow-colored carpets. No pools in sight. But Justin was a runner—what if he escaped the area without anyone noticing, and found his way to a pool? There were a *lot* of pools on this ship. I had just received an extensive education on all eight of them. And drowning was the leading cause of death for children under the age of six.

My parents listened and nodded as Todd, the director of the Little Flippers program, explained how everything worked. Each set of parents was given a pager so that they could be reached at all times if there was a problem. There was a 1:2 ratio of staff to children and a daily itinerary of activities they could participate in.

When the director finished speaking, I raised my hand. "How do you make sure the kids don't sneak out?"

Todd pointed to the door handle and explained that it was too high up for kids to open on their own. And that this was one of the few rooms on the ship where staff needed to swipe their cards to enter *or* exit the room. Which sounded like a fire hazard, if you asked me. But I didn't even want to *think* about what it would be like if there was a fire on board the ship.

"Right, but what if someone enters the room and leaves it open and a kid sprints out?" I asked, unable to stop myself.

Todd nodded, as if he were taking my rapid-fire questions seriously. "We have a strict 'enter and close' policy that all staff are well aware of. They close doors behind them as soon as they enter, with all eyes on the doorway in that brief instant, should a child try to leave the premises."

"Has that ever happened?"

Todd smiled again—he seemed used to this type of inquisition. "Once or twice, a child has made it a foot or two outside, and then has been redirected safely back to the play area. If we find a child has difficulty abiding by our guidelines, then we will discuss with the parents whether Little Flippers is the best place for them. Safety is our number one concern."

My dad placed a hand on my shoulder and whispered, "Maybe give the director a little breather, prosecutor? Our friends have assured us this is a safe environment for the twins."

I shrugged. "Okay." But I still couldn't stop picturing Justin running out and diving into a pool, his little, helpless body sinking to the bottom, never able to be resuscitated. My heart sped up as I pictured his small fingers, the vision as real and horrific to me as if it were actually occurring.

I breathed in and out, trying to erase the picture and bring myself back to the present. My mind had become a constant battlefield of unwanted images ever since the twins had been born six weeks early. But my instant, overwhelming love came alongside a fear so great it often felt paralyzing. When the twins came home after a month in the PICU, I stood for hours just staring into their cribs, checking to make sure they were still breathing.

Now any time we entered a new environment, I couldn't stop myself from imagining worst-case scenarios. These thoughts kept me up at night, and I would scroll for hours, looking up stats on SIDS and other accidental deaths. I would caress the dark, soft fuzz on their heads, unable to stop picturing all the ways those heads could get squished. When my parents baby-proofed the house, I babyproofed their babyproofing. It took me months to trust myself enough to hold the twins; I was so scared I would drop them and they would die.

The therapist I had briefly seen after Logan's death had labeled this "catastrophic" thinking and told me that it was completely normal. But she hadn't given me a way to *stop* the thinking. Because there was no way to stop it. Catastrophes *did* happen. As I was all too aware.

I glanced back over at Shari. Justin was already clinging to her leg, and Matt was even holding on to her hand. She was a bit annoying, sure, but she did at least seem to be good with kids.

My mom caught me staring at Shari and put a hand on my back. "You're a really good sister, you know that?"

I shrugged and mumbled "Thanks," caught off guard by my mom's compliment. And wishing I could accept it.

Because I wasn't a really good sister. If I was, Logan would still be alive.

THREE

Jules's face lit up when she saw me. "Olivia!" she said, running across the boardwalk to me. The cluster of metal bracelets on her arm chimed as she threw her arms around my neck. "So good to see you!"

I did my best to match Jules's excitement. "You too," I said, coughing a little as I took in a giant mouthful of her fruity perfume. "It's been forever." It took me a second to connect this flawlessly-put-together person with the gap-toothed girl I had dug for worms with at summer camp.

Jules looked like she had walked straight out of a Regal Islands pamphlet. Her long black hair was thrown up into a messy-yet-sophisticated bun. She had on giant round sunglasses that perfectly matched the expensive-looking tortoiseshell flip-flops she was wearing.

"I know. Want to walk around and catch up?" Jules asked. "My friend went on this cruise last month and said you need to find your group ASAP."

I had promised my parents I would say hello to the Lees before heading back to my room, where my work schedule called out to me. It was already seven p.m., and I had planned on a solid five hours of work today. Plus, wandering around and asking people to be our friends sounded . . . awful. I had no idea people met one another on cruises; Jules was making it sound more like *Survivor* than a vacation. But it would seem overly rude to say no, so I put on a smile. "Sure."

Jules hooked her arm through mine, as if no time had passed. Like we were still nine years old, braiding each other's hair and screaming "GIRLS RULE BOYS DROOL" at the top of our lungs.

"Bye, parents!" Jules said with a wave.

My mom caught my eye and smiled, seeming pleased I was taken care of.

"Bye, sweetie! And Olivia, I cannot *wait* to catch up!" Cindy, Jules's mom, had so much emotion in her voice, it was as if we were leaving for a year—not a few minutes.

As we neared the stairs to the next level, Jules thankfully let go of my arm so that she could open her purse.

"I am *so* excited for this week," she said, pulling out something thin and shiny. "No drinking age at sea," she said. "Let's celebrate!"

She tossed the—what I now realized was a flask—to her lips and then offered it to me.

Seriously? Jules had brought a *flask* on the cruise? But I shouldn't have been surprised. After all, Jules was the one who almost got us kicked out of camp, after she had begged and pleaded and finally convinced me to create nail "art"—all over the side of our cabin. She had told me nail polish remover would get rid of it, and for some reason I had believed her.

"Oh, I'm good," I said, as if I had already celebrated with my own flask beforehand.

Jules narrowed her eyes at me. "Don't tell me you're a narc," she said.

"I'm a narc," I replied, deadpan.

Jules let out a laugh that was far too loud and then grabbed my arm again. "Well, we're gonna have to change that this week, aren't we!"

Were we? I was quite fine with the way that I was. Aside from the gross Manischewitz tasting, I had tried vodka exactly once, with Shruti, as part of a controlled scientific experiment. And surprise, surprise—it was also gross. I'd never had a desire to try any type of alcohol again.

As Jules opened the flask and took another swig, the distinct, antiseptic scent found its way to my nostrils. I didn't know why, but it felt nice in a sort of familiar way, more like being on the streets of NYC than any other part of this ship.

When we stepped onto the next floor, we were greeted by a gaudy sign that read "Welcome to the Brooklyn Bridge Promenade." Jules and I rolled our eyes and kept walking, past the top of the freaking Ferris wheel and a camera that allowed you to get "featured in Pool Time Square" (whatever that meant). Jules stopped at a balcony that overlooked the boardwalk below.

"Have you *seen* the selection on this ship? So many hotties."

I had no idea how to respond. So I did what I had always found to be best in these types of social situations—state a tangentially related fact in a vaguely excited tone. "There are definitely a lot of people on this ship!"

"Right? I've already found like thirty people I want to hook up with."

Internally, I couldn't turn off the alarms going off in my brain. *This* was who I was stuck with this week? I was going to be Jules's chaperone as she got wasted and hooked up with strangers?

Not that this was much of a surprise. Jules had been the outgoing one when we were younger; she was the bunkmate who everyone gathered around late at night, as she explained all about French kissing and the difference between tampons and pads. She always had at least one camp boyfriend and usually forced some poor, shy boy on me as well. That way we would both have "camp boyfriends," even though most of my camp boyfriends and I never exchanged more than a few "hi"s.

We walked around to the back of the deck, through the mini golf course and around the perimeter of the basketball court. Jules was looking every which way, judging any clusters of cruise-goers who looked around our age. "Too young." "Camo pants—hard pass." Jules wrinkled her nose at a guy looking her up and down. "*Way* too old."

"Let's go up a few floors," Jules said. We got in the elevator and Jules waved her finger around, deciding on the fourteenth floor. "So you're at Bleeker now, right? Is it true every guy there wears pink polos with popped collars?"

I laughed. "Ugh, unfortunately, yes. There is some truth to that."

I had transferred to Bleeker Prep after Logan had died. My parents had been convinced that I needed more "structure" than my public high school offered, as if Logan wouldn't have died from a heart attack at seventeen if they had instead shelled out $35,000 a year for a school with a fencing studio and an art gallery. Not that I was complaining—I had been more than happy to transfer, to no longer be looked at as the "girl whose brother had died," like a fragile piece of glass about to shatter at any moment. All that my friends at Bleeker knew about my family was that I had two younger brothers.

"And starring in every musical, I assume?" Jules asked.

I cringed on instinct but tried to cover it up with a short laugh. "Nope; gave up my Broadway dreams long ago."

"Oh," Jules said, her smile fading. "But you were so good!"

"Ha, maybe for a nine-year-old."

I saw a flash of recognition in Jules's eyes, and I knew she must be thinking back to the last time I had seen her, at Logan's funeral. The last time I had ever tried to sing in front of a group. I prayed that she would drop the subject. I was relieved when Jules launched into a monologue about her own life.

"MHS is fine, but a total dating desert. Lily's off at Rutgers, so I'm an only child now."

"Do you know where you'll be applying to college?"

Jules squinted a bit, and I could tell I had said the wrong thing. College was basically the only thing my friends and I talked about at Bleeker.

Jules shrugged. "I'll figure it out next year, but probably Rutgers. Lily seems to like it, and it's not crazy expensive."

I nodded, trying to conceal my surprise at her lackadaisical attitude. I didn't know *any*one who was going to just "figure it out next year." My friends and I had all compiled lists of schools with our college counselors during the fall of our freshman year. Those lists had been updated each semester based on GPAs and test scores. Brown had remained number one on my list, despite my counselor's constant reminder that "the Brown medical program is a reach, for anyone whose name doesn't end in Gates or Walmart." To appease her, I had created a carefully curated list of backup options. But I had done my research; with my test scores and extracurriculars, and the essay I had rewritten fourteen times over the past two years, I had a pretty good shot. Now all I needed to do was secure the internship with Dr. Klober. Which meant I needed to get back to my room, stat.

Jules walked over to a grab-and-go café, which overlooked a little library below. She turned to me, her eyes bright. "Bingo," she said. "They look fun. And smart! Because they're in a library."

I looked down and spotted the immature group I had noticed at the muster drill. It didn't exactly seem like they were in the library for educational purposes; they were tossing around a water bottle, with their backs facing the stacks of books.

"Okay, so how did you want to do—" But before I could finish my question, Jules had already grabbed some ketchup packets from the café and was *throwing* them at the group?

"Yes!" she cheered when a packet hit the tallest guy—the one who had been doing all the cheering and stomping back at the muster drill—square in the back.

He looked confused and then glanced up and spotted us. "Is this yours?" he asked, seemingly concealing a smile.

"Oh, jeez, sorry!" Jules squealed. "Guess I dropped that!"

"Quite a long horizontal distance to drop something," the boy mused.

"I'm so clumsy," Jules said, shaking her head and trotting down the spiral staircase that led to the library. I glanced around, wondering if it was too late to sprint back to my room without anyone noticing. But they all were staring at Jules and me, so I dragged my feet as I scurried behind Jules, like a puppy being yanked on a leash.

"I'm Jules," she said, extending her hand.

"Troy," the guy said, shaking her hand. He was wearing a hot pink bathing suit and a white T-shirt, and had a towel thrown over his shoulder. "And this is Sebastian, Ash, and Charlie. We all go by he/him and Ash goes by they/them."

"This is Olivia," Jules said, putting her arm around me. "And we go by she/her."

"Where are y'all from?" Troy asked.

"New Jersey," Jules answered for us. "You?"

"Kansas City," Troy said. "As in the OG Kansas City in Missouri. Not that other dumpy one."

Jules laughed.

Troy swung around the towel he was holding. "We were actually just about to head over to the hot tub—care to join?"

"Sure," Jules practically squealed. "That sounds fun."

No no no. I did not have any more time for "fun" today.

"And I believe this is yours." Sebastian—the dark-eyed, wavy-haired guy who had volunteered at the muster drill—bent over and picked up one of the errant ketchup packets Jules had thrown and placed it in her hand. As he leaned over, a stray lock of hair fell over his eye. He wiped it away and smiled at Jules, which revealed not only an adorable dimple but a perfect set of teeth. This was clearly a boy who went to his six-month dental cleanings. He was absurdly cute—and he looked like the type of boy who *knew* he was absurdly cute. I had a strong feeling he would be Jules's next target. And that Jules would be successful.

Jules giggled and slipped the packet into her back pocket. "Thanks! See y'all in a bit."

I had tried to convince Jules to go to the hot tub without me, but she had merely laughed. "These might be our people! Don't abandon me in my time of need."

So I headed back to my room to change into the one swimsuit I'd brought—a faded navy one-piece that had to be at least three years old. As I tugged the swimsuit over my hips, I glanced at the neat stack of papers lying next to my schedule on the desk. So much for five hours of research that day. But I needed to at least get started, which meant I was going to step into the hot tub, fake a yawn fifteen minutes later, and leave.

When I showed up at Jules's room, she looked at my swimsuit and furrowed her brow. "Did you bring any bikinis?"

"Don't have any. My family hasn't really been on vacation in . . . well, forever."

"Luckily, my mom and I happened to find this amazing sale at Nordstrom right before we left." Jules pulled open one of her dresser drawers, which was overflowing with strings and tiny triangles of fabric in every possible color and tropical pattern. She waved her hand in front of the drawer. "Take your pick!"

"Oh, that's fine," I said, instinctively crossing my arms against my chest. "But thanks." I had only grown up with brothers, so I had never been one to share clothes—especially bathing suits. Why would someone want to share something so rife with germs? Who knew what kinds of infections could be passed along?

Jules's smile faltered. I could tell she was already disappointed, that she must have had some grand idea of what it would be like going on vacation with a friend. Someone to drink with and point out hot boys with and try on cute bikinis with. I felt a pang of guilt, knowing Jules must have expected a more easygoing sidekick. Instead, she was stuck with . . . me. The world's worst vacation friend.

I thought about what Logan would do if he were here. Throw on one of the skimpiest bikinis, then confidently strut around the ship until I "no longer looked like I had a permanent wedgie."

I reached into the drawer and selected what appeared to be the least revealing option—a red polka-dot halter-neck top with a high-waisted bottom. "Actually, this one looks nice," I said. "If it's okay if I borrow it."

"Omigod, yes, that one will look great on you!" Jules squealed. I took the suit to Jules's tiny bathroom. It was identical to mine, except that Jules's counter was already covered with every type of toiletry and makeup product imaginable.

I stepped out of my swimsuit and put on the bikini top. I looked at myself in the mirror. My skin was pale; I seemed like the wrong person to be wearing a bathing suit or showing any skin.

"You look *hot*," Jules said when I reappeared. I couldn't remember the last time anyone had ever described me as "hot." I was sure Jules was just being nice, worried I might bolt at any minute. But it was still kind of her, the same Jules I had loved being around at camp. Even as a kid, she had always had total confidence in her appearance and did her best to make others feel the same.

Jules linked her arm through mine again. "C'mon. Let's go find those Kansas City cuties."

FOUR

The late March sky had already turned dark, which meant the carnival attractions of the ship were all ablaze in neon lights. As we made our way through a (fittingly) packed Pool Time Square, we were accosted by bright flashing signs advertising the upcoming attractions on the ship—*Kinky Boots*, a buy-one-get-one-free steak night at the Empire Steak Building, the infamous Coney Island Mermaid Parade. One giant screen featured a live feed of the promenade, where a very inebriated man was flashing his chest and sticking his tongue out as his very embarrassed wife attempted, unsuccessfully, to tug him away.

Jules and I walked past a shirtless man in a cowboy hat—I guess meant to be the Naked Cowboy, a well-known street performer in the actual Times Square—who was taking pictures with giddy middle-aged women. Next to him, a Frank Sinatra impersonator was belting out "The Way You Look Tonight." Jules and I laughed as we passed a group of adults who were busting out ridiculous-looking dance moves.

It definitely wasn't New York, but it was . . . *some*thing.

We heard Troy's voice echoing across the deck long before we approached the hot tub.

"Ladies, welcome!" Troy boomed. The air was humid and smelled distinctly of chlorine. The hot tub was turned up high, the sound of bubbles echoing through the night.

Jules threw her towel on one of the deck chairs and practically hopped into the tub, letting out a deep sigh as she settled in. I carefully laid out my towel on a chair next to hers, slowly slid off my flip-flops, and then, with no procrastination tools left in my belt, climbed in and sat down next to her. The water was hotter than I'd expected. I glanced over at the giant flashing Regal Islands display. It was 9:04. I just had to put up with this until 9:30, when I would fake a yawn and get back to work.

"So small talk is boring," Jules started. "Wanna play Two Truths and a Lie?"

I sank down farther in the hot tub, praying this game wouldn't take longer than a few minutes.

"Sure," Troy said. "I'll go first."

He held out one large finger. "I'm the leading quarterback on our school's football team."

Troy definitely looked like a football player, but Ash snorted, clearly outing Troy's lie.

"I have six younger siblings and"—he paused—"my parents are former army generals."

"Name your top three football plays," Jules said.

"Yeah, do tell," Ash said with a grin.

"Ah, it's so hard to pick just three," Troy said, scratching his chin. "Probably . . . the crouching tiger . . . and the . . . double

42

bologna sandwich, and the . . ." Troy looked around and finally broke, a huge smile forming on his face. "Okay, fine, you got me. I'm a musical theater guy; I've never held a football in my life."

Jules and I laughed. I liked Troy immediately. He seemed like a giant, real-life teddy bear; the type of person who would bring positive energy wherever he went.

"Okay, I'll go next," Jules said. "One of the regulars at the Starbucks I work at is Bon Jovi, I've never gotten high, and I've been to all fifty states."

Jules said all three statements quickly; she had clearly prepared in advance. And her lie couldn't have been more obvious. I internally winced, secondhand embarrassed for Jules. Did she really think it looked cool to brag about doing drugs?

"You have definitely gotten high," Troy declared.

"Fine, fine, you got me," Jules said, holding her hands out. "I like the green."

Everyone started laughing—except for me. I guess Jules wasn't the only person who liked "the green." I wondered just how uncool they'd think I was if they knew I'd never even seen "the green" in actual, real life.

I realized Sebastian was staring at me, noticing my straight face. Did I really want to out myself as the baby of the group already? No one in this hot tub really knew me, except for Jules. And even Jules didn't know much about me, except for what I was like as a kid. So maybe it would just be easier to play along. After all, I wouldn't get caught. I mean, no one had brought drugs out to international waters. Right? Right???

I settled on biting back a bit of a grin, as if I had some dirty secret to hide.

43

"Okay, I'll go," Charlie said. "My parents are white. I'm the only Black guy in our grade. And I'm a killer trombone player."

"Bro, that last one's a little subjective," Sebastian said.

Jules met Charlie's eyes and studied his face. "It's the second one, isn't it?"

Charlie smiled. "Got me. There's one other Black kid in our grade, Damian. And yes, I'm adopted."

Wow—we were getting deep here, from the get-go. I had to hand it to Jules. She had always been great at group dynamics; at taking a group of strangers and immediately transforming it into a group of friends. This power was why I had been so drawn to her as a kid. All I had to do was follow by her side, and she did all the hard work (small talk—ugh). It baffled me what she had gotten out of our friendship, but maybe she liked having a beta to her alpha; someone willing to go along with her antics.

No one said anything for a moment. Ash was sitting on the other side of Charlie, so finally they said, "All right, I'll go. My middle name is Strawberry. I work at a record store. And I've never seen *The Matrix*."

Jules turned to me. "Your turn to guess, Liv." It took me a second to realize that by "Liv," Jules was referring to me.

Wait, what had they said? "Um . . . the last one?" I guessed.

Ash shook their head. "Nope."

"Is your middle name not Strawberry, then?" Jules laughed.

"Nope. It's Avocado."

"You're joking," Jules cackled. "No way!"

"Way. My parents were total hippies. And probably pretty high when I was born."

Ash's *parents* got high? I would bet a million dollars my parents had never gotten high. They were quick to change the channel whenever drugs were so much as mentioned on TV, as if we could somehow get high through the screen.

That led to a drawn-out discussion about everyone's parents—who did drugs, who did drugs but pretended not to, who wouldn't know a marijuana leaf if it was staring them in the face.

"All right, Sebastian, you're up," Troy said.

"Okay," Sebastian said, scratching his chin and looking around. He seemed to be the type of person who was used to taking his time, used to people waiting on his every word. He reminded me of Jack Klidel, a guy in my grade who everyone—girls, guys, teachers—seemed to have a crush on. They all giggled and blushed whenever he so much as glanced in their direction. Honestly, it was embarrassing.

"I played Melchior in our high school's performance of *Spring Awakening.*"

My ears perked up. *Spring Awakening* was my favorite Broadway soundtrack, next to *Rent*.

"I can run a sub-five mile."

As a runner, even I had to admit that was pretty impressive. Unless, of course, that was his lie.

"And I got suspended for performing a Celine Dion song on the roof of our school."

This boy sang, ran, and loved Celine? I had to admit that I was intrigued, even if there was only truth to two of those statements. But not intrigued enough to forget that it was already ten, way past the time I had mentally agreed to spend in this barrel of boiling water with a group of strangers.

I had been so consumed by my own thoughts that it took me a moment to notice that rather than responding with hoots and jeers to Sebastian's list—as the crew had done to the rest of the obvious lies—they had gone silent and were looking around with odd expressions on their faces.

"What, too soon?" Sebastian asked with a small grin.

Jules cut the tension in the air. "No way did your school do a production of *Spring Awakening*."

"Way," Sebastian responded back, mimicking Jules's tone. He was smiling, though, clearly flirting with her.

"And you played Melchior? Prove it," I said, surprising myself with my own audacity.

Sebastian turned his magnetic smile over to me. "'All that's known, in history, in science,'" he chanted in a crisp, confident tone. I felt a cascade of shivers erupt down my spine. I wrapped my arms around my chest, sure it was just the evening drop in temperature.

"All right, all right," Troy said, clapping a hand over Sebastian's shoulder. "You got him. Seb's a musical theater nerd too."

"Sub-five?" I asked, raising a brow.

At this, Charlie smirked. "By a few seconds; don't be too impressed."

"So it's the last one, then," Jules surmised.

"Yeah, I didn't get suspended," Sebastian said. "Just a stern talking-to."

My head was spinning, trying to take in all this information about Sebastian. But before I could begin to process the pieces, I realized Troy was calling on me. "Liv, you're up."

Liv. I guess that's who I was this week.

Since I was the last to go, I should have come up with something to say by then, but I had nothing. What about me was interesting? I followed rules and did what I was told.

So I blurted out the first thing that came to mind. "I can't run a sub-five mile, but I can run sub-six." At that, Sebastian met my eyes and grinned. Oh no—it looked like I was trying to impress him. I was not trying to impress him. Was I trying to impress him?? I looked around the hot tub and then cast my eyes across the deck, landing on the giant flashing Regal Islands logo. I needed to say something else, fast. Something that had nothing to do with Sebastian.

"I tried to talk my way out of coming on this cruise because I was supposed to participate in a science research fair this week." Welp, there I went, outing myself for the complete nerd that I was. "And . . ." I was coming up blank. Finally I spit out the least interesting thing I could think of. "I like pineapple on my pizza."

At that, the tub erupted in chaos. "What?" "Gross!" "Pariah!"

But Sebastian met my eyes again. "A girl after my own heart," he said. "Unless that was your lie."

I opened my mouth to shoot back some snappy repartee—*I liked pineapple pizza; my personal tastes were not a bid after Sebastian's heart.* But I simply opened and closed my mouth like the fish out of water that I was, unable to think of any clever retort.

"The first!" "No, the second!" "Definitely the third."

Five pairs of eyes were on me. Which was when—completely mortified—I realized I had told three *truths*. God, what was wrong with me?

"It's definitely the second," Troy repeated, and I forced myself to face him, so that I was no longer gaping like an idiot at Sebastian. "No way you tried to attend a research fair over going on a cruise."

"I dunno, I buy it," Ash said. "She seems smart."

Before they could debate any longer, I shook my head. "Sorry," I said. "Those were actually all truths."

"Ah, I like this girl," Troy said. "Way to shake things up."

I was grateful for Troy's kindness, for twisting my embarrassing mistake into a purposeful act of deviance.

"So, sub-six, huh?" Sebastian said. "Guess we'll have to test out the track together."

"There's a track?" Jules asked before I could answer.

"Yeah," I said, ignoring Sebastian's invitation. It must have been killing him that I wasn't drooling over his grins and glances, which probably worked on pretty much all his other targets. Which I'm sure was why he kept singling me out. Guys like him couldn't *stand* their charms not working on someone. "It's a freaking quarter mile long."

"Speaking of pizza," Ash said, even though we were long past that topic. "Who wants to get some non-gross-pineapple-free—no offense, Liv—pizza at Roy's Famous New York Pizza?"

"We do!" Jules eagerly volunteered.

"Actually, I've got to get back to work," I said, regretting my choice of words as soon as I saw the way five faces all creased in confusion. I could sense the shift in the air, the way I had thrust myself into the spotlight as the group's resident nerd. Why couldn't I have just lied? Or been more vague?

"Work?" Sebastian repeated, his confusion now forming into a sly smile. "On . . . vacation?"

The bubbles in the hot tub had quieted down, and the deck was much emptier than it had been an hour ago. Sebastian's words hung in the air, and my face flushed as the rest of the crew waited for my answer.

"Forced vacation," I clarified. "I have an important research paper due this week."

Sebastian took in the new info and nodded. "That's too bad."

"Actually, not really," I said, stepping out of the tub and wrapping a towel tightly around myself. "It's a pretty interesting paper."

"What's it on?" Sebastian pressed, clearly trying to drag out my public humiliation.

I leveled him with a cool glare. "Science." And with that, I slid on my flip-flops, offered a meek wave to the rest of the group, and began speed walking back to my room.

I was still fuming when I climbed into my bed. One night into the cruise, and I was already being made fun of for being a loser. I had no idea why Sebastian had to call me out, pick on me like a schoolyard bully.

More important, though—why did I feel the need to justify myself to this person I'd just met?

I took a deep breath to reset and reminded myself of my goal this week: to write the best science research paper possible and score the internship with Dr. Klober. Yes, I had to get this done in the middle of the Caribbean Sea. But I was Olivia Schwartz—I had gotten a bad case of the flu at the end of my sophomore year and had still aced all my final exams, even on maximum-strength cough syrup that made me see double. (Shruti had said I was "high as a kite but spouting Shakespeare vocab and AP chem definitions like a machine.")

I sat down at my desk and glanced forlornly at the schedule that I had screwed up, not even a day into the cruise. I couldn't believe I'd already fallen behind, all so I could be publicly humiliated.

Although, maybe now that Jules had found a crew—a crew that drank, that liked "the green," that was certainly a lot cooler than me—she wouldn't need to rely on me anymore. She must have been so disappointed in how I'd turned out. Then again, she probably took pity on me. Assumed I was broken because of Logan's death. People did that. A lot. But this was who I *was*, and I liked it. Yes, I had been a little more carefree as a child. But that was because I was a *child*.

My stomach grumbled as I sat down at my desk, so I opened up the front pocket of my suitcase to grab a granola bar. As I reached for it, my hand grazed over the hard cover of the journal that Logan had given me.

It didn't take much to picture what Logan would do if he were here—his easy smile and the way he would have swept all my papers off the desk, stood up on the bed, and declared it time to christen the room with a performance of *Rent*. He would have loved this ship, all the crazy activities and new people to meet. He would have felt right at home.

But he wasn't here. And I needed to stick to my schedule so that I could figure out why. The thesis for my project: What causes a perfectly healthy teenager to die from a heart attack at seventeen?

I opened up my binder to the first article, "Leading Risk Factors for Heart Failure in Adolescents." Then I lined up my highlighters—pink for facts and blue for themes and purple for vocab I'd need to look up later.

I unwrapped the granola bar and took a big bite. It was time to get to work.

FIVE
DAY TWO AD

Justin's eyes nearly popped out of his head when we entered the kids' pool area. It was the size of a standard water park, with seemingly hundreds of different candy-colored contraptions, all with the same end goal—to get you wet: in-ground geysers and slip-and-slides and water gun stations and, of course, four different kids' pools. Overhead, four intersecting waterslides towered more than one hundred feet above us. I shuddered thinking about what it would be like riding down those completely enclosed tunnels. If Logan was here, he would surely have found a way to convince me to go on one with him.

"Is the pool water cold?" Matt asked me as I wriggled a floatie onto his arm.

I dipped a toe into the pool to check the water's temperature. "Nope!"

Matt's little button nose was scrunched up in his typical worried fashion, the same facial expression I made when I got worried—which was often. Meanwhile, Justin had the same spark and excitement that Logan had had. Which was part of the reason why I had grown to love the boys so much—even though I was initially determined not to, sure that my love for them would be a betrayal of my older brother.

I'd been furious with my parents when they'd gotten pregnant with the twins—three *months* after Logan had died, as if they were simply replacing their son with a new one. We had spent those eight months (the twins had been born six weeks early) tiptoeing around one another—me, rewatching old videos of Logan in my room, while my parents put up teddy bear wallpaper and installed car seats in their SUVs.

But then the twins were born. I had taken one look at their helpless, terrified eyes and teeny tiny fingers behind the plexiglass PICU walls, and I was a goner.

Justin gleefully skipped into the water, flapping his arms wildly. It took a few minutes, but after I ducked my head under and made a few silly faces, Matt waded in and was smiling too. And I had to admit—the water and sun did feel pretty refreshing.

Toddlers (and their already-drunk-looking parents) floated around us on oddly colored circular pool floats. Upon closer inspection, I realized the floats were meant to be everything bagels. I bit back a smirk.

I grabbed a beach ball emblazoned with the face of the Statue of Liberty and began passing it back and forth with the boys.

We took turns shouting out what the ball was and then making the sound the ball would make. "Train!" "Choo choo!" "Airplane!" "Whooshhh!" "Kitty cat!" "Meowww!"

It was their favorite game, one I had invented when they were learning to talk. And then a deep voice behind me shouted out, "Pig! Oink oink!"

The boys lost it, their brown eyes shining through their laughter. I turned around to find—Sebastian?

"Oh, hey," I mumbled. This was the last person I wanted to run into—especially now. I could only imagine the picture he must be piecing together of me. Leaves hot tub at ten to go work. Wears old bathing suit that doesn't fit. Meows like a cat in public.

"Hey, Liv," Sebastian said with a smile, as if the night before hadn't ended in a massive, passive-aggressive tête-à-tête. "How's the science going?"

I rolled my eyes. "Can we cool it with the mockery?"

Sebastian drew his brows together. I seemed to have caught him off guard. He lowered his voice, and his eyes looked guilty. "Sorry, I—"

"Who are you?" Matt interrupted.

"Oh, hey," Sebastian said, bending down to meet Matt at eye level. "I'm Sebastian. What are your names?"

"Justin!" Justin shouted eagerly.

"And the worried-looking one is Matt," I said.

But even Matt now had a shy smile on his face. The twins loved hanging out with older guys. They absolutely adored their behavioral aide, Theo, who was a sophomore at Seton Hall University and came over to our house once a week to work with them.

"Where are you from?" Matt asked, continuing his interrogation.

"Kansas City," Sebastian answered. "Do you know where that is?"

"Um," Matt said, putting a finger against his lips in concentration. "Missouri?" he asked, pronouncing it like "Ma-zor-ee."

"Wow—correct!"

"Missouri starts with *M* just like Minnesota and Mississippi and almost but not exactly New Mexico," Justin added, not one to be outshone by his brother.

Sebastian laughed. "Wow, you guys really know your states!"

I shook my head. "There's this, like, bird cartoon on YouTube they're absolutely obsessed with; we've listened to his rendition of the state song at least a thousand times."

"Oh, is it the one that goes . . ." Sebastian started to sing, "Alabama, Alaska—"

Matt and Justin immediately joined in. "Arizona, Arkansas!"

"Oh no," I groaned. "Now they'll never stop."

"Sorry," Sebastian said when they had finished, shooting me an apologetic grin. "Would anyone like an airplane ride across the pool?"

Was he seriously volunteering to spend time with two little kids on his vacation? Was this what boys were like in the Midwest? Because this definitely wasn't what they were like in New Jersey.

"Me, me!" the twins shouted.

"Oh, it's okay, you don't have to—" But before I could finish, Sebastian was jetting across to the other side of the kiddie pool with Matt on his back. When he zoomed back, he dropped Matt off. "Flight 1047 is now landing safely at JFK Airport. Your captain would like to thank you for flying with Sebastian Air, and we hope you enjoy your stay at the Regal Islands *NY Sea*."

"My turn!" Justin shouted, throwing himself onto Sebastian's shoulders.

"I'm sorry," I mouthed. But Sebastian just shot me a giant grin, his eyes gleaming, and announced his takeoff.

"Can I ask Sebastian to be my friend?" Matt asked, always one to ask permission—for anything from requesting someone's friendship to ordering a soda at a restaurant.

"Sure, bud," I said.

After a few more airplane rides, I glanced over at the Regal Islands flashing display, which showed that it was already 11:45. Time for me to get back to work.

I turned back to the boys. "Boys, say goodbye and thank you to Sebastian."

"Thank you," Justin shouted, followed by a demure "Thanks" from Matt.

"Anytime, guys," Sebastian said.

I toweled off the boys and helped them put on their sandals. Then we walked with Sebastian toward the elevators, passing a "subway car" where a group of performers was shouting, "What time is it?"

"Showtime!" Sebastian yelled back.

I shook my head. "Don't encourage them."

But it was too late. We watched as the group burst into an embarrassing subway-style breakdance routine.

Sebastian turned back around to face me. "I'll see you tonight?" he asked. "Unless you'll be busy with work—which is totally cool," he quickly added.

He was clearly trying to be nice, so I offered a small smile in return. "I'll have to see how much I get done, but I'll come if I can."

Sebastian smiled again and waved. I gave a half nod back in his direction.

Okay, so he wasn't *as* bad as he'd come across the night before. But I could tell he was working hard to gain my approval; that he was the type of guy who couldn't stand not being liked by everyone. But I really hoped he didn't have some endgame in mind where we became friends. Because if he did, he was surely going to be disappointed.

The boys zoomed back to their room with their arms spread out, still in full-force airplane mode. I ran after them, doing my best to stay close enough to prevent any crash landings.

"Are you coming to lunch with us?" my mom asked when she opened the door. The boys flew into the room right past her.

"I can't," I said. "I've got a lot of work to do."

"Sure you can't take off thirty minutes to eat?" My mom's voice was warm, but her eyes were tinged with sadness. She and my dad were always good at respecting my work time—which was the majority of the time. But we *were* supposed to be on a vacation, and I hadn't meant to hurt my mom's feelings.

"Cindy told me the *Magnolia* cupcakes are to die for," my mom added, putting an extra emphasis on Magnolia. "Maybe even as good as the real ones." I could see how hard she was trying, and I felt bad for being difficult. It was just lunch.

I forced myself to smile. "Sure, I guess thirty minutes can't hurt."

Ten minutes later, the five of us were walking across the tan-and-orange carpeted floor and taking the elevator up to the main buffet, Penne Station (I just couldn't with the NYC puns).

The cafeteria was packed when we got there. The smell of microwave pizza and fried food wafted through the air. Long lines of people zigzagged through the enormous room, filling their plates at the two dozen different stations—from salads and sandwiches to soups to make-your-own burritos, omelets, and sundae stands. I still couldn't believe how big and wasteful this ship was. There was probably more food here than in many small countries.

After we filled our trays—salads for my parents, a turkey sandwich for me, peanut butter and jelly for the twins, and four suspicious-looking droopy cupcakes (the twins would be allowed one-half each)—we found a round table in the back.

"Can I have a soda?" Justin asked. The twins were obsessed with soda. Their diet was pretty intense—very little sugar and no dairy and a host of other limitations. Which was definitely to blame for their intense addiction to anything sweet.

"You get one a day," my dad said. "So if you have one now, you can't have one later."

"I want one now," Justin said, so he and my dad got up to go fill his cup.

I munched on my sandwich and glanced out the window at the unnaturally blue sea. The boat felt so stable that I often forgot we were continuously moving, all 55,000 tons some-how not sinking. I knew from physics that this was due to buoyancy—the ship displaced an equivalent amount of water as its mass. But it still seemed crazy.

"Is it okay I made a friend today?" Matt asked when my dad and Justin returned.

Uh-oh.

"I made a friend too!" Justin chimed in.

"Oh yeah?" my dad asked. "Who's this friend?"

"Bastian," Justin said.

"SUH-bas-tian," Matt corrected him. "We made friends with him at the pool. He knows Livia. He's from Kansas City in Missouri, not in Kansas."

This boy was going to grow up to be a great PI.

My mom turned to me. "Is this one of your new friends? Cindy told me you and Jules already found a great group."

I swallowed. "I wouldn't exactly call him a friend. But yeah, Jules and I met him yesterday. And then we saw him at the pool."

"And is he your age?"

"Yup," I said, crumpling up my napkin in my hand. Could this conversation be over already? It seemed to be dangerously bordering on discussing the fact that I had met a boy. Which I did *not* ever discuss with my parents. Not that there was ever anything to discuss.

"And how is Jules doing?" my mom asked, thankfully changing the subject. "Is she still making those beautiful earrings?"

"Mom, she was into making jewelry when we were *nine.*"

"Yes, come on, Diane, get with the times," my dad said with a grin. "Jewelry is out. Tattoos are in."

I rolled my eyes at the dad joke, although he wasn't that far off. *She's more into smoking the green now* was more like it, but I figured my parents preferred discretion to the truth.

"Well, I'm so glad to hear you girls still get along."

"Yup," I said, twisting my napkin further. I took another bite of my sandwich and glanced out the giant floor-to-ceiling windows at the moving waters below. The boat was so big, but it was also contained. I was going to have to be careful. I didn't want my parents to run into Jules when she was drinking. I could only imagine what kind of scene they'd make.

When Logan was in high school, I was used to being awakened late at night by the sound of the front door creaking open, always immediately followed by the flicking-on of my parents' light and heavy, disappointed steps down the stairs. Then the yelling would start, and the fighting would snowball from there.

All high schoolers drank, Logan assured me. But to my parents—super-straitlaced, out-of-touch, teetotaling nerds (as he referred to them)—the fact that he went to parties was the end of the world.

Which was part of the reason why I had always avoided parties. I had no problem with nerdom. Obviously. And it just seemed easier than dealing with my parents' disappointment. I didn't have many invitations to avoid, of course—or a burning desire to see kids from my school any more than I was legally required to.

"Did you have a chance yet to look through the list of off-shore excursions?" my mom asked. "If you want to do any, we need to let the concierge know by eight tonight to get the ten percent discount."

I shook my head. My plan was to spend as much time on the ship as possible so I didn't fall behind on my paper.

My mom reached into her bag and pulled out a glossy Regal Islands pamphlet. "I circled a few I thought you and the boys might like."

I began flipping through the pages to appease my mom. Each day there was a list of different excursions, separated by category: "For the whole family!" "For the adventurous!" "For the fitness junky!" Most seemed significantly more expensive than was warranted—typical, for a cruise seemed intent on suckering you with upcharges. My mom had a train tour circled for St. Kitts ($26 per person), as well as a few beach days (no additional charge, with free transportation to and from the ship).

I was about to hand the brochure back to my mom when I saw the final list—Antigua.

"Explore a slice of time, frozen in history. Sail out to sea aboard a fully stocked catamaran (drinks and meals not included). Then throw on some scuba gear and follow our certified dive experts through a shipwreck tour of the 1762 *Beaumont*."

A shipwreck—just like Logan had always dreamed of taking me on. I had to go.

But then I saw the price—$125 per person.

"Can I do this one?" I asked, pointing.

My mom and dad glanced down. I could see their eyes both grow in surprise, then quickly return to normal.

"Sure, honey," my mom said. "That looks really fun."

I was shocked that my dad didn't protest. But I guess my parents were just relieved that I was interested in something.

"So tell us about your research paper," my dad said. "Have you figured out a way to eviscerate the competition?"

I smiled and launched into a summary of what I had read so far. The night before, I had stayed up until one and managed to read through two of the eight journal articles I had brought. One of them was written by Dr. Klober herself, who was a leader in innovative cardiac surgery. She had been one of the first doctors to perform heart surgery through the *wrist*.

My parents nodded along as I spoke. God, I was *so* grateful they weren't helicopter parents, like the parents of some of the kids in my grade. At the same time, though, they were always eager to discuss my work, quick to offer encouragement or guidance if I needed it.

"So basically, I want to come up with a program to help to prevent heart disease in teens," I finished.

"Oh?" my mom asked, and I could sense the hesitation in her voice. She knew why I was interested in this topic. She was on high alert, no doubt, to avoid all mentions of Logan.

Because that was the thing about my parents. We were close, but there was a thorny underside to our relationship—Logan. They never wanted to talk about him.

Especially in front of Matt and Justin—because the twins didn't know he existed. My parents thought they were too young to be told about death. They believed that the idea would frighten them, make them worry about their own mortality.

I didn't know much about child psychology, but when they explained their position, I had agreed, wanting to do whatever I could to shield the boys from pain.

It still hurt, though, not being able to talk about Logan. I planted my feet on the floor and pushed my chair back from the table. "Is it okay if I head back to my room?"

"Sure, hon," my mom said. "Thanks for gracing us with your presence."

I let out a loud sigh when I got back to my stateroom, giddy to finally have a quiet, uninterrupted afternoon of research. I know how that makes me sound, but I'm filled with a sense of calm when I have a solid stretch of time with no other commitments—and not even cell service (my dad, of course, refused to pay the extra charge for the ship's data plan)—to focus solely on work.

I began clearing off the desk, which now featured a towel animal in the shape of a dog, a boat-shaped piece of chocolate, and the same pamphlet my mom had just shown me. I flipped to the page with Antigua and then gingerly tore out the section about the shipwreck, which I taped above my desk. A good reminder of why I was spending a week stuck out at sea.

Then I uncapped my pink highlighter and inhaled the chemical scent that I loved. While I did my best writing on my laptop, I always did all of my reading and research on paper. Shruti made fun of me, but my brain just worked differently when I saw words in print. And also—nothing beats the smell of highlighters.

I opened up the next article, which discussed the biological underpinnings of heart disease. My heart rate slowed down and my body relaxed as I highlighted key phrases and annotated the text. When I read about medicine, I think the same brain areas are activated for me as for other people when they watch Netflix or do drugs. I get captivated by the journeys these doctors go on, the incredible discoveries they make.

As I read, I tried to brainstorm possible ideas for a program that could help reduce the incidence of heart disease. Because in addition to the research paper and PowerPoint presentation summarizing our findings, Shruti and I also had to come up with a detailed program that Dr. Klober's hospital could execute, to combat the issue we had researched.

I found my mind wandering, picturing what it would be like to spend a summer shadowing Dr. Klober and coordinating a real live hospital program. Meeting with patients and watching actual surgeries. I had spent years waiting for my actual life to begin, the one where I was studying medicine at Brown, being taught by renowned professors and researchers. The closer I got to the goal line, the more impatient I felt.

But this all relied on winning the research fair, which meant my paper needed to be perfect. I looked at the thick stack of articles in front of me and then glanced to my left, where I could see a calm blanket of blue water. I grabbed the curtain rod and yanked it to the right, covering up my view and darkening the room. Then I leaned back and flipped to the next article.

Just as I was about to get started on my fifth article, there was a knock at my door.

I opened the door, expecting to find my parents. But instead, Jules was standing there. Her eyes were sparkling and lined with eyeliner, and she was wearing a delicate open-crochet crop top.

"Figured I'd come over to help you get ready!" Jules sang out, waving a striped bag in the air.

I bit my lip and glanced back at the articles on my desk. If I wanted to be caught up on my schedule, I was supposed to have read through all the articles at least once by that evening. It was already seven, and I wasn't even halfway done.

"I'm actually not sure if I can go out tonight," I said. "I have this really important research fair I'm preparing for this week."

"Okay, but," Jules said, shoving a piece of paper in my face, "check this out."

I took the paper from Jules. ULTIMATE TEEN CLUB COMPETITION, it said up top in big bold letters.

"So . . . ?"

"So?" Jules laughed. "Come on, Olivia. I'm sure you've changed since we were nine, but I *know* competitions are your kryptonite. I mean, you're pretty much the only fourth grader I've ever met who drew up a ten-page, three-pronged plan of attack to win the camp Olympics."

Jules wasn't wrong—I did love a good competition. I blamed my parents. The few family traditions they had honored when Logan and I were younger were major Jewish holidays. For Passover, they always took off from work and concocted elaborate hiding places for the afikomen, the piece of matzah that was hidden before the Seder. The search would take hours, but Logan and I wouldn't relent until we had found the towel-wrapped matzah.

"Plus, Sebastian was asking about you. I promised him you'd be there."

He was? "When did you see Sebastian?"

"We were all at the hot tub this afternoon," Jules said, and I winced, feeling a small pang of unease forming in my stomach. I *wanted* to be working. I did. But they'd been *talking* about me.

"Troy was trying to convince us all to do this silly competition thing tonight," Jules explained. "Sebastian said not to bother you, but he seemed *sad*."

I looked back again at the page detailing the competition schedule. There was one challenge each night. The challenges had start and end times—convenient ways for me to make an easy exit. Even better, the competition had two emcees—which was a sneaky way of saying chaperones. If I was going to hang out with Jules and the crew . . . I was going to need all of the above.

I sighed. "What are the chances that I convince you to drop this?"

"About equal to the chances that I let you wear a track tee tonight," Jules said, eyeing the faded Bleeker Prep track tee and pair of running shorts I was wearing.

Two minutes later, Jules had somehow managed to cobble together a moderately decent outfit for me—pairing a white tank with my shorts and a thick belt, which I never would have thought of. Then she opened her clutch. "Do you want any makeup?"

"I'm okay, thanks." I rarely wore makeup, and it seemed a little unnecessary to put any on when we would probably just end up back in the hot tub again.

"Come on, it'll be fun! Like old times."

When we were at camp, Jules had assigned herself as the bunk's personal stylist, always doing our hair and makeup before dances. Logan would eschew camp rules and break into our bunk to join us, always asking for extra-sparkly eye shadow. I smiled, thinking back to how much fun the three of us used to have.

"Okay, but nothing too heavy?"

Jules nodded and opened up one of the containers. "So who are you planning on hooking up with?" she asked as she dabbed some sort of glitter on my cheeks. It was cool to the touch and felt a little slimy.

I shrugged. "No one? They're not really my type."

"So what *is* your type?"

"I mean . . . I guess I don't have one? I've never really dated."

"At all?" Jules eyebrows shot straight up, as if I had told her I didn't really eat food.

"Nah, there aren't many datable guys at my school. I figured I'd wait until college." That was my plan. After all, Brown—or wherever I ended up—would have already done the work of curating a group of people with similar drives and goals. Which I couldn't exactly say to be true for Bleeker Prep. There, we were pretty much all paired together because our parents had an extra $35,000 a year to spend on our education.

"Well, that's silly. You should for sure hook up with Sebastian. He is *so* cute."

My mind flashed back to his dark eyes and the way his face lit up when he was carrying the boys on his back across the pool.

Fine, he was objectively cute. Very objectively cute. But that didn't matter.

"He'd never go for someone like me." I remembered the way his face scrunched up the night before when I told him I was working on a research project. The same way the guys at my school saw me—intense. Smart. Not datable.

I wasn't like the girls the guys dated, who got up and blow-dried their hair every morning and put on makeup and never raised their hand to tell Jack freaking Klidel that *actually* his interpretation of *Othello* was one-dimensional and completely biased by his privileged, cis-male lens. Which it was! Even our English teacher was too distracted by Jack's biceps—which were suspiciously large for a sixteen-year-old—to tell it to him straight.

"Oh girl, don't play that game. You're adorable, and funny, and smart. And also—this is a freaking *cruise*. Everyone's just looking to have some fun."

I think we have different definitions of fun. "Why don't *you* have some fun with Sebastian, then?" Sebastian would definitely go for Jules—she was gorgeous and way more outgoing and fun than I was. And way more experienced, I was sure.

Jules shot me a conspiratorial grin. "Because I gave up on cis boys in the eighth grade."

I hadn't realized that. It had been so long since we had really talked. "So then why did we choose this crew to hang out with? Let's go find you some cute girls!"

Jules laughed. "I said *cis* guys. I actually tend to go for people like Ash. Who is *super*hot."

Ash was pretty cute. "Perfect. We've got our cruise couple! You and Ash have a wonderful time."

"Nuh-uh, I'm not letting you off the hook that fast, Liv." Jules pulled out yet another makeup palette and a small brush, which she began running over my eyebrows. I didn't even know they *made* eyebrow makeup.

"Ta-da!" Jules spun me around so I was facing the mirror above my dresser. "You look amazing! What do you think?"

I looked at my reflection. My cheeks were shiny, my lips were pink, and my eyebrows were sleek. I didn't look like a girl who had voluntarily spent her first day of vacation in a dark room with her nose buried in books. I looked like . . . someone who had fun, someone who might take a few risks sometimes. And maybe that wasn't such a bad thing. I could almost see Logan smiling back at me. If he were here, he'd snap his fingers, meow like Mimi from *Rent*, and twirl me around, belting out that it was time for us to go "ou-ou-out tonight!"

I rubbed my glossy lips together and smiled back at Jules.

"I like it."

SIX

Jules and I found the crew waiting for us in the "teen club," which was even worse in real life than I could have imagined. It looked like it was designed in the seventies, like an old airport lounge had been thrown up on by a few disco balls. Whoever designed it had definitely never met a real teenager—or been one themselves.

Sebastian smiled at me when we walked over. "You made it."

I shrugged. "Yup." I looked around. There were a whopping three other kids sprawled out on the purple-and-orange faux-velvet lounge chairs. Michelle and Dan were standing up front, and their faces lit up like Christmas trees when they spotted us.

"Looks like we have some additional contenders! Welcome to the first night of the Regal Islands Teen Club Competition. Get ready for a week of physical, mental, and emotional challenges."

Emotional? What were they going to do, call up our therapists and put them on speakerphone?

Michelle explained the rules for that week. There would be one competition each night, and the winning team would be awarded ten points. The team with the most points at the end of the cruise would win a free meal at Regal Islands' "most exclusive" eatery—the Empire Steak Building.

"Get some steak in my belly!" Troy bellowed as he rubbed his stomach.

That night's challenge was a reverse scavenger hunt, which I'd never heard of before. Apparently, we were supposed to walk around the ship, filling a pillowcase with random objects in the hopes that they were on Dan and Michelle's list. Then we'd reconvene thirty minutes later at the teen club, hear what was *actually* on the list, and see which team had gotten the most items. Which as a planner, made absolutely no sense to me, but whatever.

Dan handed us a pillowcase. "Things you *own*," Dan emphasized with a wink.

"And remember to get creative," Michelle added with her cheery-kindergarten-teacher pep. "We're not harsh graders over here. With the right imaginative spin, we can be convinced of anything!"

Dan directed his microphone down to the three oddly matched kids. "Can you let me know what your team name is?"

The kids looked at one another and didn't say anything. Finally, a short girl with a half-shaved head said, "We're Team Dino."

"Great! Team Dino. And what about you all?" Dan asked, turning the microphone over to our side of the club.

"We're Team Pineapple Pizza," Sebastian said, turning and winking at me. I glanced away, feeling a blush creep up my neck.

"Gross," Charlie said at the same time as Dan shouted, "Fabulous! Let's get started, then. I'm going to count down from three. Make sure to return here before thirty minutes are up or you'll be disqualified. Three . . . two . . . GO!"

"Hold up," I said as the other team dashed for the door, my competitive streak activating. "Let's strategize. I think if we break into two groups, we'll be able to get a better assortment."

Troy nodded. "Good call, Liv."

"Okay, so I'll go with Ash and Troy," Jules declared.

I shot Jules a look. "I was thinking the two of us would go together." Otherwise, I would have to go to the boys' room. Or worse—they would have to go to mine.

"We've gotta split up the girls!" Jules countered. "Our stuff is too similar."

I glanced at Sebastian and Charlie. Sebastian was holding the pillowcase, a wide smile spread across his face. Meanwhile, Charlie looked as thrilled as I felt at the team divisions.

"Let's do this, crew!" Troy said before racing off with Jules and Ash.

"So, sub-six, right?" Sebastian asked, and before I could respond, he had taken off.

Charlie met my gaze and rolled his eyes, but we had little option except to follow Sebastian.

Sebastian was in flip-flops, but I could tell immediately that he was a runner. His legs glided effortlessly out of the teen club, past the kids' pools and waterslides. He stood casually in front of the elevator banks, his breathing completely even, as he waited for Charlie and me to catch up.

"Should we start in our room?" Sebastian asked.

"Whatever," Charlie grumbled.

Sebastian hit the button for the tenth floor. As soon as the doors opened, he was off again. We sprinted past identical gray doors until Sebastian finally came to a halt in front of room 1134. He flashed his key card and the door clicked open.

The room was the same size as mine, but instead of a desk, there were two sets of bunk beds, one against each wall. Clothes were strewn across the beds and the floor, and the room smelled of socks and sulfur.

"So . . . what exactly are we looking for?" I was used to regular scavenger hunts from camp. Lists of blue hats and tropical postcards and random things like analog watches (whatever those were). But I was going to need a new strategy for tonight's challenge.

"The key to these types of hunts is to get the most diverse selection of things," Sebastian said, as if he regularly participated in reverse scavenger hunts. "And then you just make up ridiculous stretches to justify how they fit."

Charlie scoffed. "You'll be good at that, man."

Sebastian shot him a full-toothed grin. "Thanks."

"So for instance," Sebastian said, grabbing a set of keys and dangling them in the air, "this may *look* like a standard key chain. But it also can count as a"—he held out each object as he spoke—"flashlight, a baby stuffed monkey, and a"—he flipped out the nail clipper attachment—"deadly dagger."

I laughed. "Shocked you got that past airport security."

I looked around the room, feeling slightly uneasy at the prospect of going through other people's things. And not just other people's, but a group of people—mainly guys—who I had just met.

"Don't be shy," Sebastian said, reading my mind. "No one brought any crazy sex dolls or anything."

I couldn't stop my cheeks from turning red. My mind hadn't even *started* going there. "I just feel weird. I don't like touching other people's stuff."

"They're just things," Sebastian said. "And it's probably better to have an outsider's perspective. You'll be able to see the full possibility of each object."

I started in what seemed to be the safest-looking spot, the night table next to one set of bunk beds. There was a guitar pick, a photo album, some random change, and an air freshener, like the type you hung up over your car's rearview mirror.

"I guess this," I said, picking up the air freshener, "could count as a Christmas tree?"

"Yes, love that!" Sebastian said, dropping it into the pillowcase.

I felt a jolt of satisfaction. Even if it was a dumb game, that didn't mean I didn't want to win.

I looked around the room, and my eyes landed on a guitar case in the corner. "Did you bring a *guitar* on a cruise ship?"

Charlie let out a full belly laugh at that. "Yes. Yes he did."

"Hey—you never know when inspiration's gonna hit!" Sebastian said. "I'd put it in the pillowcase, if it would fit."

Charlie and Sebastian grabbed a few more random objects—a stick of deodorant, a handkerchief, a toothbrush, a baseball hat.

I knelt down and discovered a small teddy bear, the kind you customize at the mall, behind the guitar case. I picked it up. "What about this?"

"Nah," Sebastian said, placing one hand on my shoulder and taking the stuffed animal with the other. I could tell I had struck a chord, and I wished I'd never touched it.

"All right," Sebastian said, glancing over at the clock. "Let's hit up your room?"

"I don't really have anything that interesting."

"We promise we won't handle your intimates," Sebastian said. "But I'm sure you have something."

I flipped on the lights in my room, relieved at how neat I kept it. Nothing embarrassing lying out for Sebastian to mock. "I mostly just have . . . journal articles."

"Well, that could be useful!" Sebastian was leaning over me, so close I could feel his breath on my neck. "'A New Approach to the Epidemiology of Cardiac Arrest.' Or . . ." Sebastian folded the article in half and dropped it into the pillowcase. "A plan to get to Mars?"

"I'm going to get that back, right?"

"Yes, Ms. Science, don't worry."

"Ugh," I said, bristling at yet another barb at my work. "Please don't call me that."

"Noted, sorry," Sebastian said, ducking his head. I immediately regretted my choice of words. I didn't know why I had to be so touchy, when he was clearly just making a joke.

Charlie took a seat at the desk. "Pretty intense schedule, Jersey."

"Yeah." I didn't know what else to say. Did he want to make fun of me too?

"Excited for the shipwreck?" Sebastian asked, pointing at the paper I'd taped up.

"Yup." *Not that you'd understand why.*

When I turned around, Sebastian was at my night table, holding my journal. "What about this?"

In one swift movement, I grabbed it from him and shoved it into my desk drawer. "No," I said without bothering to give an explanation. That journal was definitely not leaving this room.

I opened up the drawer I had designated for dirty clothes and found the bikini top Jules had lent me. That I could do without, so I tossed it into the pillowcase.

"Nice, but we're definitely going to need some frilly under-wear," Sebastian said. "I promise to be a gentleman and not look." He turned around and held the pillowcase out toward me.

I scoffed. "Sorry to disappoint, but I didn't bring any frilly underwear on this trip." *And I don't own any, anyway*, I didn't bother adding.

"Okay, how about something with like, days of the week or animal prints?"

I pulled out a pair of plaid pajama shorts and threw them into the pillowcase. "Happy?" I asked.

"Elated," Sebastian said, shooting me a grin.

I checked the clock on the night table. "Shoot—we've got two minutes to get back."

Sebastian twisted the pillowcase, swung it behind his shoulder, and took off toward the elevator. I ran behind him, not even bothering to check whether Charlie was following us. I was many things, but a time-disqualified loser was not one of them.

Despite many cleverly spun tales from Sebastian and Jules, Team Dino won. I couldn't help feeling slightly deflated, already thinking ahead to the next night's competition and hoping we would take the lead.

As soon as we had left the teen club, Jules was whipping out her flask. "Let's celebrate second place?"

"Yesss," Troy said. "Our girl has brought the goods!"

Jules passed me the flask. I shook my head. "No thanks."

"Suit yourself!" Jules said before taking a long drink. The rest of the crew passed it around. Sebastian was the only one, aside from me, who didn't drink from it.

"Wanna head up to the observation deck?" Ash asked. "The sky's supposed to look real crazy tonight."

"Yes, good idea!" Jules cheered. We began walking toward the elevator. I silently hit the button for the ninth floor and prayed no one would notice. I didn't say anything, not wanting a repeat of the night before.

"I'm gonna call it a night," I said when the elevator doors opened. I just had to make it through the next three seconds and I would be free.

"Wanna grab some celebration ice cream?" Sebastian asked.

I shot him a look. "We lost."

"Okay—loser ice cream, then?" Sebastian stepped out, just as the doors began closing behind him. After the doors had shut,

I heard Jules whistle. I shot her a glare dark enough to make its way through the closed doors.

I crossed my arms. "Don't you want to go get drunk with everyone else?"

"Don't think I'm really in the best headspace for that."

I wondered what he meant by that, and if he wanted me to ask. But I didn't have time to get into that right now. "I really have to get back to work."

"Have you eaten yet?"

At that, my stomach grumbled. I had skipped dinner to work on the paper.

Sebastian laughed. "The ice cream machines are on the other side of this deck. Ten minutes tops. And then I promise I'll let you get back to work. But you're not going to be as productive on an empty stomach."

He wasn't wrong about that. As we walked past the Little Flippers Lounge, we passed a group of girls—they looked maybe a year or two younger than us. They all stared openly at Sebastian and then ran away, giggling. I was still looking at them when I stumbled, completely missing the step separating the ice cream station from the arcade area. Sebastian grabbed my arm to steady me.

"You good?" he asked, meeting my eyes.

All at once, it became apparent just how alone we were together, late at night. The stars were twinkling above us, and Jules's whistle was still ringing in my ears. If she was right—that everyone on cruise ships just wanted to have fun—then Sebastian was firing his charms at the wrong person.

I crossed my arms and held Sebastian's gaze. "Just to be clear—if you're looking for a cruise hookup, you're wasting your time with me. I'm sure you won't have any trouble finding someone else, though."

Sebastian bit back a grin. "What makes you think I'm looking for a cruise hookup?"

My cheeks were on fire now. Why did I have to shove my foot in my mouth like that? "I mean—just the way that Jules whistled, and—"

"It's all good," Sebastian said, smiling fully now. "I'm not looking for a cruise hookup either. You seem smart and fun and cool, and I like hanging out with smart and fun and cool people. But if you hate being around me, I can take a hint."

"No, it's fine, I just . . . didn't want to give you the wrong impression."

"Impressions clarified," Sebastian said, saluting me like a sailor.

I sighed, knowing it would look way too awkward to back out of ice cream now. "Okay, fine, let's get ice cream. Ten minutes on the clock, starting now."

"So—tell me more about this research paper," Sebastian said as he handed me a cone with vanilla-and-chocolate swirl. A group of "street" performers were loudly beatboxing behind us, so I took the cone and moved toward a bench that wouldn't require shouting.

"It will bore you."

"Don't be so sure about that. How do you know I don't read cardiac epistidomy papers for fun?"

I rolled my eyes. "Probably because if you did, you'd know the word is *epidemiology*."

"Tomato, tomahto," Sebastian said, taking a lick of his cone.

He was clearly still waiting for me to respond to his initial question. So I decided to go full force with the opposite tactic—doctor speak. "There are four main causes of heart disease, which can lead to cardiac arrest." I kept going, sure I would have him running for Jules's flask and the observation deck in no time.

But Sebastian nodded as I spoke. When I finished, he stared at me for a moment and shook his head. "Wow."

"Yeah, I know, I'm a nerd."

"That's not—" Sebastian ran a hand through his hair. "That's not what I was thinking at all. At my high school, no one really focuses on their future. It's really cool that you're so ambitious."

Ambitious. One time in sixth grade, I had come across a Venn diagram that listed different adjectives for girls and for boys. It was outdated in so many ways, but it had stuck with me. In the semicircle for supposedly "unattractive" traits for girls, the words *outspoken* and *ambitious* were listed. I remember reading that and thinking—okay, then. I will *never* strive to be seen as attractive to boys.

But Sebastian hadn't been using the word as an insult. He seemed genuine. I looked down at my feet. "I thought you were mocking me before."

"Not at all. I was like, this girl is ditching us to go do research? Okay, I need to get to know her."

I hadn't expected such sincerity from him, and I had no idea how to respond. I took another bite of my ice cream.

"So what made you want to be a doctor?" Sebastian asked.

I swallowed. I could tell him the real answer. But I never told new people about Logan. Because then their first impression of him would be as my dead brother, which couldn't have been further from who he was to me. He had been a living, breathing person, not someone to be defined by his passing.

So instead I said, "The same reason most people do? To save lives?"

"But there's got to be more to it than that. I mean, you could save lives in so many different ways. Why this one?"

I shrugged. No one had ever pressed me on this before. "It's the most direct; the most surefire."

"I see," he said. "You like being sure of things."

"Is there anything wrong with that?" I popped the rest of the cone into my mouth and wiped my hands. Our snack time was over.

"Nope," he said. "It just seems like you like being in control."

"You sound like a therapist."

"Well, that's good, since I want to be one."

"Really?" All the guys at Bleeker seemed to want to go into finance or law. I'd never heard any guys my age say they wanted to be a therapist. "Why do you want to be a therapist?"

Sebastian thought about that for a moment. "A few reasons, I guess. I was really affected by my parents' divorce, and I had an amazing psychologist. So I want to be able to help other kids like he helped me."

I nodded, taking this new information in. I was surprised he was telling me all of this. This wasn't the cocky *I'm cute and I know it* boy I had first thought he was.

"I'm sorry about your parents," I said.

"Thanks. It was for the best, though. They're much better parents separately than they ever were together."

The street performers had finished for the night and had been replaced by soft music from the overhead speakers. A new song began—a few somber guitar notes that I instantly recognized. "I love this song," I blurted out.

Sebastian closed his eyes. "I didn't even know what real emotion was until the first time I heard Amos Lee."

I couldn't believe he knew who Amos Lee was—I didn't know anyone who listened to him. Shruti was a music snob who loved unknown punk bands that performed in sweaty basement shows in the city. She deemed my music taste "sad white boys with guitars who all sound the same" and always smirked and changed the station when we drove around together.

We listened to the rest of the song without speaking. It just felt like a song you shouldn't interrupt, like something holy.

"How does he *do* that?" I asked when the song was over.

Sebastian shook his head. "He's lived a lot of life. Of love. Of heartbreak. I just think that activates new areas of the brain that never were turned on before. I'm not religious, but that song is definitely a spiritual experience."

"Exactly!" I had never heard anyone else voice my feelings about music so precisely. I hadn't sung since Logan had died, and there was a hole in my chest that I could feel, aching for the comfort that singing used to bring.

"Anyway, I promised I wouldn't keep you longer than ten minutes, and I'm a man of my word," Sebastian said, placing a hand over his heart.

"Right," I said, realizing that for a few minutes I had forgotten the time and the stack of papers in my room. "Well, thanks for forcing me to eat."

Sebastian reached a hand over to me and pulled me up from the bench. I couldn't ignore the way my heart fluttered as our fingers briefly joined together.

"See you at the competition tomorrow?"

"On one condition," I said.

"That you finish your work in time?"

I shook my head. "That we win. I don't really *do* losing."

Sebastian let out a loud laugh. "You're really something, Liv. See you tomorrow."

My parents' lights were off when I got back, so I skipped saying good night and headed straight to my room. I scrubbed at my face with the small bar of Regal Islands soap for ten minutes, wishing I owned makeup remover.

As I toweled off my face, I thought back to how I'd felt around Sebastian that night. He wasn't the totally awful spotlight-seeker I had initially pegged him as. He was actually pretty kind and easy to talk to.

But I felt the familiar rolls of anxiety kneading in my chest. I still wasn't caught up on my work, and I had so much to do.

I grabbed my journal and began to jot down my goals for the week, a focusing technique I had learned for when I felt overwhelmed by my thoughts.

1. Write the world's best research paper

2. Get to Antigua

I closed the journal and ran my fingers over the island on the cover and Logan's sloppy Sharpied letters.

Then I flipped my binder open to where I'd left off when Jules barged in earlier that night. I couldn't let anything—or any*one*—distract me from the much more important mission at hand.

SEVEN
DAY THREE AD

The train taking us through St. Kitts made yet another sharp turn, forcing my highlighter to make a big purple streak across my journal article. I puffed out an exasperated sigh through my nostrils. We'd been on the train for over an hour, and I'd only managed to read three paragraphs. I had never been good at getting work done in cars, and I was getting nauseous from the train's constant starts and stops.

My mom laid a hand on my shoulder. "Do you have to be studying right now?" she asked gently.

"Yes, because you made me go on this cruise, when I was planning on working on this paper all week." I knew I sounded like a petulant teenager, but what mom seriously yelled at her kid for studying?

As the train entered a narrow bridge, I sucked in my breath. There was no way a bridge like this could support such a big train. I kissed the air twice, said "Thank you God," and squeezed my eyes tightly shut until we had somehow safely made it across.

When I opened my eyes, I found a woman in a bright tropical shirt with a tray of bloodred drinks in front of my parents. "Would either of you like a St. Kitts margarita?"

"We're just fine, but thank you," my mom said, wrinkling her nose.

My dad laughed. "Noon seems a bit early to start drinking."

I rolled my eyes. Of course my parents weren't going to drink—on a train—regardless of the time.

We bumped our way onto an extremely narrow, one-way road. Or at least by all science and reason it should have been one-way. But when the train screeched to a halt to let a speeding car pass by, I realized that I was wrong. Then the car slowed down, and soon the driver was . . . having a conversation . . . with the driver of our train. And we weren't moving anytime soon.

I sighed again and checked my watch. "Do you know when we're getting back?" As long as we made it back to the ship by two thirty—which was the end-time listed in the Regal Islands daily itinerary—I would have a full three hours to work before I had to send over the outline I had promised to Shruti that night.

The train employee leaned over and smiled. "We're on island time, sweetheart," she told me. "Relax, enjoy yourself!"

There it was—*relax*, my least favorite word in the English language. But I smiled back, not wanting to come across as the textbook definition of an ungrateful teenage tourist.

"This isn't a real train," Justin said far too loudly.

I began rubbing small circles on Justin's back, as his behavioral therapist had taught me to do at any signs of overstimulation. I had assumed he and Matt would be terrified to be thrown into a completely new environment, but they had been handling the trip like champs. They were usually well-behaved, but if things strayed too far from routine, that could cause overstimulation. I hated seeing the pain on their faces when that happened. I knew exactly how it felt when the tightening in your chest made it hard to breathe.

"This is a special train, sweetie," my mom said. "An island train."

"Not like Amtrak," Matt added.

Matt was right—it certainly wasn't like Amtrak. The train had an open roof, covered only by a thin yellow tarp. Green hills rose in the distance against deep blue skies dotted with puffy white clouds. Groups of rocks along the coast separated the land from sea.

As we rounded a corner, an adorable village came into view. Each building was painted a different shade of pastel and had the same rust-red shackle roof. It looked just like the villages Logan and I had researched online, when we had looked up Antigua.

I shut my folder, giving up on the notion of getting any real work done while we bumped to and fro. I closed my eyes, letting the breeze wash over my face, and thought back to the last long train ride I'd taken. When I was seven and Logan was thirteen, my parents took us on a twenty-two-hour train down to Florida to see our grandparents. My parents preferred the train, because they could still get work done while we traveled—a gene they had passed down to me. They had booked a private car and buried themselves in their laptops. Meanwhile, Logan kept me entertained. He stood up on an empty row of seats and narrated the train's sudden starts and stops in a low voice to make me laugh and stop worrying that we were about to die at any moment.

"Remember that train ride we took to Florida with Lo—" But before I could even finish saying his name, my mom had raised her eyebrows and mouthed, "Not in front of the twins." Right. Because that was the rule.

I bit my lip and looked out the window, keeping my thoughts to myself. I smiled, remembering how Logan had taken advantage of our empty train car, putting on an entire musical and making me forget that even on vacation, our parents weren't really there with us. He flew from pole to pole, transforming the train car into a Broadway theater. People paused on their way through our car, stopping to watch him perform, until we had an entire audience standing around clapping.

"Look, Livvy, look," Matt whispered in my ear, jolting me back to the present. In front of us, a mother goat was crossing the tracks with three baby goats behind her. My heart seized as I thought of Mr. Snuggles Factory back home. I missed that damn cat so much.

"And look—" My mom pointed, just as the train came to a stop.

"Sheep sheep!" Matt cheered.

"Close—goats," I said, brushing back a stray curl that had fallen in front of Matt's eye and inhaling a whiff of his honey and lavender–scented shampoo. My parents had packed all the twins' products, including their organic, vegan, GMO-free shampoo, the same brand they had been using since they were babies. We used to give them little sink baths, because they were far too small and fragile for the real tub.

Matt snuggled into me further and continued whispering "Look, look" whenever we passed a new animal. We spent the rest of the ride identifying different animals (the twins had quite a knowledge base, thanks to Birdie, a magical talking parrot who was the star of a wildly popular YouTube show for kids).

When we pulled back into the parking lot, I couldn't help realizing I had somehow managed to enjoy myself.

But with that realization came the instant onset of guilt that enveloped me whenever I found myself having a good time with my family.

Because that meant I was forgetting him, letting Logan's presence slip further away. Just like my parents intended.

I couldn't let myself forget this *wasn't* my family—not my whole family. And it never would be.

When we finally made it back from the excursion—at three thirty, an hour late—I rushed to my room. I closed the blinds, put on my theta wave playlist, and buried myself in work.

Two hours later, I had managed to cobble together a half-decent outline for the paper. I sprinted over to the business center so that I could send it to Shruti. As soon as I emailed her, a chat message popped up.

Shruti: omg hi hi is it really YOU
Olivia: it is really me

Shruti: so how's the boat

Olivia: tacky. big. somehow floating on water

Shruti: ugh fine. thanks for sending the outline.

Olivia: np. you'll have it back by tonight? 10pm?

Shruti: yes, madam. promise me you won't work on it before
then?? i don't want another sophomore year chem lab
disaster . . .

I *had* been planning on working on it some more that night.
But Shruti did have a point. I didn't have regular internet access,
and she'd be furious if I wrote an entirely new paper that ignored
all her edits. Again.

Olivia: promise!

Shruti: good, go have some fun. what's the man situation at sea?

Olivia: i don't understand the question

Shruti: DID YOU FIND A HUSBAND FOR YOU AND ONE FOR ME

Olivia: oh no. boat wifi. crashing waves. iceberg. losing signal.

I logged off.

EIGHT

Since I was banished from work until later that night, I decided to try out the track. I laced up my sneakers, put on my running playlist, and took the elevator down to the sixth floor, where the track was.

This floor was quieter than the others, consisting mainly of the spa, a basketball court, a mini golf course, and a 10,000-square-foot fitness center—which looked completely empty. The cruise ship and people around me blurred into the background as my world was narrowed to just my steady breathing, my chest expanding in and out, and the sound of Journey.

Which is why I loved running. The intense physicality of it was the only way I could pause my racing thoughts.

I loved the control I had when I ran. The contained atmosphere of the track, with its red-rubber surface and clean white lines. How each lap was exactly 400 meters, making an even 1,600 after four laps. How I could go home and analyze my times online and see steady improvement. How the more I ran, the better my mile time got.

I started running in fourth grade, after I had definitively proven the area of my brain responsible for hand-eye coordination was missing. Logan had been the athlete—a star basketball player, but also able to pick up any sport on a whim.

Meanwhile, I couldn't catch a pop fly or dribble a basketball or throw a lacrosse ball if my life depended on it. I figured people were either born athletes, like Logan, or . . . born like me. And I was a pretty poor runner as well, at first. But that was fine—running was only about me. At least I wasn't letting the rest of some team down.

Logan came to all of my elementary school "races," and screamed his lungs out cheering for me, even though I always came in dead last. But toward the end of the season, something clicked. My breathing got steadier. My footwork got smoother.

I kept running after the season ended, with Logan by my side. We ran endless laps together at the high school down the block, through that summer and into the next fall and winter. By spring of fifth grade, I was good.

After Logan died, I ran more and more. The track was the one place I could finally be alone. I didn't have to talk to anyone, to answer for the millionth time "how I was doing." (Badly, was always the real answer, but no one wanted to hear that.) I never wanted to stop running. Because stopping meant my thoughts would return, the constant questioning would return, meant that Logan was really and truly gone.

So I kept going, long after my legs had turned to lead. Bloody blisters sprouted up across my toes, and my quads turned solid. I liked feeling them, a reminder that a part of me was objectively strong, even if inside I felt like I was made of Jell-O.

I had just finished showering when, like clockwork, I found Jules at my door.

This time she had come prepared. She held out two floral mini-dresses for me to choose from. They looked identical, and neither was something I would normally ever wear. I chose the path of least resistance—the one that zipped up back, instead of the one with a million different strings somehow holding it together.

"Good choice," Jules said, throwing off her shirt and bra and putting on the strappy dress. I shielded my eyes to give Jules some privacy, and she laughed.

"So what happened last night with Sebastian?" Jules asked, raising her eyebrows.

"Um, nothing?"

Jules groaned. "We've only got a week here, girl! Name one reason why you won't hook up with him."

I wondered if Jules had some secret affiliate relationship with Regal Islands, if she got a cut from every match she coordinated or something.

"Because we live one thousand miles away."

"Right now, you live one thousand *feet* away. Do you always jump to worst-case future scenarios?"

I took the dress into the bathroom. "I jump to most realistic future scenarios," I shouted from behind the door.

Jules groaned. "I think I have a way to fix that."

"Oh yeah?" I asked as I walked out of the bathroom.

Jules shot me another mischievous grin and pulled her flask out. "Tequila."

"Oh, thanks, but that's okay, I—"

Jules cut me off. "I know, I know, you don't drink. Because it's illegal and what if your parents find out and what if you get sick and—"

I rolled my eyes. Of course Jules had to turn this around on me, mock me for being too much of a wet blanket. But I had to admit her reasoning wasn't so far off.

"How about just one tiny sip?" she asked, dangling the container in front of my face.

"I'm really okay," I said, crossing my arms in front of my chest. This was going to be a *long* week.

Jules looked around my room, her eyes landing on the Brown University pendant I always carried around for good luck.

"What about when you get to *Brown University*?" she asked, affecting a haughty accent.

"What about it?"

"I mean, you know even people at *Brown* drink."

"Not everyone parties, Jules."

"That's where you're wrong. Lily's friend Sam goes there. It's not like high school, where the smart kids don't drink. *Every*one there drinks. And Sam told Lily that it's always the really sheltered kids that end up going way too hard and not knowing how to manage classwork and parties."

I thought about Francheska, the valedictorian two years before. She had gotten into Harvard, then had taken a year of medical leave after the first semester. Which had turned into two—she still hadn't returned. Rumor had it that her workload had been too intense, which had led to an Adderall-and-whiskey addiction.

"What if you thought of tonight as a—trial run, before college?" Jules asked. She really did know how to speak my language. "No one here knows you. You're not going to get arrested. I'll make sure you don't go too hard. Then when you get to college, you'll be one step ahead of all the other nerds." Jules laughed. "Excuse me—the other smart kids. Plus, connections are one of the most important parts of college. And you're never going to get to know people unless you go to parties."

I had to admit that it wasn't the *worst* plan I'd ever heard. Bleeker Prep was more insular than most high schools. Which was one of the reasons I loved it. If they found out you drank or used drugs—even off campus—you got kicked out. But I knew that wasn't what college would be like. I wouldn't always have that safety net. I'd have tons of research projects, and I'd need to figure out how to get my work done and go to parties. And I *did* love planning in advance. I didn't want to end up like Francheska.

"Okay, fine. One sip."

Jules's face lit up. "Really? That worked?"

I reached over and took the flask from Jules. My parents would *kill* me if they found out what I was about to do. They'd never even talked to me about alcohol. They just assumed I knew to stay away from it. Because I wasn't Logan.

I unscrewed the cap and tipped it back to my mouth, not exactly sure how much one drink entailed. The liquid burned its way down my throat and tasted how I imagined gasoline would taste. I had to throw a hand over my mouth to keep from gagging.

When I handed the flask back to Jules, her eyes were wide. "Wow, Liv. When you commit to something—you commit." Jules put the flask to her lips and took an even longer swig, downing the liquid as easily as if it were Coke.

I could still feel the metallic taste lingering at the back of my throat. It wasn't pleasant, but it was different, an initiation into a new world. This small act of rebellion had somehow made me feel a little closer to Logan.

I smiled and took Jules's hand. "To the hot tub?"

Jules and I made our way to the back of the pool deck, past the Naked Cowboy and Frank Sinatra guy (who tonight was singing Elvis instead). We found the crew in the same hot tub as the first night. Sebastian met my eyes and grinned when we came closer. I turned away, focusing intently on removing my flip-flops, and tried to resist the way my chest tightened in response.

"Finally, the voices of reason have arrived," Troy bellowed.

Charlie groaned and looked over at Jules and me. "Please tell Troy that no way in hell are we going to take part in another planned teen competition tonight. Or any night."

Jules climbed into the hot tub. I stood for a second outside it, trying to quickly calculate if it would look too obvious if I sat next to Troy, even though there was a bigger opening next to Sebastian. But Sebastian scooted over a few inches as I stepped in, which would have made it look weird if I didn't sit next to him.

I winced as the water met my charred skin. I had applied sunscreen three times that day, but I wasn't used to being out in the sun, and my body had gotten roasted during the open-air train ride.

"Someone got burnt," Charlie said, eyeing my apple-red shoulders.

I grimaced. "A little bit, yeah."

"You're a full-on lobster!" Charlie continued. "Been a little while since you've gotten some sun?"

"Yeah," I sighed.

"So who's ready for night two of domination?" Troy asked.

"Not again, man," Charlie said at the same time as Jules cheered, "I am!"

"I have an idea for how to make the competition tonight a wee bit more fun." Jules hopped out of the hot tub and returned with her flask. I bit back a groan. Jules was seriously obsessed with drinking.

Troy put a giant hand on her shoulder and squeezed. "Yes! I knew we teamed up with you two for a reason."

Jules passed around the flask, and the crew took long gulps. Sebastian smiled as he handed it to me. "Do you drink?"

I thought about the picture he must have had of me, of this uptight workaholic who didn't know how to have fun. "Yeah, I drink," I said. *As of fifteen minutes ago*, I didn't bother adding. I didn't want to drink to impress him, but the last thing I wanted was him thinking that he knew everything about me already, that I was some two-dimensional goody two-shoes. I took the flask from him and tilted it back. The liquid burned, but it went down easier this time.

And—I sort of liked the way my body was relaxing, the way my face kept forming an easy smile. It made this whole cruise thing a little easier to bear. Plus, tonight now counted as an experiment. If I wanted to prove that drunk Olivia could still manage to ace her work, then I needed to fully commit and become drunk Olivia.

As the crew joked around me, I found myself disassociating, focusing on the way the hot bubbles felt on my raw flesh, how I could see Sebastian's stomach expand and contract with his breath, how I couldn't stop thinking about his every minuscule movement. What the hell had gotten into me?

I snapped back to attention as I realized everyone was climbing out of the hot tub. "Time to go, Liv," Troy said. "We've got a competition to win!"

NINE

Michelle welcomed us like old friends as we entered. "Team Pineapple Pizza, welcome back!" She then went on to explain the rules for that night. Our crew would be competing against Team Dino—which now included two more out-of-place-looking teens—in a series of "live photo" challenges. Michelle and Dan would shout out a picture, and we'd have to create it with our bodies.

"Reminder—the final night of the cruise, the winning team will get treated to a free meal at—*THE EMPIRE STEAK BUILDING!*" Dan bellowed, as if he were announcing the Mega Millions amount for the week.

"WOOOO!" Troy cheered, stomping his feet wildly.

"Cool it, bro," Charlie said.

Dan laughed. "Looks like we've got some pretty excited contenders."

Michelle turned up the music—a playlist of loud and out-dated pop music—and read out the first challenge. "You have one minute to become a cruise ship."

Easy enough. Before I knew it, my group-leader personality was busting out. Yes, this was a silly competition. But did that mean I wanted to *lose*? No.

I positioned Sebastian, Charlie, and Ash on their sides, stretched out head to toe to form the outer edges of the ship. Then I placed Troy in front as captain and, curling up in the middle of the boys' formation, Jules and I became the hot tubs.

After an overly drawn-out "conference," Michelle and Dan announced, "And the winners of the first round are . . . Team Pineapple Pizza!"

"YEAH PINEAPPLLLE!" Troy practically burst a vein, he was shouting so hard.

Ash high-fived Jules, and Sebastian shot me another smile. I couldn't stop myself from smiling back at him, pleased with my work.

For the next round, we were supposed to become a zoo. Team Dino immediately began running around, squawking like monkeys and goats.

Jules and I walked around in a circle, holding up fake protesting signs. Charlie pretended to be an angry trapped bear. Sebastian napped in the corner as a baby bear. Troy tried to break into the bear cave.

Team Dino won that round.

The final challenge was to create a pool party. We needed to do something fun—something active, clearly, if we wanted Dan and Michelle's vote.

"What about a chicken fight?" Jules suggested. I nodded, knowing that was exactly the type of childish camaraderie that would earn us points.

Troy grabbed Jules and hoisted her up on his shoulders, and Ash followed suit, climbing onto Charlie's shoulders. Jules and Ash began swatting at one another. I couldn't help thinking that we had all been drinking, so if someone fell, they could really get hurt.

But then Sebastian turned to me and bent down so I could climb onto his shoulders, and I obliged without a second thought. I joined in the fight, batting at Jules and Ash. Pretty soon, we were all shouting and giggling and trying to push one another over.

Jules shoved me with more force than I expected, and I wobbled backward, my heart soaring as my head fell back. I inhaled sharply, picturing the medical passage I had read earlier that afternoon. When the neck snaps just below the brainstem, the spinal cord swells, causing instant paralysis—or death. But then Sebastian strengthened his grip around my legs to steady me. All thoughts of imminent death flew out of my brain, replaced by an intense awareness of his surprisingly strong biceps pressed against the outside of my legs.

When Michelle announced that we had won that challenge—and therefore that night's competition—Troy let out a cheer that could surely be heard around the ship. I cheered along with him, competitive adrenaline firing through my veins.

But as Sebastian gently lowered me to the ground and stepped to the side, I felt a pit forming in my stomach. I was suddenly disappointed that the game was over. I glanced back up at Sebastian, who raised an eyebrow when he caught my eye. I quickly turned away, my heart pounding even louder than before.

We gleefully munched on fries at Katz's Deli while passing off and finishing the rest of Jules's flask.

Jules and Ash had been going back and forth about their respective Ping-Pong championship histories, each proclaiming they were the better player. Finally, Ash suggested they figure this out once and for all, so they headed up to the game room.

After that, Sebastian leaned back and put a hand against his stomach. "I'm still sort of hungry. Pineapple pizza, anyone?"

I felt my heart rate rise. It was clear that Sebastian and I were the only ones who liked pineapple pizza, that he was trying to spend more time with me. Alone.

"Ew, no thanks, bro," Charlie said.

"Liv?" Sebastian asked, turning to me.

I gulped—it was getting late, later than I'd intended to stay out. But then I thought about what Jules had said. About how I needed to be prepared for college. Which I was sure would entail many late-night pizza runs. I needed to make sure that I could still get my work done.

"I guess I could be down for a quick slice." I glanced over at Sebastian, his wavy hair catching rays of moonlight. I had agreed because he was merely a guinea pig in my pre-college experiment, I reminded myself. And we were just getting pizza.

"Cool. See ya later," Sebastian said to Charlie and Troy.

I caught Charlie directing a look at Sebastian, but when Charlie noticed me looking, he grabbed a few more fries and shoved them into his mouth.

Sebastian and I began walking toward the elevator. The sky was dark and the stars were shining a lot more brightly than they did in New Jersey.

"How are Matt and Justin doing?" Sebastian asked.

"Pretty good, thanks," I said, surprised he remembered their names. "You were really great with them yesterday. I've never seen Matt warm up to anyone so quickly."

"It was nice getting to be around little kids again," Sebastian said. "Matt reminds me of my little cousin Peter. His family moved to California last year, so I've missed spending time with him."

"Do you have any siblings?" I asked.

"An older sister, Molly," he said. "She's a freshman at Mizzou. What about you? I mean, aside from the twins."

"I have an older brother too." The words were out before I could stop myself. I never talked about Logan, but there was just something about Sebastian that made me feel like he would understand. And the more I kept Logan to myself, the more I worried I was forgetting him. I didn't want to be like my parents.

"Is he on the cruise?" Sebastian asked. Probably because I had mentioned Logan in the present tense, a technique my therapist had taught me. Because even though he was no longer alive, he would always be my older brother.

"No," I said, looking down at the wooden planks beneath us. We were at the elevator banks now. I hit the button for the eighth floor, where Roy's was. "He actually died a few years ago."

"Oh." We got out of the elevator and began making our way toward the long row of lit-up restaurants. Sebastian met my eyes. "I'm so sorry."

"It's okay." It wasn't okay, but I always said that on instinct. Because what else was there to say?

Sebastian shook his head. "It's not. I know it's not. And I'm sure you've heard 'I'm sorry' a million times already. What's his name?"

"Logan." I wasn't sure the last time I had said his name out loud. It felt nice to hear. I had always loved his name. The way "Logan" and "Olivia" sounded together, the neat way our names started with the same two letters in reverse.

"Were you close?" he asked as we grabbed a few slices of pineapple pizza and made our way over to a booth in the back corner.

"Yeah," I said with a small smile. "Really close. He's actually sort of the reason I agreed to go on this cruise."

"What? You weren't jumping for joy when your parents offered you this"—he gestured around at the mustard-yellow decor of the pizza place—"week of class and paradise?"

"Yeah, it's not really my idea of fun. But when I realized it docked at Antigua, I agreed to go." In only five days, I'd finally make it to the shipwreck in Antigua and fulfill my promise to Logan. I hoped by then, I would know what I was looking for there.

Sebastian nodded, not taking his eyes off me, even as he brought the pizza to his mouth, so I kept going. "Logan and I—we had this silly childhood dream of going to Antigua together. And exploring shipwrecks."

Ugh—I was really full-on babbling now. Why was I telling this boy I had just met all these private things? Was this how drunk people acted? Was I drunk?

"Ah—so that's why you're doing the shipwreck excursion."

Wow—this boy had a good memory.

I nodded. "Sorry I'm talking so much. I haven't ever really drank before. Drunk before? Drinked?" I took a bite of the luke-warm pizza.

"I think it's drinked," Sebastian said, giving me another smile that set off a pinball chain of emotions inside my body. "So how is it?"

"It's . . . nice," I said. "The anxious part of my brain shuts off. I feel . . . lighter. Is this what normal people feel like?" I was *really* going all out now and telling this boy everything. He must have thought I was deranged.

"Normal people are boring," he said, staring into my eyes. "And you seem to be anything but boring."

I felt as if someone had just set off a series of fireworks inside my chest. I tried to cover up my reaction with a laugh, but it came out more as a strangled cough. "So are you saying it's not normal for a seventeen-year-old to have an eight-page Excel spreadsheet with her fifteen-year plan?"

Sebastian's eyes widened, and then he let out a loud, high-pitched laugh. "No, no, *completely* normal. So what's on that spreadsheet?"

I ticked the items off on my fingers. "Brown University— eight-year combined undergraduate and medical program. Research focus on heart disease. Residency in New York. Practicing doctor by thirty."

But Sebastian didn't seem thrown off by my word vomit. "Wow. Impressive." He folded his pizza in half and then took a few large bites. A little oil dripped onto his chin, and I had the sudden urge to wipe it off with my thumb.

I bit my lip and looked down. "And the real answer to your question yesterday—why I want to be a doctor? It's because Logan died from a heart attack. So I want to do research and figure out . . . why?"

Sebastian nodded, his dark brown eyes filled with sympathy. "That makes sense. That's a really nice way to honor Logan's memory."

I hadn't felt like I'd been honoring his memory at all. I never talked about him.

"It must have been really hard to lose him," Sebastian said quietly.

I nodded. "Yeah . . . it was." I traced the outline of my plate and did my best to swallow away the giant lump that had formed in my throat. "It is."

Sebastian reached across the table and took my hand. He rubbed his thumb over my palm, which sent a shock of electricity straight up my arm and to my heart.

"Tell me about him."

I told Sebastian all about Logan—how we'd seen *Rent* seven times on Broadway. How we used to put on tea parties with my Barbies and perform musicals for our cat. How he supported everything I did—he would always encourage me to go out for parts in school plays and shower me with praise when he saw my report cards, telling me how smart I was. Meanwhile, he'd say he was the screwup—which couldn't have been further from the truth. Sure, he wasn't great when it came to English and math, but he starred in all the school musicals and was on track to be a D1 basketball player—until the car accident his junior year, which fractured his leg in two places. How then the plan became that I would get rich and support us both. And how we'd live in a castle in Antigua.

When I glanced at the clock, I realized it was already quarter to one—fifteen minutes until the ship's curfew for anyone under eighteen. I never stayed out so late. But I had been so energized by our conversation, I hadn't even felt tired. Or concerned about how much work I still had to do that night.

When we got to my door, Sebastian pulled me in for a hug. "Night, Liv." I put my head against his chest and closed my eyes for a moment. I felt the sleepiness hitting me all at once.

"Meet me at the hot dog cart tomorrow?" Sebastian asked, his arms still wrapped around me.

I looked over at my desk, at the carefully constructed color-coded schedule, reminding me that tomorrow afternoon was blocked off for research. But when I opened my mouth, what came out was, "Four p.m.?"

"See you then." He flashed me one more grin and then turned and began walking away.

I flopped facedown on my bed, expecting to fall asleep immediately. But my mind was racing. I stared up at the ceiling and opened up Spotify on my phone. "Cigarettes and Cola" by Jet came on. I listened to it over and over as I felt my body floating away.

I hadn't talked that much about Logan since . . . well, ever. After Logan had died, I had mostly stopped talking to anyone who knew him. And then I transferred to Bleeker, where none of my friends knew about him. And the only time my parents ever said his name out loud was once a year at temple, on his Yahrzeit—the Jewish anniversary of his death. They would mechanically state his name, their faces devoid of emotion, before chanting the Mourner's Kaddish.

But tonight, it had all come pouring out of me, like it had been bottled tightly and shaken, exploding out as soon as I loosened the lid.

Talking about Logan felt . . . nice. Nicer than I'd expected. I just had this feeling that he knew where I was and that I was okay. And that he'd be happy.

And it was all because of Sebastian. He had gotten me to open up in a way I never had before. I felt anxious pinpricks shooting around my chest as I thought of the way he'd gazed into my eyes.

I grabbed my journal so that I could sort out my thoughts.

Reasons I should not get close to Sebastian:

1. *This cruise is over in seven days.*
2. *I have the most important presentation of my life in six days. I need to remain laser focused on that.*
3. *He lives one thousand miles away.*
4. *Therefore, I probably will never see him again after this cruise ends.*

Reasons Sebastian isn't the worst:

    1. He's a good listener.

    2. I feel happier around him.

    3. And fine, he is objectively cute and charming, and his smile . . .

Now I had two lists—pros and cons. Perfect. I read them over, so that I could come to the best conclusion.

The reasons in the first list were all so logical on paper. And there were more of them than there were in the second. But for once, that wasn't enough to sway me. Because I didn't know how to rationalize the way my heart slowed down when Sebastian listened and asked thoughtful questions about Logan. Or the way my heart sped up when he put his hand on mine.

I couldn't lie to myself any longer. I liked Sebastian. I liked him a lot.

Which meant I needed a new plan.

TEN
DAY FOUR AD

I woke up the next morning with a splitting headache. I had drunk a *lot*. I glanced over at my desk, at the pile of research papers that I was supposed to have gone through earlier that morning.

The door connecting my room to my parents' room opened. "You up, hon? We have to leave for our appointment in fifteen minutes."

Crap. I had forgotten all about the appointment my mom and I had made with Cindy and Jules. I had planned on getting up at eight so that I'd have time to run to the business center and read over Shruti's notes on my outline. Now I barely had time to brush my teeth. So much for that stupid plan. I wanted to kick myself for how much I had drunk, how late I had stayed out.

But I guess that was the whole point of the experiment—to make sure I didn't do anything stupid like this in college. And I would be sure not to screw up like this again this week. The research fair was in *five* days. My schedule couldn't suffer another setback.

"Yeah, I'm up," I said. "I'll be ready in a few."

I walked with my mom over to Buoyancy, the ship's spa. Today was a day "at sea," so we wouldn't be docking at any new ports. "You know what that means," Cindy had said over breakfast the morning before, clapping her hands together. "Spa day!" she and Jules had trilled together.

"Diane, Olivia, you have to join us. I have heard their deep tissue massages are to *die* for."

I had gotten a massage once before, because Shruti thought I needed to "relax" before taking the SATs. But the last thing I had done during that massage was relax—I was uncomfortable the whole time but too nervous to say anything. I spent the entire time gritting my teeth and reciting SAT vocabulary in my head.

I knew my mom wasn't a fan of strangers touching her bare back either. But she also wasn't one to turn down a friend. And we didn't really have a good excuse.

"Girls, so glad you made it!" Cindy said. Of course she was the type of mom to refer to any woman under ninety as a "girl."

Although it was nine, the spa was dark, lit only by candles. My head felt like it was about to split into two, though, so I was grateful for the darkness.

"Welcome to Buoyancy," the woman behind the front desk whispered. *Amanda* was sewn in giant, curlicue letters on the left pocket of her starchy white polo. "Do you have an appointment with us today?"

"We do," Cindy responded in her cheery, near-shouting voice, which only exacerbated my headache. "We were wondering if we could add on our friends, Diane and Olivia?"

I grabbed a brochure and glanced at the list of services. When I saw the prices—$80 for a pedicure, $140 for a massage—my eyes practically shot out of my head. No way would my mom agree to this.

"We were thinking about the Soho Relaxation package," Cindy said, pointing to the special advertised on the desk. "How does that sound?"

The special was $240—*per person*! I knew the Lees had money, but I didn't realize they had *that* much money.

My family was comfortable, and my parents did well enough to afford private school and private aides for the twins. But when it came to anything aside from education or basic necessities, my parents made it clear that had to be earned through chores or babysitting.

The biggest fights my parents had with Logan were always over money. The year of the accident, it seemed like every week my dad was yelling at Logan. Once he accused him of taking money from his dresser drawer. Logan denied it, and I never doubted him.

"It looks like we have room for a party of four in thirty minutes," Amanda said. "But you'll have complimentary access to the steam lounge if you don't mind waiting."

"Oh, that's fine, you don't have to wait for us—" I started.

"No, no, the steam lounge is all the rave," Cindy said with a wave of her hand. "Do not worry!" As if I had been worried about them. I had so much work to catch up on, and I did not have all day to just lie around in the spa.

Amanda checked us in, and we were instructed to head to the back, to change into robes. My mom, unsurprisingly, headed into the toilet stall to change. If some families were naked families, then my family was a three-layers-with-a-ski-jacket family. Except for Logan. He was always the first person in a game of Truth or Dare to run butt naked through our camp. Before anyone had even dared him.

Cindy and Jules removed all their clothes and stepped into their robes. I turned around and quickly removed my clothes and put my robe on.

When we walked into the lounge, we were greeted by soft elevator music and air that had clearly just been sprayed with eucalyptus.

"Mmm, I love steam rooms. Time to sweat all our toxins out!" Cindy said.

My mom nodded politely. I was pretty sure she knew there was absolutely zero scientific backing to the idea that sweat eliminated toxins—forced perspiration actually caused the kidneys to retain *more* water, holding the toxins in—but I kept my mouth shut.

A woman who looked identical to Amanda appeared at our side—she must have literally tiptoed in. "Can I offer you two a eucalyptus martini?" she asked my mom and Cindy, using her soft, soothing spa voice. I glanced up at the clock. It was nine thirty.

"Ooh, yes please!" Cindy said, clapping her hands together. "These are delicious," she told my mom. She cupped her hand over her mouth and stage-whispered, "I've been coming back every day for them."

"Sure, I'll try one," my mom said. Wow—the ocean air must really be getting to her. I had to clench my teeth to stop myself from gaping.

The woman handed the drinks to my mom and Cindy, then gave glasses of sparkling water to Jules and me.

"Cheers!" Cindy and Jules exclaimed together as they clinked their glasses to ours.

"So," Cindy said, after taking a large sip of her drink, "I want to hear all of the goss. Jules has already told me all about Ash, and it appears that you have a suitor as well?"

My face turned so red it felt purple. I knew Jules and her mom had some type of weird *Gilmore Girls*-type relationship— Jules said they got *weekly* massages together—but my mom and I certainly did *not*. We talked often about tests and grades and schedules, but not about . . . feelings. Much less dating, not that there was anything to discuss.

My mom turned to me. "This is news to me." My mom had forced a small smile onto her face. I could tell she was trying to act like a "cool mom" around Cindy.

"Oh," Cindy said, throwing a perfectly manicured hand up over her mouth. "Did I accidentally spill the tea?" Wow. Jules's mom was like a carbon copy of her. She didn't even look that much older; they could have passed for sisters.

"No," I mumbled, not wanting to embarrass Cindy or Jules. "It's fine. It's nothing, really."

"Well, it's not *nothing*," Jules said in a singsong voice. "And Sebastian is pretty freaking cute."

"I'm not surprised," Cindy said. "If you're anything like your mom, you're going to turn out to be quite the little heart-breaker."

"Cindy! That is not true." Now it was my mom's turn to exclaim, and my turn to snap my head toward her. My *mom*? A heartbreaker? I knew she and Cindy had met in high school. But as far as I knew, my mom had been a nun before she'd met my dad in college.

Cindy wagged her finger. "Don't think I forgot the *three* prom invitations you turned down, just so you could go with me, because Chad dumped me the week before."

My mom had been asked to prom—by *three* different guys? I had never really thought of my mom as a young person before. She had always just seemed like a *mom*, like she came out of the womb as an adult.

"That's not quite how I remember it," my mom said, but a small smile played out on her lips. The martini seemed to be doing its job. She seemed relaxed for once, her feet tucked under her and her hair thrown up in an uncharacteristic ponytail. "And I'm pretty sure Billy only asked me so that he could spend more time with you."

"Ooh, Billy McClaren, that sends me back," Cindy said. "So, Olivia, tell us about this Sebastian."

I glanced at my mom. She was looking at me cautiously.

She seemed so vulnerable and open that I felt my heart clench. And I was bursting to talk about what was going on with Sebastian, so . . . I took a deep breath.

Just as I was about to open my mouth, the martini woman walked in. "We can take the first two guests."

"Girls, you can go ahead. That'll give us moms a chance to catch up and finish our 'tinis!"

Jules and I followed the woman back to one of the private rooms. "How ya feeling?" Jules asked.

"Bad," I said. "Head very throbby."

"Thought that might be the case." Jules reached into the pocket of her robe and then took my hand. She slid two pills into it.

I gave her a look.

"Relax—it's just Advil."

I grabbed a water bottle from a table we passed and swallowed the pills. Then I downed the rest of the water bottle before letting out a yawn. "Thanks."

"Baby's first hangover—I'm honored to witness it."

I stuck out my tongue at Jules and then looked over my shoulder, just to make sure our moms were still out of earshot. Luckily, they hadn't seemed to notice the blinding headache I was suffering from.

Jules and I entered the massage room, which was also dark and playing soothing music. I wondered if that's why people liked spas so much—maybe they were a secret hangover cure.

"Your masseuses will be with you in one minute," the woman whispered before stepping out.

Jules tossed her robe on the chair and then lay down on the massage table—*stark naked*. What the hell? Was that the protocol?

"Um, do I have to . . ."

Jules laughed. "Relax, you can keep your robe on if you want. It's just a lot more comfortable if you don't."

Clearly, we had different definitions of comfortable. I readjusted the belt on my robe, tightening it around me, and lay down on the second table, which was a few inches away from Jules's.

Jules turned her head so that she was facing me. "So, did you and Sebastian . . ." Her voice trailed off, replaced by excessive eyebrow wriggling.

"Did we what?" I couldn't stop myself from looking around again, just in case anyone could hear us.

"You know," Jules said, her eyebrows still dancing. "DO it. Do IT! Did you do it???"

"Jules!" I felt my already sun-flushed face become an even deeper shade of red. "We just met! Of course not."

"What's wrong with having sex with someone you just met?" Jules's normally sunny face had darkened. "It's not the 1950s, you know."

I could tell I had offended Jules, so I quickly tried to back-track. "No, no, I just meant . . . there's nothing wrong with that. It's just, I've only ever kissed two other guys before. So I'm not really . . . I mean, I wouldn't even know . . ."

"Relax," Jules said, reaching over and shoving my shoulder lightly. "I'm just messing with you. Anyway, there are so many things you can do aside from sex. Do you know how to give a good blow job?"

"JULES!" I looked around once again and then dropped my voice to a whisper shout. "Our *moms* are in the other room."

Jules just shook her head and smiled. "Exactly. The *other* room. And so what? My mom knows I have sex. She doesn't care."

I scoffed. "Well, our moms are *very* different. And anyway, Sebastian and I haven't even kissed. He already told me he's not into me, so . . ." But there was a part of me that wanted Jules to tell me I was wrong.

"Well, that's a big fat lie," Jules said with a laugh. "His thing goes"—she raised her arm and stuck her pointer finger straight up in the air—"as soon as you enter the tub."

"Jules!" I was mortified, but also—I had no clue about any of these things. Jules was the one with experience, not me. And if she thought he liked me . . . maybe he did.

Just then, the door opened, and two *male* masseuses walked in. "Let's maybe finish this conversation another time?" I asked, not wanting Jules to mortify me in front of two strangers.

"Mm-hmm," Jules said as the first masseuse began placing hot stones on her back. "Now it's time to relax."

ELEVEN

When I got back from the spa, I printed out Shruti's notes and dove back into my research. But I had to keep rereading the same lines over and over, my brain still foggy from my hangover. I knew that wasn't the only thing that was making it hard to focus, though. My mind kept drifting back to the night before, to Sebastian's dark eyes as he listened intently while I told him about Logan. To the way it felt when he grabbed my hand and rubbed his thumb over my palm. I wondered what the science on that was. If I had cell service, I'd look up what physiological triggers were responsible for that, so that I could turn them off. Because these feelings were distracting me from the important work I needed to get done.

Heart disease. Leading triggers. Most at-risk demographic. Focus, Olivia.

By two, I had finished typing up a first draft to send to Shruti. I was caught up, technically. But I was still coming up absolutely blank, trying to think of ideas for what kind of program to recommend for the hospital. Every article I read mentioned maintaining a healthy diet and exercise routine. Yeah, we had grown up on frozen food, but Logan was a pretty healthy eater and exercised a *ton*. I wanted something better than that. Something that was novel, that would actually make a difference. The winner of the fair would actually get to set this program up, under Dr. Klober's guidance. So this couldn't just be an assignment that I half-assed. It could save real people's lives.

I read through my notes and then read through them again. Finally, at two thirty, I headed to the business center. Maybe talking things through with Shruti would help zap my brain into action.

After I sent my work over to Shruti, I opened up the chat, glad to see she was online.

Shruti: how's paradise

Olivia: actually not so bad

Shruti: really?? two days ago, you said, and i quote, "i'd rather die a million deaths than spend a week on a floating mall"

Olivia: well the people here are sort of cool

Shruti: you met a boy!??!?!

Shruti: . . . ???!?!?

Shruti: WHATS HIS NAME

Olivia: sebastian. but its not like that. anyway, was wondering if you had any ideas for the hospital program?

Shruti: should we do something related to healthy eating? exercise, etc?

Olivia: eh . . . everyone's going to be doing stuff on healthy eating and exercise, so let's not do that. i really want to create something that targets a different area

Shruti: . . . aren't most heart attacks just caused by genetic factors and obesity, though?

Olivia: not all. i want to be unique—to help the people no one else helps.

Shruti: okayyy whatever you think is best. but we need to decide by tomorrow, so i have enough time to make the presentation

Olivia: don't worry, i've got it under control. i'll send over my notes tomorrow!

I had come close to telling Shruti about Logan after I had known her for a year. But then one day at lunch, I overheard her talking about a kid in our grade whose father had just died. "I mean, he died from a heart attack—which isn't that surprising, because you know, he *was* overweight."

"Does that mean he deserved to *die*?" I burst out.

"What? That's not what I was saying at all," Shruti said, but I was already halfway out of the cafeteria.

People always immediately found some way to rationalize death—"He was born with only one functioning kidney" or "Her grandma was sick for a long time" or "He was clinically depressed." As if a reason kept them and *their* families safe.

It was *always* possible, in retrospect, to find someone to blame, some detail to harp on, some way to rationalize the death. Didn't it ever occur to anyone that if it were *them* in the ground, people would be doing the same thing? Summing up their entire life to one simple fact or fault and writing it off.

Because none of us were immune to death. It was out there and it was coming for all of us and, in the end, there was nothing we could do to prevent it.

"Liv!" a deep voice boomed from behind me. I turned around to find Troy walking toward me.

"Hard at work on your paper?" he asked.

"Yup," I said, impressed he remembered. "What brings you here?"

"Wanted to shoot my parents an email and let them know we were all alive."

Troy sat next to me and signed in to his email account. He let out a groan, but he was smiling. "*Twelve* unread messages. All from my family."

I laughed. "From the last three days?"

"From the last twenty-four *hours*," Troy said. "I've been emailing them every day."

"Wow." I thought about the two-week science camp I'd gone to the previous summer. My parents had texted a few times to check in, but we hadn't sent a single email. I couldn't imagine being part of a family that emailed every day. "So what's your family like?"

"Big. Loud. The best," Troy said, and I could tell he missed them.

"How many siblings did you say you had again?"

"Six."

"That sounds so fun."

"It's awesome." A huge smile filled Troy's face. "Like living at a big summer camp. Total chaos all the time. I can't imagine growing up in another family."

"What was it like having parents who were in the army?"

"We moved around a lot when I was younger. We never really fit in anywhere we went, and we didn't stay long enough to become close with anyone. So my siblings were always my best friends. And still are."

"That's nice," I said. "Moving around so much must have been tough though."

"Yeah, when I have kids, we'll be doing the whole white-picket-fence thing and staying in one place." Troy sent a few rapid-fire emails, then turned back to me. "What about you? Do you want kids?"

"I'm not sure," I admitted. I had a big plan for my life, but had decided I'd figure out the kid question later on down the line. "All I know is that I don't want to do what my parents did."

"Which was?"

"They got pregnant with my older brother when they were still in law school, so they were never around when we were growing up. And then they had the twins much later in life and gave up the law careers they'd worked so hard for. So just, timing-wise, none of this was ideal."

I had never understood how my parents—who otherwise seemed like mostly rational, smart individuals—had gotten pregnant during their first year of law school. I knew how difficult law school was—there was no way that pregnancy could have been planned. And I was pretty sure that com-muting into the city while raising two kids wasn't the life my parents had imagined.

Troy nodded. "Not sure family planning is ever ideal, though, timing-wise. But then you meet your kids and you're like"—Troy's eyes lit up—"who cares, 'cause look at this perfect angel face I created? And then in my parents' case, at least, they did that *six more times*."

I laughed, feeling like someone had twisted around a wet rag inside my chest. "Ha, not sure that's exactly how my parents think."

"I wouldn't be so sure about that, Jersey. I'm sure your parents love you a ton. Not everyone is great at showing that, though."

Troy went back to his inbox. His fingers clacked the keys loudly. After a few minutes, he let out a giant sigh of relief. "Done!" Then he swiveled his chair around so he was facing me and smacked his palms on his knees. "So—what's going on with you and our boy Seb?"

I left out a half laugh, half snort. "What? Nothing, I—"

"Relax, I'm screwing with you," Troy said. "It's chill."

"We're just having fun," I said, mimicking what Jules had said. "So where is your cruise partner?"

"My very very hot boyfriend, Chris, is back home," Troy answered. "Or rather, Hawaii."

I hadn't realized Troy was in a relationship. I guess I had never thought to ask.

"What's he like?"

"Well, I'm not sure if I've already mentioned, but he is very very hot," Troy said. "We met in a gender-bent community theater production of *Fiddler on the Roof*. He was Yente. I was Golde."

I snorted at that, imagining this giant of a guy playing the role of Golde. "I'd pay good money to see that performance. I love *Fiddler*."

"Do you do theater?" Troy asked.

"Used to."

"Why'd you stop?"

I shrugged. "Didn't really have time."

"Ah yeah, Seb told me you're one of those superbrainy girls."
Sebastian had been talking about me?

"Oh yeah? What other lies has he told you about me?" I was suddenly desperate to know every single thing he'd said when I wasn't around, so that I could analyze each piece of information and figure out how he felt about me.

Troy pretended to zip his lips. "Bro code," he said.

"Ughhh," I said. "Fine, then. Can you at least tell me what Seb's really like?"

Troy crossed his arms against his chest. "Whatcha want to know?"

"He seems smart. Is he?"

"Yup. He works really hard but tries to hide it."

I laughed. That sounded like him. "I'm sure he has tons of girls chasing after him back home." I did my best to recite this line as casually as possible. I was a cool cucumber who couldn't care less about what girls Sebastian did or did not involve himself with.

Troy let out a small laugh. "Nah, he doesn't really roll like that. He's more of a one-girl type of guy."

My heart slowed down a bit at his answer. "So he's a good guy?"

Troy put his hands up. "I can't be held accountable for anything that boy does. But yes, I think he's a good guy. And *you* seem like a good girl. So, you know, just be good . . . together."

125

I speed walked straight from the business center to the elevator bank, wondering if Sebastian would even remember to show up for the hot dog—appointment? plan? date?!—we had made. I felt oddly nervous, like showing up for a test I knew I hadn't studied the right amount for. Which was silly, because I had just seen Sebastian the night before and I didn't want anything out of this relationship. There were literally no stakes.

I walked past the Starbucks and kitschy gift shops. Carnival music and kids' yells filled the deck. When I got closer, I spotted Sebastian waiting for me, his hands in the pockets of his khaki shorts. When he saw me, he looked up and smiled, and all my worries evaporated.

"Hey," he said. "Can I buy you a genuine NYC hot dog?"

I eyed the familiar blue-and-yellow Sabrett umbrella, the same ones that dotted every New York street corner. The air smelled vaguely of meatballs, not the wonderfully familiar odor of burnt onions and dirt that seemed to radiate from all New York hot dog stands.

I raised my eyebrows. "*Can* you is the real question."

He laughed. "We'll have two, with everything on it," he told the smiling boy manning the cart, who looked no older than us. Absolutely nothing like a real New York City hot dog vendor.

We walked across the fake moss and found a table. I bit into my hot dog and had to cover my mouth to stop myself from spitting it out.

"Just as good as the real ones?" Sebastian asked.

"Oh yeah," I said, my voice dripping with sarcasm. "Can hardly tell we're not in New York." I set the hot dog down next to me and wiped my mouth with a napkin. "So how was your day?"

"Pretty chill," Sebastian said. "Just happy to be out of that tiny-ass cabin. How was yours?"

"Not too bad. Got massages with Jules and our moms."

"Nice." Sebastian took another bite of his hot dog. "So wait—you're telling me this *isn't* what New York hot dogs taste like?"

"Ugh—no. There's like a special type of water . . . a lot more pollution in the air . . . just general anger and annoyance . . . that all combine to make the perfect hot dog. Which this"—I gestured to my nearly untouched hot dog—"is most certainly not."

"So what *is* the big city like?" Sebastian asked.

"It's . . ." I closed my eyes, picturing the sparkling sidewalks and the honking taxis and the energy that was impossible to put into words. "Magical. The sidewalk glitters, and the air smells of slightly burnt sausages, and people always look like they have somewhere important to be and are late getting there. It's a city filled with . . . people with purpose, with life plans."

You didn't just "end up" in New York. If you didn't have a plan, you wouldn't survive there very long. "And then the art, the live music, the shows . . . there's nowhere like it."

Sebastian nodded slowly, taking it all in. "I love that," he said. "I've heard a lot about New York, but I've never heard it described so . . . poetically."

I felt my cheeks turn red, so I quickly covered up my embarrassment with a joke. "Meanwhile, this ship—it's just an insult to humanity."

"So why are you here, then? If you have NYC right in your backyard?"

I sighed. "It's really the only type of vacation that allows my parents to relax, since the twins have the kids' center and special aides."

Sebastian nodded. "That makes sense."

"And we haven't really taken a vacation in . . . like eight years, since before . . ." My voice trailed off. But from the way Sebastian was looking at me, I could tell he didn't need me to finish the sentence. "What about you? Why the *NY Sea*?"

"Well—I wanted to see the Big Apple, but *apparently* I came to the wrong place," Sebastian said with an adorable smirk.

"Way to avoid the question, mister."

Sebastian wriggled his eyebrows and finished off his hot dog. "I know I'm no classy New Yorker like you, but this does taste pretty good."

I felt a little bad for being so snobby. "I mean, if you squint your eyes really hard and . . ." But I just couldn't. It was sacrilegious. "Ugh, never mind, this is zero percent like New York." I looked around at the squeaky-clean promenade, the flashing purple lights and fake palm trees (PALM trees!) and beige-and-brown tiled floor. The vintage red convertible parked outside the casino. "But . . . it's sort of magical in its own way? Like, just a completely different world from real life."

"Sort of like a . . . vacation?"

"Yeah, exactly."

"Guess you'll have to show me around the real Big Apple sometime," Sebastian said, meeting my eyes and holding my gaze.

I giggled. I never giggled. Sebastian wanted me to show him around the city? Sebastian wanted to *see* me again, after the cruise? I couldn't stop my mind from leaping forward in time, picturing how cute Sebastian would look in a cable-knit sweater and plaid scarf, the crisp winter air freezing his breath and snowflakes getting caught in his long lashes.

"Sure, but you're going to have to make me one promise— like swear-on-your-life promise—if we're gonna do that," I said.

"Sure, anything."

"When we're in the city, you can never, ever, no matter what the situation . . . refer to it as 'the Big Apple.'"

Sebastian shook his head and crinkled his eyes. Then he held out his hand. "It's a deal, Ms. Hardened New Yorker." I met his hand with mine. He didn't exactly shake my hand so much as . . . caress it?

Was Jules right? *Did* Sebastian like me?

Sebastian looked over at the Regal Islands display. "I think the crew's headed to the surf simulator now."

"Oh." That would give me more time to get back to work, and I should have felt relieved. But instead, I felt like a small anchor had been dropped inside my chest. "Were you gonna meet up with them?"

"That depends," he said. He lowered his voice an octave and met my eyes. "Do you want me to?"

I swallowed, shocked and elated by how direct he was being. The best response I could muster was a meek "No, I mean, if you want to go hang with the crew—"

"Didn't you have to get back to work?" He raised an eyebrow.

"Nope. Did all of my work for today." The lie was out before I had time to stop myself. I took a small breath and tried to reset. I sat up straighter and leaned in toward Sebastian, trying to channel some of Jules's confidence. "I think I need a break from this awful music. Can you play me something better?"

Sebastian scoffed, and I could tell that I, for once, had been the one to catch him off guard. I felt a small jolt of satisfaction.

"I guess you'll have to let me know." Sebastian stood up and began to lead. My heart pounded as I followed after him.

But Sebastian didn't take me to the tenth floor. Instead, we were on the eighth floor, walking past the jazz lounge and the Empire Steak Building.

"Where are we going?"

"Patience, young grasshopper," Sebastian said. We walked a little farther, and then Sebastian put his key card up to a door. The light flashed green and we walked into a small room.

The room was overflowing with musical instruments—three pianos, two drum sets, and cases for every type of instrument.

"It's the room where the musicians practice," Sebastian explained.

I put my hands on my hips. "And you got in here how?"

"I have my ways," Sebastian said, shooting me the same charming grin I was sure had gained him access to the room.

Sebastian sat down at one of the pianos and laid his fingers on the keys. "Any requests?"

"Surprise me," I said with a smile. There were a few chairs folded up against the wall, but I figured it would look weird to take one out and be a one-person audience. So instead, I took a seat a few inches away from Sebastian on the bench.

Sebastian began playing a set of high notes. Instantly, I recognized the opening chords to Joni Mitchell's "River."

"Ah, I love this song."

"You know it?" he asked.

"Of course."

"It's coming on Christmas," Sebastian started in a raspy voice, his eyes half-closed. "They're cutting down trees . . ." His voice was low and clear and beautiful. I sank into the music like a warm bath.

When he hit the refrain, I was transported back to the December when I was ten and Logan was sixteen, a few weeks before the car accident. Our last good Hanukkah together. Our parents were at work, and we had stayed up late, eating an entire box of Hanukkah gelt and blasting Christmas music. We had danced around in footsie pajamas, feather boas wrapped around our necks. And then "River" came on. Logan dimmed the lights, in "respect" of such a great song, and began singing along as the Hanukkah candles became small pools of rainbow-colored wax. There was nothing I loved more than hearing him sing. Especially because every performance was just for me.

When Sebastian finished playing, we sat there for a moment, not saying anything. Just soaking up that ethereal feeling that a great song brings, that's impossible to describe.

"Logan and I used to play that song every year on Hanukkah," I finally said, breaking the silence.

"Even though it's a Christmas song?"

"We were Christmas music fiends," I said. "There's just something about that song . . . It's so simple and yet so powerful at the same time."

Sebastian nodded. "Joni Mitchell, man. She knows what she's doing."

"Songs like these . . . They're like time machines. They have a way of capturing the present and crystallizing the moment in time. And then you can always go right back to those moments when the song comes on." *Like this one*, is what I was really thinking. I knew I'd remember this exact moment for the rest of my life.

"I love that," Sebastian said, slipping an arm around my waist and pulling me closer to him.

I felt all the air in my chest collect in my throat. *Was he about to kiss me?*

But then he removed his arm and began to play again. I reminded myself of what he'd told me the night before. He wasn't looking to hook up with anyone. He liked me because he thought I was smart.

He was playing another Joni song. "I used to play this song all the time back when my parents were getting divorced," Sebastian said softly.

I nodded, looking up at Sebastian and waiting for him to continue.

"I spent a lot of time listening to them fight and trying to mediate their conflicts. Which didn't exactly work out, so then I spent a lot of time wearing soundproof headphones and letting Joni drown out their fights."

"I thought that my parents would get divorced after Logan died," I admitted. "I did some research about the percent of parents that got divorced, to prepare myself. But then they went in the complete opposite direction and had the twins." I swallowed, willing myself not to cry. "They never talk about him. They even made Matt's middle name 'Logan,' like they were just replacing one son with another."

"Isn't that a Jewish thing, though? Honoring the departed by naming a child after them?" I was surprised Sebastian knew that.

"Yeah, but . . . they gave up their crazy jobs in the city and now they spend all their time with the boys." I thought of the train ride the day before, how my parents were doing everything with the twins that they'd never done with Logan and me. "They were never around when Logan and I were growing up. Logan basically raised me, which is why we were so close."

Another comfortable silence fell over us as Sebastian began to play again. I felt so many feelings welling up in my chest, and a sudden need to hear the sound of Logan's voice. "This may sound silly, but do you want to hear him sing?"

"I'd love to."

I had listened to the last voice mail Logan had ever left me so many times—it was the only voice mail of his I had saved. But I had never played it for anyone before.

I pressed play. "Sorry I'm so late," Logan said, sounding out of breath. "Let me make it up to you," he sang out before launching into one of our favorite *Rent* songs, "La Vie Bohème."

Sebastian laughed. "Is he drunk?"

I felt like someone had flipped a switch inside me, turning my organs ice-cold. "What?"

"Sorry—I was joking," Sebastian said.

I shoved my phone into my pocket. I remembered why I kept Logan to myself. No matter how much I told people about him, they'd never *really* understand who he was. I'd rather not talk about him at all than have someone misunderstand him. "That was just how he was," I said, bitterness dripping from each word.

"Oh—ha—my bad." Sebastian looked like a little kid who had gotten in trouble. One part of me wanted to tell him it was fine and go back to how things were a few minutes before. But the steelier side of myself won out.

"Anyway, I should get going . . . I'm really behind on my work." *Because you keep showing up, screwing up my schedule.* Sebastian flinched, and I could tell he knew what I was insinuating. There was a part of me that wanted Sebastian to apologize, to ask me to stay.

But instead, he put his hand on my shoulder and gave me a light, half-hearted squeeze. "See you later. Good luck with your research."

TWELVE

I got back to my room and buried my face in my pillow. What was I doing, sharing this much about Logan with a boy I had just met? A boy I knew next to nothing about?

I had thought he understood me, that he somehow knew Logan through my stories. But he so clearly did *not*.

I had read a study once that explained how much our own preconceptions clouded our ability to judge other people's perspectives. One participant had to tap out a simple song, like "Happy Birthday," and then the other participant had to guess the song. The other participants almost never guessed the song—their success was like 2 percent—but half of the time, the tappers thought the participant would guess right.

My words about Logan were just like random taps. And Sebastian's kind eyes and nods and questions had misled me into believing he actually understood who Logan was. You couldn't possibly sum up an entire human through words. It was like drawing a few dots on a piece of paper and expecting someone to see the *Mona Lisa*.

Which is why I never talked about Logan with people who hadn't met him.

Everyone at my middle school had wanted to talk to me and offer their condolences after Logan died. In a sick twist of events, it was like I became *popular* because my brother had died. People I had never said more than "Can you pass the scissors?" to were now proclaiming they had been my "best friend." Everyone seemed to have this morbid fascination with death—happening to someone so close to them, but without actually affecting their own lives.

But as I quickly found out, no one *really* wanted to talk about Logan. There was this immediate disconnect when I spoke about him. No one heard me talking about my brother; they heard me talking about a ghost. They all already viewed Logan as "my dead brother," even though he had been alive for seventeen years and only dead for a few days. It was like when someone died, people recast that person as someone who was always bound to die. Like his whole life that he lived was always fated to end at seventeen.

When really, he was just as human as anyone else. But no one wanted to confront that harsh reality, that our seemingly immortal lives could be cut short at any instant and without warning—and that this could happen to anyone we knew.

The more I fumed, the more my breathing sped up and the tighter my chest got.

I glanced across my room, where I had neatly laid out each pair of shoes I'd brought with me. I threw on my running shoes, hoping a good run would help to clear my head.

THIRTEEN

When I got back from the track, I paused at my door. I still felt terrible, and I just wanted to go to sleep and be done with this awful day.

But it was only six. And I knew what would make me feel better.

I turned and knocked on the adjacent door.

My mom pulled it open right away, and Justin sprinted past her and wrapped his arms around my leg.

"Livvy, Livvy, guess what!" Justin shouted.

"What?"

"I'm a BUMBLEBEE tonight! And Matt is a TREE!"

"A tree *trunk*," Matt corrected.

"The Little Flippers are putting on a play tonight," my mom explained. "But I assume you're busy?"

"Nope," I said, bending down to pick Justin up. He immediately put his arms out and began making airplane noises. "My schedule's wide open."

"Really? You and Jules seem to be having so much fun together."

"I think I need a little break from 'fun,'" I said, plopping Justin on the bed and picking up Matt.

"That's our girl," my dad said with a laugh.

"Great," my mom said. "Did you hear that, boys? Olivia's coming tonight!"

"To the show?" Matt asked. "Does she have a ticket?"

"Yup," my dad said. "Front row seats."

"Yes yes yes," Justin said as he zoomed around the room.

I smiled, knowing I had made the right decision. "What's the play about?"

"Climate change," my dad answered with a low laugh.

"Like Birdie talks about," Matt added, flapping his stuffed-animal portrayal of the character around the room. Oh, Birdie. He really got into some serious topics for toddlers.

Matt held out his arms, and I scooped him up again before dumping him on my parents' bed and tickling him. Matt's giggles were infectious, and pretty soon we were all laughing. I felt the strings in my chest loosen, and I let out a giant breath.

"Is someone knocking on your door?" my mom asked.

I felt my heart go into overdrive. Was it Sebastian? And how would I explain that to my parents?

But when I opened my parents' door, I was greeted by fruity perfume and tinkling bracelets. It took a second for my heart to slow down.

"Jules—hey," I said, trying to hide the disappointment I felt. I held up my card and pulled open the door to my room.

"Liv! I called your room, but you didn't pick up. Then I called the crew's room, but Sebastian said you weren't there. I almost asked the captain to put out an emergency signal."

I laughed and shook my head. "I was just with my family. What's up?"

"So the crew is doing a bullshit boys' night. I wanna crash it and make them do the belly-flop competition. Let's grab drinks first though—I met this supercute bartender who doesn't card."

"Sorry. I told my parents I'd go watch my brothers' play tonight."

Jules pouted. "Can't you get out of it?"

I put on my best apologetic expression. "I already told the twins. They'd be devastated."

"Ooo-kayyy," Jules said. "So—any updates on Sebastian? How is your loooove cruise going?"

"Jules!" I gestured to the thin wall separating my room from my parents' room. "My parents are right in there."

Jules rolled her eyes and lowered her voice. "Is everything okay? A few hours ago, you were in l-o-v-e."

"Yeah, everything's fine," I lied. "We hung out a bit. Nothing life-changing. Just friends, having fun, like you advised. What about Ash?"

"Oh, we're having fun . . . ," Jules said, a wide smile filling her face. "Ash told me I'm the first person to ever give them multiple—"

"Jules!" I jerked my head toward the wall again. "Parents!"

"Multiple . . . oranges," Jules finished with an exaggerated wink. "I always love being someone's first."

"Congratulations," I said. "Have fun tonight."

"I'll miss you! Meet me at the buffet tomorrow at ten, and I'll fill you in on what you missed?"

"Sure."

Jules walked out, and I closed the door behind her. I felt a sinking feeling in my stomach as I watched her go. Sure, I'd have more time to brainstorm for my project, and I had no interest in seeing Sebastian.

But there was still a part of me that felt sad to be missing out on another night with the crew. I had to admit I'd been having a good time. And there were only six nights left.

By the time the lights went down, every seat in the children's theater was filled. It was good we had gotten there early, as we had promised the boys we'd be cheering for them from the front row. If they had walked onstage and hadn't seen us up front, they would have panicked.

A petite woman walked onstage and motioned for the crowd to quiet down. "Welcome to Little Flippers on Broadway," she said with a thick Russian accent. "I'm Catherine, and I am the children's theater director. Without further ado, here are the stars of this evening, our Little Flippers!"

She pulled aside the red velvet curtain, revealing around twenty kids, a mixture of toddlers and kindergartners. Some twisted around nervously. Others had giant smiles plastered on their faces, as if they were the sole stars of the show.

The "show" was a call-and-response with Catherine. I was actually pretty impressed—she managed to tie in a lot of themes about climate change, or in kids' terms, "saving the baby koalas, bumblebees, and the—" "BIG SHADY PALM TREES!" the kids shouted in response as the ones who were assigned to play trees clapped their hands above their heads, and the bumblebees ran around the stage, buzzing loudly around them.

Throughout the next few lines, which involved a different series of hand motions, Matt stood stoically onstage, still holding his palm tree—or rather, palm tree *stump* (because it had been deforested) pose. My parents and I shared a knowing look and laughed—when Matt committed, he *committed*. Likewise, Justin continued sprinting around the stage, buzzing in everyone's ears. They made a perfect pair.

Justin was so in character that he ran straight into Catherine. "Buzzzz, you've been stung!" he shouted.

"Oh no!" she yelped, playing along.

The audience broke out in laughter.

"He's stealing the show," I said with a proud smile.

My dad laughed and my mom shook her head, but she was smiling.

I thought back to the first show I'd ever been in—a community theater production of *The Wizard of Oz*. I was playing one of the munchkins. I had been terrified to get onstage and had almost backed out at the last minute. But Logan had been playing the Cowardly Lion, and even though he wasn't in my first scene, he had ducked behind the side curtain so that he could hold my hand.

"Remember when Logan and I were in Oz?" I whispered to my mom.

She laughed. "Yes! Logan couldn't stop roaring at all the wrong times to get a laugh. I felt so bad for quiet little Dorothy. I almost apologized to her parents."

I was hit with a sudden wave of emotion. That my mom remembered the night so clearly. Including details I had forgotten. I blinked a few times and glanced up at the stage, where Justin was now running in circles around Matt, who was looking straight ahead with a serious expression on his face.

I could feel my heart expand as I watched them; they were so freaking adorable. I didn't know what I'd do without them.

But it always broke my heart that they'd never get to meet Logan. They would have loved him.

"Thank you so much for coming out to Broadway!" Catherine said when the lights came up. "Have a great night, and make sure you celebrate our stars with a special dessert!"

The boys bounded off the stage and shot straight to my parents, who wrapped them up in hugs.

"Can I have a second soda today?" Justin asked. "Since I did so good?"

"I guess we can make an exception for tonight," my dad told him. "But only tonight."

I couldn't help but think about how different their relationships were—this was all the boys knew. Hugs and parents around all the time.

Not Celeste pizza and overly exhausted parents who had a hard time remembering the dates of our games and performances.

Which was probably *another* reason why they so rarely talked about Logan.

Because they weren't keeping silent about him just to protect the twins. They were doing their best to erase that part of our lives. That part of our family.

There was a small piece of me that understood. But another, deeper part that hated them for their silence; their desire to forget.

As I lay in bed that night, I scrolled through the videos on my phone, finally pulling up the one I was looking for—Logan singing "If I Only Had the Nerve" in *The Wizard of Oz*. Even at eleven, his voice was phenomenal. Poor Dorothy never stood a chance.

I watched the way the camera zoomed in and out on Logan, the filming technique it seemed like all dads had been trained to do.

Logan's face was painted white. His natural freckles were filled in with dark brown pencil, and he had a ridiculous mop of orange strings on his head, which only added to the theater-filling laughs he earned. And my mom was right—Dorothy's voice was timid; many of her lines were drowned out by the laughter at Logan's lines.

I pulled up another video of Logan performing, then another. After he had died, I used to watch them every night before I fell asleep. But the more I watched the videos, the more I felt like I was losing him, like a song I had listened to too many times in a row. The words lost meaning. The magic disappeared with each view. He was becoming nothing more than a series of memorized pixels. So I had stopped watching them altogether, trying to preserve these precious few moments I still had of him.

But now—stuck on this floating strip mall in the middle of the ocean—I needed him with me more than ever. I was filled with joy as I watched the videos that I hadn't seen in years. And hit at the same time with a knife to my gut, seeing Logan at the same age as I was now. Knowing he was trapped in these videos, that he would never get older than seventeen. Soon, he would never again be my older brother.

I took a deep breath before pulling up my favorite video. I had been devastated after our fish had died, and so Logan had thrown an entire funeral for Mr. Bubbles. And then he had sung our favorite song from *Rent*, the heartbreaking song that Tom sings at Angel's funeral.

As Logan sang the first line, my eyes filled with tears.

This was the song I was supposed to sing at his funeral.

Because we were Jewish, his funeral had to be planned right away—which meant it was held the day after my eleventh birthday. My parents had apologized over and over, but the date didn't matter to me. I wouldn't be celebrating anyway.

When I got up in front of everyone—their liquid eyes, everyone Logan and I had ever known—it hit me that he was really gone. And that none of these "sad" people could possibly understand how I felt.

And when I opened my mouth to sing, nothing came out.

My heart began pounding louder and louder, and finally my dad came up, put a hand on my shoulder, and led me back to my seat.

After that, I stopped going to my singing lessons and I quit the school musical.

I blinked back tears as I looked down at the video of Logan. Every hair on my arms stood up as he belted out the final line.

I wished I'd shown Sebastian this video of Logan, instead of playing the voice mail. *This* was who Logan was. This impossibly beautiful and perfect soul.

I couldn't stop replaying that awful moment with Sebastian. I knew he hadn't meant to hurt me, but why had he just let me leave? And why hadn't I heard from him since? Were we—whatever it was we even were—over? Before we had even begun?

I shook my head. What had gotten into me? The problem wasn't what Sebastian had said about Logan—it was that I cared so much to begin with, about some boy I barely even knew.

I needed to nip this relationship, or whatever it was, in the bud before it got any further. Because I wasn't fond of the slick, slithering feeling in my stomach. The way my emotions were already so dependent on his. And the only way to gain back control would be if I ended things. ASAP.

FOURTEEN
DAY FIVE AD

"Okay, so what the hell is going on with you and Sebastian?" Jules started grilling me as soon as I got behind her in line for the pancake-and-waffle bar. "He asked me where you were last night, and I have never seen a face fall so hard to the ground when I told him you weren't coming."

I had to bite back a smile at that. Sebastian was upset I wasn't there? He missed me? But I quickly wiped the smile off my face, remembering the decision I had made the night before. Cutting off contact now was the smartest move before any more feelings got involved.

"I think I'm over hanging out with him." I wasn't really hungry, but I grabbed a few chocolate chip pancakes and began covering them with syrup.

"What? Why?" Jules followed behind me as I walked toward a table far out of sight—and earshot—from where our parents were seated together.

When I didn't respond to Jules's question immediately, she knit her brows together. "Did he do something creepy?"

"No, no!" I didn't want to tell Jules what had happened, but if I didn't, it sounded like she was going to invent a much worse scenario.

I took a deep breath and swirled a piece of pancake in the pool of syrup that had formed at the edge of my plate. "I just . . . I played this voice mail Logan had left me. And Sebastian asked if Logan was drunk."

". . . And?"

I knew Jules wouldn't get it. I took a big bite of pancake so that I wouldn't have to respond right away. Despite the syrup, the food felt dry on my tongue, hard to swallow.

"Well, first of all, Logan wasn't drunk. And I don't know; it's just—Logan meant everything to me. And Sebastian has no idea who he was."

"Okay . . . so maybe don't talk to him about Logan? Keep it light? Sebastian's hot. Have some drinks, lie out in the sun, get some of that Missouri meat . . ."

"Ew, Jules."

"Just try to enjoy the moment. Turn off the part of your brain that's always jumping twenty years ahead. Sebastian doesn't have to be your future husband."

Logan had always been able to enjoy himself in the moment. He *lived* for the moment. He had enjoyed every moment of his life before the accident—singing and playing basketball and being the center of attention. When that all came to a halt, he crumbled. He couldn't *conceive* of any future moments, of any moments aside from the one he was currently living in.

Meanwhile, I was the opposite. I had a hard time hitting the pause button and just being *present*. I was always jumping to the next week, month, year. Weighing each moment carefully, choosing the course that would lead to the least amount of future disappointment. Never thinking about how much I was actually *enjoying* the present.

I sighed and put down my fork. "I don't think I know how to turn off that part of my brain."

"Just—kiss him if it's fun. Don't if it's not. Enjoy the sun on your face. But whatever you do, don't end things over that." Jules stuck a fork into my mostly untouched pancakes and moved one to her plate. "That's overly dramatic; you've only known each other for like a minute. And it will ruin the vibe we've got going!"

It was hard to explain how much longer it felt, that time on the water seemed to extend on indefinitely, turning moments into weeks and days into years. That our conversations went so much deeper than they did with anyone else. That sometimes people you just met could understand you more than people you'd known your whole life. That you couldn't measure feelings rationally, by the hours or minutes you'd known someone.

Jules did have a point, though. And what was I going to do for the rest of the cruise if I didn't have any friends? Jules would be hanging out with Ash, who would be with Sebastian. I didn't want to be seen as that weird, overdramatic girl who got her feelings hurt and then hid in her room for the rest of the vacation. Who was broken because of her dead brother.

But was it possible for me to just chill out around Sebastian, and pretend like everything was totally fine? To hang out with him without taking things seriously? To not have a heart attack every time he smiled?

I spent the rest of the morning staring at my computer screen, willing a brilliant idea to somehow appear in front of me. But the screen stayed as blank as my mind.

There was a light knock on the door between my room and my parents'. "Yeah?"

My dad stuck his head into my room. "Think we're going to skip the excursions today. Want to join us at the pool?"

I looked at the mess of notes around me. Usually, coming up with ideas was the easy part. But for some reason, it just wasn't clicking. Maybe a little time in the sun could help rejigger my tangled brain cells. Or something.

"Sure." I closed my computer, put on my one-piece (which I had been handwashing each night), and walked over to the pool with my parents and the twins.

After a few rounds of Simon Says, I noticed the tips of Matt's ears were turning pink. "I think it's time to reapply sunscreen," I told my parents.

My mom started to step out of the water. "It's fine, I've got it," I said.

I walked slowly, one hand holding on to Matt's and one on to Justin's, back to the chairs where we had left our beach bag.

I covered Justin first and then handed him a towel. "Can you turn this into a swan, like they do in our room?" I asked, hoping to distract him long enough for me to cover Matt.

"Yup!" he said, eagerly getting to work.

"Does the suntan lotion fight the sun, like Birdie says?" Matt asked as I started on his shoulders. They felt hot to the touch. I should have reapplied before we'd gotten in the water.

"Mm-hmm." I could tell Matt was about to go on one of his anxious question spirals—a trait he definitely got from me. I had been trying to will away my own spiral all morning. But I couldn't stop wondering what Sebastian was thinking; if he would apologize. If I would forgive him. If anything would happen between us.

"Does the sun get mad?"

I laughed. Of course Matt was anxious about the sun getting mad. I loved how empathetic he was at such a young age. "No, the sun understands," I explained. I nodded along as Matt continued to question me about the sun and global warming. Out of the corner of my eye, I thought I saw the crew walking in our direction, and my stomach flipped. But then I realized it was just a group of guys I didn't know.

"What happens when people get too warm?"

I opened my mouth to respond. And that was when I realized Justin was no longer sitting on the chair, playing with the towel. I whipped my head from side to side. He wasn't there at all.

I felt like a stampede of horses had just trampled over my heart. Adrenaline surged through my veins, and my heart sped up. I grabbed Matt's hand and jumped to my feet.

"Ow," he said.

"Do you see your brother?"

"No."

Oh my God. How could I have let him out of my sight? What was wrong with me? I had been so distracted, thinking about Sebastian, and now Justin was *gone*. He could have slipped in the pool and drowned and—I shook my head, physically trying to erase the image of his soft dark curls waving like seaweed at the bottom of the pool. I spun around, taking in the myriad of pools and waterslides and sprinklers, my mind filling with all the ways he could have hurt himself—or worse.

"Mom! Dad!" I shouted, waving my arms around wildly. Luckily, I got their attention and they stepped out of the pool and began walking over to me.

"What's wrong?" my dad asked.

"I can't find Justin." My throat was bone-dry, and my words came out scratchy.

My mom's face went white.

"He was right here, and then I was putting sunscreen on Matt and—" As I said that, I turned around and spotted Justin, hand in hand with Shari, the twins' aide. My body flooded with such a heavy sense of relief that I felt dizzy.

"JUSTIN!" I grabbed him in my arms and squeezed him.

"Ow!" he yelped.

I was blinking back tears. "Justin—don't scare me like that."

"I'm so sorry," Shari said. "He ran up to hug me, but I immediately walked him back here."

"Oh," I said, taking a seat and taking a few deep breaths. "Sorry, I just—I freaked out."

"Don't worry," my mom said, laying a hand on Shari's arm. "Justin's always running up to greet his friends."

I gave my mom a look. This was common? Since when?

"Have a great rest of your afternoon," Shari said with a chipper smile, as if the events of the last five minutes hadn't just taken ten years off my life.

I put Justin on my lap. Tears were now spilling everywhere. I tried to get my breathing under control, but my body was still in full panic mode. I just couldn't stop thinking about what would have happened if Shari hadn't come back with Justin. "I thought he disappeared, or went in the water, or . . ."

My mom sat next to me and pushed a wet strand of hair out of my eyes. "It's okay, Olivia. Everything's okay."

But it wasn't okay. Just because he was here and he was safe didn't erase what had just happened. How had my parents reset so quickly?

"You know that drowning is the number one cause of"—I looked at the twins and lowered my voice—"*you know what*, for toddlers."

"Oh, sweetie," my mom said. "You don't have to worry about that. We were all right here."

"Along with about twenty lifeguards," my dad added with a small smile, "who I'm sure have had the wrath of God scared into them by Regal Islands' legal team, to make sure no *you know whats* happen on their watch."

I was shaking my head. My dad was *joking*? My heart was still pounding so loudly I was sure everyone on the ship could hear it. How could my parents not get why I was so scared? How could *they* not be so scared, every minute of their lives? Hadn't what had happened with Logan affected them *at all*? Did they really care that little?

"I'm going back to my room," I said, rubbing my eyes. I felt embarrassed that I'd expressed so much emotion over an incident my parents couldn't bother to bat an eye at. They probably thought I was just being hysterical. "I'll see you later."

I ignored the No Running signs as I raced in the direction of the elevators, desperate to get back to my room.

"What time is it?" a man yelled before shoving his microphone in my face. I had been so upset that I hadn't even realized I had run right into the middle of that afternoon's "subway performance." Now was *not* the time. I shook my head and continued at a near sprint toward the elevators.

When I got off the elevator, I was still shaking. I walked with my head down until I got to my room.

As I looked up, I practically ran into Sebastian, who was leaning against my door.

"Hey," he said, his voice full of concern. "Are you okay?"

I swallowed. I knew if I tried to speak, I would start crying again, so I just shook my head.

Sebastian took a step toward me hesitantly, as if he were preparing for me to shoo him away. When I didn't, he wrapped his arms around me and tucked a few strands of my matted hair behind my ear. I inhaled the slightly spicy scent of his soft cotton T-shirt.

"It's okay," he said. "Just breathe."

I tried to nod but felt like I was suffocating. My back was against the wall and I slid down. Sebastian slid next to me.

We sat there silently together. Finally, when my head felt a little better and my chest didn't feel like it was going to burst, I said, "I'm sorry."

Sebastian furrowed his brow and shook his head. "You have nothing to be sorry for." He began to gently massage the back of my neck with his fingers, a gentle rhythm that somehow slowed down the beating of my heart. After a few minutes, I stood up and opened the door to my room. Sebastian followed me in and took a seat next to me on my bed.

When it no longer felt like my throat was clogged with cotton balls, I spoke.

"I lost sight of Justin at the pool, and I freaked out."

"I'm sorry," Sebastian said, placing a hand on my arm. "That sounds really scary."

"It was," I said, relieved that Sebastian was normalizing my emotions after my parents had made me feel like a freak. "After what happened with Logan, I just . . . I'm so terrified that I'll make one little mistake and the twins will end up gone too. I know that sounds ridiculous."

"That doesn't sound ridiculous."

"I'm the one—" It was hard to get the words to form, to exit my mouth, without breaking into tears again.

I inhaled and then exhaled slowly. "I'm the one who found him."

Sebastian nodded. He didn't need to ask who.

"We were home and I was supposed to be watching him."

Sebastian drew in his eyebrows. "Wasn't he older than you?"

"Yeah, but . . . he hadn't been doing so well after the accident." Even before the car accident his junior year, my parents were always telling me to "babysit" Logan. It was the running joke. Because even though I was six years younger, I was seen as the "responsible" one.

"We were supposed to watch a movie that night, but I picked some stupid fight with him, because he"—I had to stop to laugh at the sheer ridiculousness—"because he didn't want to try out for *Little Shop of Horrors*, even though he would have made a *perfect* Seymour."

It wasn't just that night we were fighting, though—we had been growing apart all year. Logan had so many medical issues after the accident that doctors couldn't figure out, and he was always in a bad mood. I should have been nicer to him, given all that he was going through. But I was hurt and responded like a child, by avoiding him.

"He went to his room and I should have gone, I should have gone and said I was sorry and—"

I blinked rapidly, but I couldn't stop my brain from placing me right back in his room that night. After I had waited—and waited—for Logan to apologize. When he never came out, I finally knocked on his door.

"Logan?"

There was no answer.

I opened the door slowly. I found him lying perfectly still on the floor, his eyes rolled back into his head.

I don't remember what happened after that.

Sebastian pulled me into him and wrapped his arms around me—so tightly it almost hurt, but it was exactly what I needed.

"You were *eleven*. It's not your fault."

"I still knew the difference between right and wrong. If I hadn't gotten mad, or if I'd checked on him sooner, I could have saved him, I could have—"

"People get into fights. No one expects someone to die."

Sebastian searched my eyes with his and rubbed my back. I was crying harder now, and snot was getting everywhere. "You're so, so hard on yourself, Liv. No one's perfect."

"You seem perfect."

He let out a small snort of a laugh and shook his head. "You've known me for a few days. I am so far from perfect." Sebastian began tracing small spirals up and down my arm. "Where were your parents that night?"

I shook my head. "At a *meeting*."

"You should really talk with them. It sounds like there have been a lot of things left unsaid."

I nodded. I knew he was right.

"And Liv," he said, putting a finger under my chin so that I was looking directly into his eyes. "What happened with your brother was *not* your fault."

But that was the hardest part to accept. That there was nothing I could do. That Logan's death was completely out of my control.

And then before I could stop myself, I was leaning over and pressing my lips against Sebastian's. His were soft and a little salty. For a moment, it was just my lips pressing against his. He wasn't responding. I felt my body freeze. I had completely misread his signals.

But then he was running his fingers through my hair and

kissing me back, and all at once I got why people made such silly decisions when it came to love. Because I wanted nothing more than to stay in that moment for the rest of my life.

I felt the kiss from my head down to my toes. It activated neurons in my body I hadn't even known existed. It just felt—good.

It actually made me stop thinking.

When I finally pulled away, my heart was still beating so hard it felt like it would shoot right out of my chest. So much had happened in the last hour. It was like someone had mixed francium—the most reactive alkali metal—and water, a reaction so intense that even the smallest amount of francium causes a fiery explosion of hydrogen gas.

I needed to do something to regulate my breathing, to get my chest to stop from combusting.

I looked over at Sebastian. His lips were still slightly parted and his head was tilted, as if he were trying to figure out what I was thinking.

"Do you want to go for a run?" I asked.

I changed into my sneakers and then went down to the sixth floor. Sebastian was already there, lunging and reaching his arm into the air. I couldn't help finding his warm-up—or the fact that he was warming up—adorable.

"Ready?" he asked. I nodded.

Sebastian started running at a leisurely pace. I could tell it was as easy as walking for him, by the way his feet barely left the ground and his breathing stayed silent. So I picked up the pace. When I did, Sebastian met my eyes and grinned. "Ah, I see how it is," he said, quickening the pace even more.

And then we were racing around the track, maneuvering every now and then around shocked-looking walkers and little kids. I was breathing hard, and Sebastian was exerting some effort too, his breathing now audible. His calf muscles and perfect form made it obvious that he was a track runner. When non-runners run, they often go out at too fast of a cadence, their heels making heavy and inefficient imprints on the ground. But when runners run, their footsteps are silent; their feet hit the ground at a perfectly even pace. Their arms do just as much work as their legs.

The sounds of deep breathing and light footsteps filled my ears as we circled the boat once, then twice, then three times. Running had a way of calming me down, resetting everything, making me just focus on my breathing and my footwork. The track was the one place I didn't overthink everything in my life. Like what I was doing with this boy. Like how soon this cruise would be over. Like the fact that Logan was gone and always would be.

After the fourth time around, Sebastian came to a stop and then pulled me into him. "Ew, I'm disgusting," I said.

"I've never been so attracted to you," he breathed into my mouth. The words and the sensation of his lips on mine sent an electric shock straight through my body.

He placed his forehead against mine and smiled. "Let's go cool off in the pool?"

"Mm-hmm," I murmured, unable to form any real words.

We kicked off our sneakers as soon as we got to the pool. Then Sebastian wrapped his arms around my waist and I shrieked. "What are you—?" But before I could finish, he had thrown both of us into the pool, running clothes and socks and all.

I came up for air, gasping for breath.

"Refreshing, right?" he said with a grin.

"I hate you," I said.

"I bet you do." Sebastian wrapped his legs around my back and pulled me to him.

When he let go, I snapped back to reality and glanced to our left. It was late afternoon, and the pool was packed with families and senior citizens doing water aerobics. But we had the deep end all to ourselves, and there was no one around that we knew.

I floated a few inches away from Sebastian and lay on my back, making small circles in the water with my hands. Above me was all blue sky and fluffy cotton balls of cumulus clouds. It was still so jarring, being on a cruise. How vast the open sky was, and yet somehow thousands of us were contained on a 55,000-ton floating city. It was completely artificial and yet completely beautiful all at once. The juxtaposition was disorienting; it made real life seem so, so far away.

Sebastian followed my lead and took my hand in his. He squeezed and held on for an extra moment before releasing. "How are you feeling?"

I looked over at him. He seemed so earnest, so desperate to help.

"Better," I said. "Thanks for listening." I was telling the truth.

There was just something that happened when I was with Sebastian. The world felt easier to manage, less bright and loud.

"Anytime."

I looked across my body at my feet dangling above the water's surface, embarrassed to have spent so much time talking about myself. I still knew so little about Sebastian.

I flipped over and began treading water. "Tell me more about you."

"What do you want to know?" Sebastian kicked back against the wall, performing a perfect flip under the water. He popped back up and ran a hand through his wet, messy waves. "I'm an open book."

I thought for a moment. What *did* I want to know? Everything, really. If he'd been in love before. How he felt about me. What his plans were for the rest of his life.

I figured it would be best to start with a softball, though. "If you weren't a therapist, what would be your dream job?"

"Easy," Sebastian said as he glided over to me and pulled me back closer to him. "In a band. On the road all the time. Even if we never made any money."

"Worth it for the groupies alone?" I asked with a smirk.

"Exactly."

My teeth started to chatter, and I wrapped my arms around my chest. I wasn't sure if it was from the run or the pool or the insane reaction my body was having to Sebastian's.

Sebastian immediately noticed and began rubbing his hands up and down my arms. "Want to warm up in my room?"

Sebastian set the thermostat to eighty and wrapped a towel around my shoulders. He kept his arms around me, and I was grateful for the extra warmth.

He glanced down at the towel animal on his bed, which today was shaped like a monkey, before looking back up at me. "I'm so sorry for what I said yesterday, Liv. That was incredibly insensitive of me."

"It's okay," I said.

"It's not."

"No, I overreacted." I was so glad that I hadn't completely scared Sebastian off the day before, when he was the only one who really understood what I was going through.

Sebastian shook his head. "You didn't."

"I think in a way, though . . . I wanted to be mad at you."

"Why?" Sebastian asked, cocking his head to the side.

"I just . . . I like you a lot." My heart pounded louder as the words escaped my lips. Even though we had kissed, the actual confession felt loaded, heavy, like a bowling ball balanced precariously at the top of a ramp.

Sebastian put one hand around the nape of my neck and tugged gently, so that my nose was resting against his. I could feel his eyelashes brush the top of my cheeks.

"I like you a lot too," he said.

His words released the pressure, the bowling ball suddenly flying down the ramp, all of its potential energy now kinetic.

"I've never felt like this before," I confessed. "I have no control of the outcome."

"What if you just enjoyed the time we had together, without trying to plan ahead?"

"That's hard for me. I'm a Planner. Capital *P*."

"That's the story you tell yourself, sure. But what if it wasn't?"

I laughed. "You are such a shoo-in for therapy school."

Sebastian extended his arms behind him and leaned back. "We think of ourselves as people with these rigid, fixed identities. But we're so much more malleable than we give ourselves credit for."

"You're only proving my point."

He grabbed the end of my towel and pulled it away. I felt the sudden drop in temperature, but it sped right back up as he began planting a trail of kisses on my shoulder, up my neck, finally landing on my lips. I sighed. I had never known kissing could feel so good. Every spot of my body that Sebastian touched lit up when his lips were on mine, as if his lips emitted chemiluminescence, the trait that gives fireflies their magical glow.

I was in such a deep trance that I nearly jumped when the phone next to the bed started to ring. "Just ignore that," Sebastian said. I didn't need to be told twice.

But as soon as the phone stopped ringing, it started ringing again.

"Sorry," Sebastian said with a sigh. Then he reached over and picked up the phone. "'Lo?" He paused. "Yeah, yeah, just changing. I'll be there soon."

He hung up and turned to me, an apologetic look crossing his face. "The crew's playing mini golf." He brushed his fingers down my arm. "Mind if we pick this up a little later?" His voice was low, and I felt nervous pinpricks shooting around my chest at everything his question implied.

"Okay," I responded immediately.

We got up and walked out of the room. Everything had changed so quickly that I hadn't had time to process what was going on before agreeing. Why was he leaving so suddenly? If he had to meet the crew to play mini golf . . . why hadn't he just invited me?

Before I could linger on the thought too long, Sebastian leaned in and kissed me again. The pinpricks transformed back into butterflies. "Sorry, they've been giving me shit about disappearing on them. Let's meet back at Roy's at ten?"

"Sure," I said, trying my best to act like a cool and collected girl who was used to making out with guys. And who could survive eight hours on her own. "See you then."

FIFTEEN

When I got back to my room, I flopped onto my bed and closed my eyes. My head was spinning as I replayed the afternoon. The way Sebastian had kissed me. Our run. The pool. The way Sebastian had kissed me again.

But every time I landed on our first kiss, the memory was sliced through with another image.

Logan.

On the ground.

Me standing there, not doing anything to save him.

It's not your fault. It's not your fault. It's not your fault.

I had heard that chant countless times after the accident.

But the people who said that didn't know the real story.

How petty I had been. How angry. How I hadn't run to Logan's room right away.

There was nothing you could have done.

And that's when it hit me. There *was* something I could have done.

CPR.

That's what my hospital recommendation could be. CPR training. For kids.

After all, 80 percent of heart attacks happened at home, and children were often the only people around. CPR can add on crucial minutes to someone's life, keeping them alive until the ambulance arrives. If all kids knew how to perform CPR, so many lives could be saved.

If I had known CPR, I could have saved Logan.

I grabbed my laptop and flew to the business center. I couldn't wait to tell Shruti my idea.

Olivia: i came up with an idea for our hospital program!!!

Shruti: you're there!! i have been dying to hear from you. WHAT IS GOING ON WITH YOU AND SEBASTIAN? have you kissed? more than kissed? what's his last name? i need to do some major stalking

Olivia: did you get my message?? i have an idea!!

Shruti: . . . olivia? is our connection working?

Olivia: so i was thinking we could suggest that CPR become mandatory in all high school AND middle school classrooms. because, did you know that every minute someone whose heart has stopped goes without CPR, their chance of dying increases by 10 percent?

Shruti: i guess that could work . . .

Olivia: you're not convinced

Shruti: how would you teach something that complex to little kids, though? CPR is pretty . . . intense. especially if someone's heart has actually stopped. can you really expect a child to break through someone's ribs?

Olivia: maybe not a really young child but . . . yeah, i guess i
should think about this some more
Shruti: in the meantime, updates please??
Olivia: after i figure this out!! talk to you later!

I pulled up a bunch of websites on CPR and printed out the
info so I could read through it later. Shruti had a point—CPR
was a pretty intense skill to teach to kids. I was going to have
to give this plan some more thought. But I knew in my gut that
it was the right way to go. I just had to read more about it and
come up with a plan.

I went to sign off but found Google's search box flashing
before me. Before I knew it, I was googling *long-distance relationship success rates* and *high school relationship success rates*
and *how do you know if someone is actually interested in you.*
But there were no concrete suggestions, just a bunch of silly
quizzes to take with your boyfriend, and Sebastian wasn't even
my boyfriend.

I closed the sites. I'd have to figure out the answers
another way.

SIXTEEN

I read the notes I'd printed out, but I still didn't have any ideas for how to implement my plan. Instead, my brain was working double time, trying to figure out what was going on with Sebastian, and why he had just . . . left, in the middle of our make-out.

I slammed my notebook shut and picked up the phone. I needed Jules's opinion, stat. Did Sebastian actually like me?

Jules picked up on the first ring. "Hello?"

"It's me. Whatcha up to?"

"Was just about to call you. Wanna head to the bar and convince the bartender I know to refill my flask?"

"Sure," I said. "I'll meet you at your room?"

"Yay, see you soon!"

I slipped on my flip-flops and took the stairs up the two flights to the floor where Jules's family was staying. I knocked on Jules's door, and she swung it open, greeting me with a big smile and a whiff of her fruity body spray.

I had barely made it inside her room before she began firing questions at me. "Okay, so *what* is going on with you and Sebastian? Ash told me you've been hanging out all day."

I shook my head. "I mean, we hung out this afternoon, and"—I couldn't stop a giant smile from spreading across my face—"we sort of kissed."

"AHHHH!" Jules screamed, grabbing me and shaking me by my shoulders. "I SO called it!! I'm shipping you two so hard."

"But then he kind of like, left? To go hang with the crew and play mini golf?"

"Yeah, Ash ditched me too. They're supposed to be on a, and I quote, 'no chicks' cruise." Jules rolled her eyes, but then she smiled. "I guess Sebastian and Ash have already sort of . . . broken that rule."

I felt the knot in my chest loosen a bit. "Okay, so it's not just that I'm the world's worst kisser?"

"Absolutely not. The crew is just being clingy." Jules reached across her desk and grabbed her flask. "Let's go fill this up. We don't need make-out buddies to have a good time."

The Manhattan Cocktail Bar wasn't open for the evening yet, but Steph, the bartender Jules had befriended, snuck us in. Steph had a shaved head and a septum piercing, and hardly looked old enough to legally be serving alcohol. Then again, she wasn't exactly legally serving it—we were minors. The bar was dark and filled with mahogany wood, and the walls were papered with photos of famous old-time NYC movie stars. Floor-to-ceiling shelves were filled with liquor bottles, which I was sure cost a premium (finally, something true to NYC).

Jules slipped Steph her flask, which Steph filled to the brim with rum before sliding two full shot glasses our way.

"To Liv's new love affair!" Jules sang out.

"To Liv's new love affair!" Steph repeated. I just shook my head, but I was smiling as I downed my shot. The liquid was smooth and syrupy, not nearly as bad as whatever had been in Jules's flask the first night.

Jules turned to me. "Okay, tell me everything. How was it?"

"Amazing," I responded immediately, remembering the way Sebastian's warm lips had felt against mine. "Well, I mean, I don't really have much to compare him to. But . . . I think he was?"

Jules nodded. "When you know, you know."

"I just can't believe he left, mid-make-out," I moaned. "Does that mean I was bad?"

"No, no," Jules assured me. "He seems like the kind of boy who it would be impossible to have a bad kiss with. According to Ash, he's got a bit of experience under his belt."

My stomach flipped. *Experience?* What did that mean? Jules handed the flask to me and I immediately tipped it back, swallowing the sugary liquid. I winced as the rum made its way down my throat. Steph laughed and slid over a glass of water.

Jules must have sensed the inner turmoil she had caused, because she immediately backtracked. "I mean, like, experience with long-term relationships. He seems to be a relationship guy. Those guys are *always* the best in bed, because they're not just hopping from one girl to the next. They've had someone actually *teach* them what to do."

169

Jules had been trying to calm me down, but instead had started an even bigger fire in my head. Good in *bed*? Did that mean Sebastian expected me to have sex with him? We had just kissed, but we were going to meet up later. Lord, what had I agreed to?

I took another swig from the flask before handing it back to Jules. "Well, it's good one of us knows what to do, because I've never done anything other than kiss. And I've only kissed two other guys before."

I thought back to my last two kisses. One was in a game of Truth or Dare, and the other was a very explicit setup by Shruti. She had been trying to win back her debate camp boyfriend by setting me up with his friend, who had greasy black hair and very garlicky breath. Suffice to say, that plan did not pan out.

Jules put a hand on my shoulder. "Don't worry. You're a fast learner."

"Thanks," I said, wishing kissing were as easy for me to ace as a biology exam. "How about Ash? How are they?"

A dreamy look filled Jules's face. "So, so good. Easily in the top five best kisses I've ever had."

"Top five? How many people have you kissed?"

"Impossible to say, really. But . . . more than five?"

Jules passed the flask back to me. I hesitated, but then took another sip. I needed the courage if I was going to see Sebastian again that night. I hadn't felt nervous around him until . . . well, now. Now I was questioning everything I thought I knew about him. Who was he when he wasn't on the ship? And what were his intentions with me?

Steph had been setting up the bar for the night, but now she was back. "I'll give you another refill in exchange for some cruise gossip. I'm desperate for some tea—it's been a desert out here since Tim and Brian got kicked out for coning." Jules and I stared back blankly. "Hooking up with cruise kids."

Jules caught Steph up on the previous few days. The whole time, I couldn't stop thinking about why Sebastian had just left. And why I hadn't said anything.

"Who kisses someone and then just *leaves*?" I asked Jules and Steph. The rum had kicked in, and I could tell I was repeating myself, but I didn't care.

"Cis guys are the worst," Jules said. "Don't say I didn't warn you."

"Agreed," Steph said, winking at Jules.

"And this is why I don't believe in monogamy," Jules said, and I caught her exchange a look with Steph.

"Yup—it's our obligation to take advantage of being young," Steph agreed. "To figure out who we are and who we want to be, before we settle down."

I thought about my parents, how young they were when they got married and then had Logan. I wondered if they wished they had explored more or waited until after they were settled in their careers before getting pregnant.

"Just be careful choosing who to give your heart out to," Steph said, turning to face me. "Leaving in the middle of your first kiss? Sounds like he might be trouble."

"Ugh, but he's such *cute* trouble," Jules said, putting her arm around me and pulling me into her. "Right, Liv?"

"I need to fix this." I noticed my voice was coming out louder than intended and I was mixing up words. But I no longer felt nervous about Sebastian. Now I felt *angry*. And in need of *answers*. "Wanna go for a walk?"

"A walk to . . . the hot tub?" Jules asked, reading my mind.

"I mean, if our feet so happen to wander near the perimeter of the tub . . . we are all only passengers on one boat of life," I said, sure I was making complete sense.

Jules grinned widely at me. "Let's go."

When Jules and I got out of the elevator, we practically sprinted over to the hot tub. So much for our casual walk. My head felt fuzzy and my legs felt light as they glided across the deck.

Sure enough, we found the crew in the tub. Sebastian's arms were stretched out and sprawled around the edges. He was fully man-spreading, not seeming to have a care in the world.

"Look who it is," Troy bellowed. "Welcome to the tub, ladies."

I immediately glanced at Sebastian to gauge his reaction. He met my eyes and gave me a small smile, betraying no emotion. No *We just made out* eyes. No concern at our busting in, uninvited.

But I couldn't miss the way Charlie's face darkened when we approached.

"We got a little refill," Jules said, dangling her flask in the air, "and thought it would be unladylike of us not to share."

Ash looked at Jules, and I could practically see the sparks flying. "I'll take some of that please," they said, reaching over and taking the flask.

Charlie still hadn't said anything, but when Ash offered him the flask, he took a long swig.

"So are you two gonna get in, or what?" Troy asked.

"We're not in our bathing suits," I said.

"Guess we'll have to improvise!" Jules said, slipping off her skirt and top and revealing a lacy bra and matching underwear. Very, very *small* underwear. Honestly, I wasn't even sure they counted as underwear.

But of course Jules would come perfectly prepared in matching lacy lingerie. And then I realized—maybe she had been wearing that for *Ash*.

Oh no. All I had brought on the ship—all I *owned*, really— were childish patterned underwear and boring, white cotton bras from Target. Pretty much the opposite of sexy.

Charlie shook his head and handed the flask to Troy. Ash was gazing unabashedly at Jules. And so was Sebastian—who looked for a moment too long, before glancing back at me.

Despite my burned skin and ill-fitting bra and my old and very not-matching underwear—and the fact that it wasn't even dark out yet—I followed Jules's lead.

As I took off my shirt, Sebastian's eyes widened. He met my eyes again and held the stare. I felt my insides turn to marshmallow fluff at his unconcealed interest. I stepped into the tub right next to him—the second-guessing part of my brain apparently now fully deactivated by the rum.

When Sebastian slipped his arm around my bare waist and pulled me closer, I inhaled sharply. My body felt weightless in the water, and the combination of the hot, bubbling water and my bare skin directly against his made me feel like I had just been electrocuted.

"Hey," he whispered to me. His breath was so close that it tickled my ear. "I'm glad you came."

"Me too," I said. He pulled me in closer and kissed my shoulder. Everyone's eyes were on us, and I felt like I was floating. I was so glad to be back next to him, to see that everything was okay between us. Better than okay.

SEVENTEEN

By the time we'd finished Jules's flask, it didn't take much for Troy to convince us to attend that night's competition.

Jules and I grabbed our clothes and began running back to my room to change into dry ones. The distance from the hot tub to the room didn't seem that far, and it felt kind of . . . fun to not care about what other people thought. We giggled as we ran half-naked across the deck and into the elevator. When we got in, the sole occupant—a middle-aged man—saw us and then planted his eyes intently on a spot above our heads, which only made us giggle more.

"Have a nice night," Jules said brazenly, locking eyes with the man, as we got out of the elevator and began skipping toward my room.

"Oh no," Jules said, throwing a hand over her mouth. I could tell she was grinning, though. "Your parents," she stage-whispered.

"No!" I said, sure she must be messing with me. But then I followed her gaze. Sure enough, my parents were coming from the other direction.

My dad had his arm around my mom's shoulders, and they were laughing. My mom was in a turquoise, sleeveless dress, and my dad was in *shorts*. For once, they looked like a couple, rather than the parents they had been since they were twenty-five.

As my parents got closer, I sucked in my breath, racking my brain for an excuse. I should have realized the likelihood of this occurrence, seeing as we were next-door neighbors. But I wasn't really thinking. The boat felt huge, like its own world.

But it wasn't. I was a mere twenty yards away from my parents.

Wearing nothing but my bra and underwear.

When my parents spotted Jules and me, they became parents again. My dad dropped his arm, and my mom drew in her eyebrows.

I froze. My parents probably hadn't seen me half-naked since I was in diapers. Plus, I was sure we reeked of alcohol. My parents would book the next flight out of Martinique if they found out I was drinking.

"Hi, Mr. and Mrs. Schwartz!" Jules said cheerily, as if she weren't walking around like she had just left a Victoria's Secret photo shoot. "I spilled ketchup all over her clothes!" Jules explained before they could say anything. "And then when I was trying to clean up the mess, I got ketchup all over mine too! So then we jumped in the pool to try to clean off, and now . . ."

Shockingly, my parents nodded. I doubted they wanted to know the real story. I tightened my fist around my very ketchup-free dress.

"Anyway, we're just gonna go—get changed," I said, grabbing Jules's hand and frantically waving my card in front of the reader.

"All right, well, have a good night, ladies," my dad sputtered out.

As soon as the green light appeared and the door clicked—which felt like a full ten minutes but was probably only a few seconds—I threw open the door and yanked Jules in behind me.

After I shut the door, Jules and I collapsed on my bed in a fit of giggles.

"I can't believe we didn't get in trouble!" I felt relieved, but at the same time I also felt—hurt. I didn't want to get in trouble, but I also wanted to believe that my parents cared at least a little about my health and well-being.

"Of course we didn't, silly. Your parents *love* me," Jules said.

"That's true."

"And Liv, I hate to admit it, but—your parents are *hot*."

I rolled my eyes. "They are not."

"They are definitely PWFs."

"I don't even want to know what that means."

"Parents Who Fuck," Jules spelled out, blatantly ignoring my request. "I mean, you don't just *happen* to get pregnant at forty. My friend's parents had an actual schexdule on their refrigerator—" Jules was slurring now. "Schexadal. Sex—schedule! They did it all the time! And they *still* didn't get pregnant. So to end up pregnant with not just one but *two* babies—"

"Jules, the amount of sex you have does not share any correlation with the number of functional fetuses." Or was it fetii? Because it was radii, not radiuses . . .

"Livvy, enough with your sciencey science. Your parents. Are Hot. And have sex. Speaking of which, you know who else is hot and should have sex?"

I shook my head no, but I already knew the answer.

"You and Sebastian!" Jules raised an eyebrow. "You couldn't stop smiling around him, even if you tried!"

"Not true," I said, but I was smiling as I answered. I couldn't help it. "But . . . I think I like him."

"Duh," Jules said. "I've never seen a couple more disgustingly obsessed with one another." Jules grabbed my hand. "Let's go find our lovers."

We arrived at the teen club at the same time as the crew and found that the space had been transformed into a nightclub for the evening. There was a remote control sitting on a table, along with a note that said *Welcome to Teen Night: Challenge Four! Starring YOU as the DJ!* Under the paper was a book of songs with their corresponding numbers, like the type you'd find at a karaoke bar.

Sebastian placed a hand on my shoulder as I flipped through the book. "Did you talk to your parents?"

I shook my head. "Not yet." I thought of the way they had ignored me a few minutes before. The same way they had dismissed me that afternoon at the pool when I was so clearly upset.

Jules shoved the flask in front of my face. "Excuse me, lovebirds! Can I interest either of you in some very quality alcohol?"

"Yes, please." I wanted a break from my brain for the night. My anger at my parents and the work I had to do for the research paper and my concern over what the hell was going on between Sebastian and me. I took a long swig from the flask before offering it to Sebastian, who did the same. I needed to follow Jules's advice and have some *fun*. Focus on Sebastian in the here and now and how good being around him made me feel.

The door opened and Michelle and Dan bounded in. Jules quickly slipped the flask back into her purse. A few minutes later, Team Dino—which had now expanded to a group of eight—trudged in.

"Welcome to Competition Number Four: Dance Dance Execution!" Dan shouted. "Each team will get to select a song, which at least two members will have to improvise a dance to. There will be five rounds, and we'll be assigning points for creativity, technique, and"—Dan began making jazz hands—"passion!"

Troy pulled everyone in for a huddle. "We need a win tonight, crew." He turned to me. "We're nothing without you. We tanked in last night's belly-flop challenge."

"Ouch." Even though I was drunk, I still found myself calculating our odds of success. A loss the night before meant Team Dino was one challenge ahead of us. There were only four nights of challenges left—including this one—as the final night of the cruise was set aside for the winning team's dinner. Troy was right—we needed a win.

We won the coin toss, which meant it was our chance to perform first. I grabbed the book and, using the remote, entered the numbers I had found. "Out Tonight" began to play from the speakers. Michelle turned the volume up, and I stepped onto the dance floor. Jules smiled and followed me out.

I closed my eyes and rolled my shoulders back, letting the energy from the song direct my body. Logan and I had choreographed a dance to this song, and I still knew every move by heart. Logan would grab my hand and twirl me in so many fast circles that I'd feel nauseous, but I'd be having so much fun I'd keep on twirling anyway.

Sweat dripped down the back of my neck as I danced faster and faster, letting the music fully remove me from my body. "Ou—oot tonight!" I howled along with Mimi. My hair was in a ponytail now, so I threw the hair tie to the ground and tossed my head down, shaking out my chlorine-matted hair. I grabbed Jules and twirled her in a circle, and she began howling too.

I felt joyful tears clawing at the sides of my eyes. I could feel the music in my veins and Logan there with me. I howled again. I'd never felt so alive.

And then the song was over.

I collapsed into Sebastian's open arms and caught my breath as two members of Team Dino chose a country song, which they performed some form of line dance to. Sebastian tightened his arms around me and I melted into him, rubbing my face against the spiky stubble on his chin.

"And the winners of the first round are . . . Team Pineapple Pizza!" Dan shouted.

I bit back a grin as the crew erupted into cheers and foot stomping around me. Then Troy grabbed the remote, and I laughed when I heard the opening chords from a *Fiddler on the Roof* song.

Troy transformed into Tevye, and he held out a hand to me and began to lead. I didn't know the dance, but Troy was smooth, and somehow my feet found a way to match his rhythm.

"You doing okay there, Jersey?" he asked.

"Doing great!" I yelled back. Then I leaned in and whispered, "It's okay that I'm with Seb, right?"

He laughed and spun me around. "As long as you're having fun, my sweet summer child."

"All right, Team Dino, show us what you've got!" Michelle sang into the mic.

Team Dino seemed out of their realm—they were far too sober for this kind of competition. The entire team came out to the floor and performed a lackluster version of the Macarena.

We won that round as well.

Jules snatched the book of songs before anyone else could. "Okay, you musical theater nerds, new rule—no more show-tunes tonight!" she declared.

"Amen to that!" Ash said. Jules keyed in a number and the room began vibrating.

Jules and Ash began to shake their heads back and forth to the techno song, Jules's hair flying everywhere as Ash ran their fingers down Jules's arms.

Adrenaline still pumping through my veins, I grabbed Sebastian and led him to a corner, out of sight of Michelle and Dan. I pulled Sebastian up against my back and placed his hands on my hips. In response, he leaned in and began kissing my neck. I had never been kissed on the neck by anyone before. I'd had no idea what I was missing out on. It felt good. *So* good.

Before the song had ended, I was leading him to the elevator bank. I didn't need to stick around to know that we had won.

EIGHTEEN

This time I was the one throwing Sebastian into the pool. He laughed when he popped up and then tangled his hands in my hair and began to kiss me.

I knew that there were still families out and that everyone could see us, but I lost myself in Sebastian.

He put his hands around my waist, and we glided together to the far end of the pool. Sebastian placed his body against mine so that my back was pressed firmly against the wall. And then Sebastian was kissing my neck again and his hands were going lower. I couldn't see anyone from where we were. "If *I* can't see anyone, no one can see us, right?"

"Mm-hmm," Sebastian said. "That's definitely how physics works."

I was only halfway through AP Physics, but . . . my brain couldn't really compute physics problems at the moment. It was too focused on Sebastian's hands, and how good they felt, and how I'd never felt so in the moment before.

"Just relax," Sebastian whispered. And for once, those were the only words I wanted to hear.

I wrapped my legs around him, and then he was kissing my neck again and I was leaning back and on another planet. And he was rubbing his hands up and down my sides, and I just wanted more of him.

"Maybe we should go back to your room?" I asked. Because there were some things I really, really wanted to do that I knew I really, really shouldn't do in public.

When we got to Sebastian's room, Sebastian closed the door softly behind us. Then he turned to me and tucked a strand of hair behind my ear. "Oh hey," he said with a grin.

His voice was irresistibly raspy, and his Adam's apple jumped in and out while he spoke. Two words in, and I could already feel my knees buckling.

Sebastian slipped his hands around my waist and pulled me in toward him. But instead of kissing me, he kissed the tip of my ear. "How are you feeling?"

"Gooood," I said, drawing out the word. "And I decided that I have fallen for you, mister."

"Oh yeah?" he asked. "You sure about that?"

"Should I be?" I asked, pulling back a little.

He immediately pulled me back to him. "I hope you are," he said, kissing my temple. "Because," he said, taking a breath and pressing his lips against my collarbone, "I think you're pretty great."

I clenched my teeth, trying not to make it obvious how delirious he was making me. "I think you're pretty great too, Seb." I was drunk, and saying his entire name felt like too much effort. And I liked the way "Seb" sounded.

He wrapped one arm around me as he maneuvered us over to the bed. He lowered me down gently, and then he was on top of me.

Kissing while lying down—well, this was a lot different from kissing standing up. Now our tongues were directing what our bodies were doing. I loved the way the weight of his body felt.

I had never kissed anyone like Sebastian before. His hands were so confident, so steady. I could tell he knew exactly what he was doing. But then Jules's voice popped up. *They've had someone actually* teach *them what to do.*

I shook my head, trying to get myself to stop overthinking things, for once. And anyway, was it really so bad that he knew what he was doing? My other two kisses had been slimy and gross and lacking any sense of passion. I had been completely present, feeling the way the boy's tongue battled against mine as if in a sword fight. I had felt my lips become chapped. I had wondered when it would be over.

But this—it felt like our lips were made of neodymium, a metal that made up the most permanent magnet known to physics.

I never wanted this kiss to be over.

Or this cruise.

"I can't believe I've only known you five days," I said, my breath coming out in short bursts. "It feels like so much longer."

"Well, it's more like five 'cruise years,'" Sebastian said.

I laughed. "Yeah, I guess it is."

And then he was kissing me again, and I lost track of any sense of time—real or cruise.

I lay in bed that night, twisting around the towel animal (which today was a dove) in my hands. I had never liked anyone like this before. I hadn't even realized that it was possible.

I slipped on my headphones and put "Cigarettes and Cola" back on repeat.

I thought back to the night around a year before Logan had died. He'd invited me to his room and had me sit down. It was all very formal, very un-Logan.

"Olive, I have two important pieces of news." He was wringing his hands and looked nervous. Logan never got nervous.

"Yeah?" I asked.

"I'm gay."

I smiled. "Like Kurt on *Glee*."

He laughed. "Yeah. Like Kurt. Do you think that's weird?"

I shook my head. I couldn't believe Logan had been nervous to tell me. "No, of course not. So what's your second piece of news?"

His smile immediately expanded, like a tide rushing in all at once. "I'm in love."

I tucked my legs under me. "Wow," I said. "Tell me everything."

Logan and I had talked all night. He told me all about Patrick. The way they had cautiously flirted, unsure of whether they were just friends or something more. Their first date to see the latest Batman movie. How relieved they'd felt when they both admitted how much they'd hated it. How they had turned on a bootleg recording of *Spring Awakening* as a consolation, and had their first kiss as Henry and Eugene had theirs.

I had been a little nervous that Logan might shut me out, but pretty soon, the three of us were together all the time. I loved Patrick. He drew me funny pictures and always seemed to have chocolate stashed on him.

I wished Logan were here now, so I could sit him down. And tell him I had met a boy. I was desperate to hear what he would have thought of Sebastian. I was sure he would have loved him, though.

I inhaled deeply, breathing in Sebastian's oaky scent that lingered on my clothes. I felt so happy that I could burst.

My music changed, replaced by Amos Lee's dreamy, somber voice. Sebastian's words came back to me, about how these types of songs only came from heartbreak.

I felt a hot sense of fear slowly creeping through my veins.

Because for once, I wasn't in control of the way the situation would play out.

NINETEEN
DAY SIX AD

The next morning, I looked out the small window in my room. We had just pulled into St. Lucia, another island with sparkling blue-green waters and lush greenery. My heart sped up as I realized just how close we were to Antigua. Only two more days and one more island to go.

We hadn't signed up for any excursions that day; we'd just be spending the morning at the beach. I had never liked the ocean much—too many unknowns (jellyfish! crabs! drowning!)—and my plan was just to smother myself in sunscreen, read through my notes, and figure out an idea for the CPR program.

Before it got too hot, I wanted to squeeze in a quick run, so I put on my headphones and turned on the playlist I had made that week. Running on the sand was much harder than running on a track or a trail, but it was also way, way prettier. The sparkling sea was out to my left, and each step I took left an imprint in the sand. I lost myself in my music as the sun hit my peeling shoulders. *I could get used to this life.*

I was shaken out of my running trance when I realized someone was shouting my name—and maybe had been for a while. I paused my music and glanced to my right, where I saw Troy waving and bellowing.

Troy? Even though we were all docked at the same ports, for some reason it hadn't occurred to me that I might see the crew at one of the islands. It felt nearly as magical as running into someone in the city, although obviously it was a lot smaller of a coincidence here.

"Hey there, speedy," Troy said as he jogged up to me. "Sorry to interrupt your run."

"No problem," I said. "I could use a little break. How'd the rest of the competition go last night?"

"We won!" Troy said, pumping his fist in the air. "Want a celebratory beer?" I looked behind Troy, where I could see Ash, Charlie, and Sebastian. And a few very unconcealed six-packs.

I laughed. "Probably not the best mid-workout refreshment." I wondered if Sebastian had seen me; if he'd come to say hi too. I definitely didn't want to interrupt their morning; I could only imagine the level of stink-eye that Charlie would direct my way if I butted in on their precious crew time.

But then Sebastian was walking over, beer in hand. "Hey, Liv," he said, and I felt my heart rate speed back up to sprinting-across-the-finish-line level.

"Hey," I said. And then we all stood there for an awkward moment.

"So I'm just going to finish my run, but it was nice running into you," I said. "No pun intended."

"I could actually use some exercise myself," Sebastian said. "Mind if I join?"

I eyed his beer. "Are you sure about that?"

He tilted the can up to his lips, finished it off, and handed the empty container to Troy. "At your service, sir," Troy said, rolling his eyes.

"Race you to the lifeguard stand?" Before I could agree, Sebastian was off. Even with him being barefoot, and who knows how many beers in, his legs glided effortlessly in the deep sand. His breathing remained steady, despite the ambitious seven-minute pace he was setting.

I was used to running with the other girls on my team and leading the pack. It felt different—nice—to have someone else set the pace, to run alongside Sebastian and know that I could keep up with him.

When we got to the lifeguard stand, Sebastian came to an abrupt halt and put his arms out, which I practically tumbled over. But instead he pulled me in toward him, and we came together for a long kiss, our lips both dry and salty.

"You're a really good runner," he murmured.

"You're not so bad yourself," I said back into his mouth.

I nervously glanced to my right, but luckily, we were still too far from where my family had set up for me to be able to spot them.

Sebastian grabbed my hand, entwined his fingers in mine, and led me out to the ocean. I kicked off my sneakers and followed him into the water. He took me out far—farther than I'd ever been on my own—until we were both treading water. And then he was wrapping his legs around mine, and his hands were everywhere.

"Aruba, Jamaica, ooh I wanna take ya," he sang into my ear, before kissing down the tip of it and to my neck.

"I'm going to drown if you don't stop."

"Okay," he said, kissing me deeper.

We had been in the pool together, and the hot tub, of course, but the ocean was different. We were half-naked, and the water was slapping at our skin and the energy in the air was just—charged, like a toaster that was half plugged in and potentially going to set the house on fire (the infamous Schwartz household Hanukkah disaster; I took the fall for Logan).

I wanted to stay out there forever.

I felt myself being pulled under by Sebastian's irresistible spell, until we were literally being pulled under. A giant wave crashed over us, and I was tumbling underwater, trying to catch my breath but instead inhaling water, the waves tossing me around like a sock in a dryer.

Finally, I came up for air and began gasping, trying to fill my lungs with oxygen. And then Sebastian was by my side again. "Sorry about that," he said into my neck. "I got a little distracted." His eyes were soft, and I couldn't be mad at him for letting his guard down. "You're so fucking sexy, Liv, you know that?"

I had never heard my name and the word *sexy* uttered in the same sentence. I was so shocked by his words that I snorted a little water out of my nose—a definitively *un*sexy thing to do. "I think you're drunk" was all I managed to say back.

"Possibly," he said, wrapping his legs back around my waist and trailing his fingertips down the ridges of my spine. "But it's still true."

"Maybe we should . . . go a little closer to shore?" On the one hand, I liked being out far with him—the danger seemed to only make things feel better, and I didn't have to worry about anyone seeing us. It felt like we could do anything. And there was a *lot* I wanted to do.

On the other hand, I really, really didn't want to drown that day.

"K, hop on," Sebastian said, bending over. I climbed on his back, laughing at how childlike it felt. Logan used to carry me like this all the time when we went to the beach.

When we made it back to shore, Sebastian clasped the running watch on my wrist so he could check the time. "My scooter tour starts in ten. Wanna come?"

"Sure," I said, not bothering to ask what a scooter tour entailed. I just knew I wasn't ready for our time together to be over.

Luckily, my parents hadn't asked any questions when I asked for their credit card and permission to go on the tour. But this meant that I actually had to do it.

I nodded along as our instructor, Ashley, explained to the four of us—Sebastian, me, and a tanned, CrossFit-looking couple in their twenties—how the motorized scooters worked and what hand signals to use if we needed help.

Apparently, this was an *underwater* scooter tour, some terrifying combination of snorkeling and Jet Skiing, neither of which I had ever done before. You didn't even wear a life jacket—instead, you were *strapped in* to this death contraption.

But of course, I hadn't thought to ask about any of this before agreeing or signing the waiver. The waiver that mentioned that underlying conditions could cause a risk of cardiac arrest or stroke. And of course, when you're young, you generally don't *know* about underlying conditions. Until it's too late.

So now I was far out at sea, with an instructor who couldn't be more than a few years older than us, and four deathmobiles ready to go.

"Any questions?" Ashley asked with a smile.

What if the scooter breaks and I can't swim back up? Or it gets stuck underwater along with me strapped to it? How the hell am I supposed to trust this thing?

I kept my mouth shut, hoping someone else would chime in, but no one did.

"Great, then we're all set!"

As soon as Ashley gave the signal, the CrossFit couple hopped right onto their scooters. Their scooters' engines roared as they zoomed underwater, but a moment later, the sound died out completely and they disappeared.

"I'm just going to try out the mask for a minute," I said, stalling. I put the mask on and took a few practice breaths, trying to adjust my body to the feeling of wearing a mask. My throat immediately seized up, and I had to yank the mask off. No *way* could I do this strapped on a scooter. Underwater.

"Trust your breath," Ashley assured me. "You'll be fine. Just breathe in and out." *Oh yeah, Ashley? Do you know for sure that I'll be fine? What about that waiver you had me sign, that denied all liability for any potential injury or death? Do you know I don't have any underlying conditions? Can you guarantee it?*

I took a few deep breaths and then looked at Sebastian.

"We don't have to do this if you don't want to, Liv." He said the words so gently, I knew he meant them.

"No, I do want to." For whatever reason, I did. I trusted him. If he said it was okay to dive onto this deathmobile, then it would be okay.

"Follow after me on the count of three?" he asked, and I nodded.

When Sebastian dove under with his scooter, I didn't calculate how long it might take to suffocate or think about getting tangled up in seaweed a mile underwater. I softly kissed the air twice, said "Thank you God," and then took the biggest breath I could manage. I squeezed the trigger and jetted straight down after him, gripping the handles as tightly as I could.

And then—wow.

The waters were nothing like the Jersey shore. Here, they were green and filled with rainbow-colored coral.

I jetted around, watching the colorful fish and sea life swimming around me.

When I turned my head to the left, I nearly gasped. Less than a foot away from me were two gold-and-red-speckled sea turtles. I felt tears prick the back of my eyes.

Logan and I used to love going to the Atlantic City Aquarium. The first spot we'd always hit up was the turtle tank, where he would invent elaborate backstories for each turtle in the tank.

That's Lola. She's a hot lil piece who was married to old Mr. Moneybags, but she had him murdered so that she could steal all his money and shag Timmy. But then Timmy left Lola for Joe, so Lola hired Mr. Pickles as a hitman, who you can see over in that corner, currently plotting Timmy's and Joe's assassinations.

He would have made an excellent script writer for *The Real Housewives.*

Would have.

I had never imagined that snorkeling would have this big of an impact on me. It's just—there was all of this life going on that I wasn't aware of before. Which made me wonder how much other life was out there that I couldn't see. If Logan was still existing, somewhere on a different dimension. Maybe under the sea.

I blinked back tears as I floated alongside the turtles. I followed the turtles up and down, left and right, fully mesmerized by the beautiful speckles on their flippers and the symmetry of the lines on their shells. They didn't seem to have any worries in the world. They swam slowly, nowhere to go, nowhere to be.

I came back up so I could take a few breaths but then dove straight back down again. When I made it back down to the turtles, I released my death grip on the trigger. I just floated there, alongside the glittering sea life and Sebastian, never wanting to return to land.

I guess this is why people went on vacation.

It was all so beautiful.

Logan would have loved it so much.

TWENTY

I walked back to where my family was spread out on the beach. My hair was a wet, matted mess, and I was still soaked from head to toe.

"Did you have one hundred dollars' worth of fun?" my dad asked with a wry smile.

"Yeah," I said. "It was . . . amazing." *Amazing* didn't even begin to do the trip justice. It was impossible to put words to what I'd just experienced.

"That's great, honey," my mom said. "We're so glad you're enjoying the trip."

I wanted to tell them about my time under the sea with Logan. The sea turtles and how many memories they had brought back. But I knew they wouldn't want to talk about Logan in front of the twins, and I didn't want to risk ruining the perfect day.

So instead I just nodded. "Me too." Then I spread out my towel and lay back, letting the sun dry me off.

I closed my eyes and went back underwater in my mind, already feeling nostalgic for the past hour of my life.

If I had every single moment of my life planned out, there would never be any space for the unexpected—the magical moments that take your breath away, that you remember forever. Like the sea turtles. And Sebastian.

How many experiences like these had I missed out on, because I was too busy planning each and every moment of my life, never just letting myself *be*?

Maybe that was the whole point of this trip, what Logan was trying to show me. I needed to allow a little wiggle room in my plans, a little space to let the unexpected in. Logan still wanted me to have joy in my life, even if he wasn't there to bring it to me.

As my family gathered our belongings to head back to the ship, I wondered if we'd run into Sebastian and the crew.

I took Justin's and Matt's hands and began to walk across the sand. We had only made it a few steps before Justin was bending down and reaching for something shiny. "Justin—no!" I grabbed his hand, not wanting him to cut himself on a piece of metal or get infected with God knows what.

"But Birdie says litter kills the sea creatures," Justin said earnestly.

"Okay, why don't you point the litter out to me and I'll collect it, then?" I loved that the boys were already such good citizens at this young of an age. I had to hand it to Birdie, for knowing how to educate young kids about such an important and scary issue in a way that they not only understood, but that also gave them actionable tools to actually *do* something about. Because collecting beach litter was definitely doing more than most adults or politicians were doing.

And then it hit me.

Birdie!

That was how I could teach kids CPR! It was the perfect idea for my hospital program. Birdie—or some other kid-friendly cartoon—could do a video showing a family member having a heart attack and then could teach the steps to perform CPR.

Justin and Matt watched all of Birdie's videos over and over; they had every single word and hand gesture memorized. If they had seen a video on CPR—well, maybe not while they were *this* young, because their hand-eye coordination and strength weren't there yet. But I bet if they were just a few years older, and if they'd seen a CPR video dozens of times, that they'd be able to do it. They would know exactly what to do, *and* they wouldn't be scared. Because Birdie would've told them all about it, normalized it, prepared them.

I wanted to sprint back to my room to get to work, but I kept my promise to the boys and continued collecting litter along the way. I couldn't stop smiling, though. This was definitely a program that would get me the internship. And save lives.

I was so lost in concentration typing up my Birdie idea that it took me a moment to realize someone was tapping on my door.

I went to open it and found Sebastian leaning against the frame, a large grin on his face. I felt my heart speed up a few beats at his smile. At the fact that he was there. That he wanted to see me again.

But then I shook my head, forcing myself to snap back to reality. I had *work* to get done. Sebastian would still be there in a few hours. For now, I needed to focus.

"I've just got to finish up this outline," I said.

"No problem," Sebastian said. But rather than offering to come back later, he took a seat on the bed next to me.

Sebastian slung an arm around me, and I inhaled, feeling the same light, prickly sensation I always felt when we made contact.

Focus, Olivia, I reminded myself.

"The incidence of cardiac arrest could be severely lowered in key demographics," Sebastian stated in a loud, sportscaster voice. "Really fascinating stuff you've got here, Liv."

"It is!" I said.

I went back to typing, and thirty seconds later, Sebastian was slipping down the strap of my tank top and kissing my now-bare shoulder. "I find your tibia," he said, kissing my shoulder—which was nowhere near my tibia—"and your extensor carpi radialis"—he was now creating a trail of kisses down my arm—"incredibly sexy."

"Despite having no idea where those bones are," I said, but my voice came out tight and high-pitched.

"Absolutely not," Sebastian said. "I most certainly failed biology."

I breathed in and out, trying to summon up the willpower to resist. But finally I slammed my laptop shut and leaned back. Nearly instantaneously, Sebastian was crawling on top of me.

"Does it turn you on when I speak medical to you?" he asked, his voice low and throaty.

"Oh yeah, so much," I said with a smirk.

"It still counts as studying, then, right?"

"Mm-hmm," I said as he kissed my neck again.

"Is it okay if I have a soda with dinner?"

"Crap!" I was out from under Sebastian in an instant, standing up and readjusting my tank top. The twins and my parents must have just gotten back to their room, and I could hear them talking through the shared wall.

Sebastian looked at me, confused. "My family is back," I whispered. I gestured with my thumb to the wall.

For a moment, I pictured what might have happened if my parents had knocked on the door and met Sebastian. I was sure they'd love him—I mean, the twins already did.

"Ah," he said. "Let's switch locations, then?"

But the moment passed quickly. Of course it would be crazy to introduce a guy I'd been dating for all of thirty seconds to my parents. "Let me send these notes to my friend, and then I'll meet you back at your room?"

"Deal," Sebastian said before quietly slipping out of my room.

I waited a few minutes after Sebastian left, in case my parents were listening, and then brought my notes to the business center.

Olivia: GUESS WHAT

Shruti: OMG DID YOU LOSE YOUR V CARD

Olivia: outdated patriarchal invention and also no—better

Shruti: omg what???

Olivia: i came up with the best idea for the hospital program!!!

Shruti: oh. major letdown

Olivia: if you think SAVING LIVES is a letdown, then fine

Shruti: so what is this genius idea??

I explained everything to Shruti—how the boys knew all of Birdie's videos by heart. How the problem with CPR wasn't just teaching the technical moves, but staying calm and remembering what to do in the moment. How I was sure a channel like Birdie's would love to promote something so positive, that could help so many families.

Shruti: not bad, Schwartz. send me over your notes and any relevant links so I can make the powerpoint?

Olivia: i still have to put the script together, and i was thinking of even creating some graphics of Birdie teaching the moves. so i'll probably need another day

Shruti: oh, i thought your carefully outlined schedule had me on call today to do the presentation

Olivia: it did, but is it okay if i send it to you tonight?

Shruti: i just have that stupid family bbq tomorrow . . . and the presentation is in three days

Shoot. Right. Although there was a part of me that was a little annoyed, because I had an entire family trip this whole week, but I was still getting my work done.

Olivia: kk don't worry, it's my fault it's late. i can do the powerpoint and send over the notes for you to memorize for the research fair

Shruti: are you sure we're gonna be done in time? that's cutting it pretty close

Olivia: 😝 isn't that your style, though

Shruti: har har har, fine. there's really nothing i can do to help today?? even something little? i could draw some of the cartoon!

Olivia: nope, i've got it. promise we'll be done in time

Shruti: everything else there good? how's your crab friend?

Olivia: ha ha. sebastian is good. great. i really wish you could meet him. he's just . . . not like the boys in new jersey

Shruti: i mean, he must be pretty great for you to be missing deadlines 😝

Olivia: very funny

I knew Shruti was joking, but her words still stung. Sure, I hadn't stuck to the exact schedule. But had I not done the research, come up with the idea, and agreed to do the entire PowerPoint? Did she really need to give me crap for enjoying myself, for once? Especially since I was *still* getting all of the work done? Had I not sent her notes for every class that she missed, then helped her prep for every test, while she zoned out and cried after her debate camp boyfriend broke up with her? Couldn't she cut me some slack?

I signed out of the computer and then headed to Sebastian's room. When I knocked on the door, Charlie answered. "Hey," he said, clearly not thrilled to see me.

"Oh—hey," I said, for some reason not expecting to find Charlie there, even though of course this was his room too. "Is Sebastian here?"

Charlie rubbed his forehead. "Oh, um, no, he's—out," he said.

"Out?" I repeated, crossing my arms. "Like out . . . at sea?"

Charlie let out a small bitter laugh. "Can I take a message?"

I didn't know what the hell Charlie's problem was with me, and I was in no mood to deal with this right now. "Can you please just tell me where he is? Why are you acting so weird?"

"Look, Liv," Charlie said. "Just . . . maybe don't spend so much time with him, okay?"

Why was he telling me this? "I'm so sorry; am I interrupting precious bro time or something?"

"Actually, yes, you are. So maybe just let him chill with us for a single fucking afternoon?"

"Sure—enjoy," I said. The door slammed behind me, my eyes stinging from the tears that had so quickly formed. What the hell was Charlie's problem? Had Sebastian put him up to this? Was he trying to end things with me, let me down gently?

I headed straight for the elevator, staring at the ground and blinking back tears—where I ran right into Sebastian.

"Whoa!" he said, backing up. "Liv?"

"Hey," I said. "Sorry, I was just going—"

"Hey, what's wrong?" he asked, squinting at my tear-streaked face and putting a hand on my shoulder.

Sebastian's eyes began blazing when I repeated what Charlie had said to me.

"Shit, Liv, I'm so sorry Charlie was such a dick. He's . . ." Sebastian trailed off and he sighed. "He's a good guy. I think he's just pissed at me for not spending every second with the 'crew.' And also, a little jealous."

"Jealous?" I asked. "Of what?"

Sebastian shook his head and smiled down at me. "Of me, silly." He wrapped his arms around me and pulled me toward him. He tucked a piece of hair behind my ear and kissed me. "Because I'm with you."

"He is *not* jealous of you. He hates me."

"He does not hate you. Anyway, I'll see you at the hot tub tonight?"

"Yeah, sure," I said, doing my best to hide my disappointment. I had thought that before, we'd agreed to meet up after I sent my work to Shruti. I had been hoping to hang out now, to not waste any of the little time we had left together. But clearly Sebastian had other plans.

"See you later." I gave a slight wave and then walked back to my room. At least this would give me more time to work on the presentation.

"You'll never believe what happened with Charlie," I said as I collapsed onto Jules's bed. I had spent the last hour trying to put together slides but had finally given up, unable to focus. All I could think about was why Charlie had been such a jerk to me. And why Sebastian hadn't seemed to want to hang out. So I had closed out of the presentation and headed to Jules's room to get ready. I knew she would be just as indignant when I told her about Charlie.

"Weird," Jules said after I finished telling her what happened. Her tone was measured, like a teacher who knows the answer but is refusing to give it to you.

"Weird?" I repeated, raising an eyebrow. "More like extreme douchebaggery."

Jules shrugged. "I dunno, I mean, they all came here to hang, and I guess they just want to spend more time together as a crew."

"Yeah, but he didn't have to be such a dick to me. I mean, he's not Sebastian's *dad*. Seb's allowed to hook up with whoever he wants."

"What are you actually upset about?" Jules asked as she put in a new pair of sparkly earrings.

I scrunched my eyebrows together. "What do you mean?"

"I dunno; you just seem really upset that Charlie wants to spend more time with Sebastian. What's the big deal?"

"The big deal is that we only have three days left together! Charlie has the rest of their senior year."

"Yeah, but . . . you just met him. Charlie and Sebastian have been friends much longer."

"I know," I said, twisting my fingers together. Jules didn't get it. "I just really like him. Like, *really* like him."

Jules swallowed. "Okay," she said slowly. "But . . . you live so far away. Do you think you'll like . . . date, after?"

The way Jules asked the question made it sound like she thought the idea was absurd. Like I was deranged for even considering it.

"Is that so crazy?" I asked.

Jules let out a long sigh. "I just think you should be careful."

"What does that mean?"

"Sebastian is . . . I mean, he's excessively charming. He doesn't seem like the type of guy to . . ." Her voice drifted off.

"Didn't you say he's a serial monogamist?"

"I mean, yeah, but from what I've heard, he also . . . tends to always be involved with a girl. And not always long-term."

"Oh," I said, swallowing and immediately feeling like an idiot. What had Jules heard? What wasn't she telling me? "Have you and Ash talked about what's going to happen when the cruise ends?" My voice came out weak.

Jules laughed. "Maybe we'll text after, but it's just a cruise hookup. Everyone knows these things never last."

I felt my heart squeeze. Was this just common knowledge everyone shared, except for me? Was that how Sebastian felt? Did he assume I felt that way too?

Jules saw my face fall. "I mean—I'm not saying that's the case with you and Sebastian. But regardless, just make sure you're having fun, okay? I know you like to have a ten-year plan for every aspect of your life, but . . . sometimes a ten-day plan is all you need. These are memories we're going to look back on as old ladies."

I didn't need any more memories to look back on. When I committed to something, I wanted long-term results. I fingered the thin comforter on Jules's bed. "It just doesn't *feel* like a hookup, you know?"

A soft smile played out on Jules's face. "Aw, hon," she said, reaching over and putting a hand on my shoulder. "They never do."

My palms felt clammy as Jules and I walked over to the hot tub. I wasn't excited about facing Charlie again, the death glare he was sure to direct my way the whole night. But I definitely wasn't going to let him win or miss out on one of my final four nights with Sebastian.

When we arrived at the hot tub, we found the crew—but no Sebastian.

"Where's Sebastian?" I asked, trying to sound as breezy as possible. But I felt a sinking feeling in my stomach.

There was a brief pause as Troy and Charlie exchanged a look. "I think he's in the business center, checking in back home," Troy finally said.

"Question," Ash said. "This guy I met said he can get us a seven-hundred-fifty-milliliter bottle of Malibu for thirty dollars or a one-liter bottle for thirty-five dollars. . . . Which should I get?"

"Well, the one-liter bottle is half a cent cheaper per milliliter," I responded.

Four heads whipped toward me. Ash whistled as Troy said, "Shit, that was fast."

I sank down farther into the hot tub. I hadn't been trying to show off. I loved doing mental math, and this really wasn't that hard since seven point five went evenly into thirty, four times, and it was easy to divide anything by one liter, or one thousand milliliters—you just moved over the decimal point three times. But I knew that explanation would only make me look nerdier.

"Liv's our resident genius," Jules said, putting an arm around my shoulders. "She got, like, a perfect score on her SAT."

"Jules! I did not," I protested.

"Oh, my apologies—she missed one question on reading." I could feel my cheeks heating up. My mom must have told Cindy.

"Whoa, really? That's sick," Troy said. I shot him a small smile. I knew he was being sincere.

"Speaking of cool, guess what Steph hooked me up with today," Jules said.

"Shrooms?" Troy guessed.

"Close—brownies. *Special* brownies," Jules said, her eyes twinkling.

I shifted uncomfortably. "Isn't that . . . illegal?"

"It's baked into the brownies. I don't think anyone's ever been arrested for that."

"It should be legal, anyway," Charlie said.

Troy laughed. "If it were up to Charlie, *all* drugs would be legal."

"Really?" I asked, raising my eyebrows.

"Yeah." Charlie spoke slowly, as if he were patiently answering a five-year-old. "Addiction is a disease, not a crime. Criminalization is just the government's way of bringing back Jim Crow laws. And since when has prison ever *helped* someone?"

I shrugged. "I just think doing drugs is a choice."

Charlie let out a dark laugh. "Where are you from again? The Jersey suburbs?"

"What does that have to do with anything?"

"You're sheltered. Do you understand the complex socioeconomic and big pharma factors at play?"

Before I could answer—or mention that Jules was *also* from the Jersey suburbs, so his point was moot—Sebastian appeared and climbed into the hot tub.

"Yooo," he said, sliding an arm around me. I let out a small sigh as I sank into him. "Oh no—did you get caught up in one of Charlie's pharmaceutical conspiracy lectures?" His speech was slow and the words came out slurred.

Troy began waving a hand in front of his face. "Bro—are you smashed already?"

"Hey, it's always drinks time when you're on a cruise, am I right?" Under the water, his hand was playing around with the hem of the bikini bottom that I had borrowed from Jules. I felt my heart rate speed up and a sudden urge to sprint out of the hot tub and go somewhere alone together.

I breathed out, trying to keep a steady face. "Time does feel . . . different here. Every day sort of feels like a year."

"Cruise years," Ash said. "That's what my family calls them."

"Are you a cruise family?" Jules asked, raising a brow.

"A bit," Ash admitted. "We've been on"—they began ticking off the places on their fingers—"four Regal Islands cruises, and three on other cruise lines."

"Wow," I said. "That's a lot of time to spend on floating malls."

Charlie actually let out a small laugh at that.

"So are you the one who organized this?" I asked.

"Nope, that was all Seb," Ash said. "He convinced us we needed a 'crew cruise.'"

"A *crew*se, one might say," Troy said.

"Really?" I asked, turning to Sebastian. "This was *your* idea?"

Sebastian shrugged. "What can I say? I guess I'm a fan of floating malls . . . and lax drinking ages. And cheap-ass prices."

"And running away from your problems," Charlie muttered under his breath.

I looked from Charlie to Sebastian, but before I could ask what that meant, Troy was jumping in. "So who's ready for *karaoke* tomorrow? I'm going to bring this ship *down*."

Sebastian scoffed. "We all know I'm going to win, man."

"Oh yeah?" I asked. "What are you going to sing?"

Sebastian winked at me. "It's a surprise."

There was a bit larger of a crowd at the teen club that night—fifteen or so people sprawled on the lounge chairs and couches. A few were chatting, but most were looking around nervously.

"Welcommmme to teen night number FIVE!" Dan shouted into his completely unnecessary headset mic. "Tonight, you are all in for a treat. We've set up a complex obstacle course across the ship. Whoever wins tonight will be one step closer to a night you can't forget at the Empire Steak Buildiiiing!"

"WOOOO!" Troy cheered. A few people snickered.

Michelle explained the challenge—there were eight stations set up around the ship. Every station had a Post-it note in each team's color, which contained the clue for how to find the next station. We'd all be hitting up the same stations, but in a different order.

"Your first clues are hidden right in this room. On your mark, get set, goooo!" Dan and Michelle shouted together.

Everyone got up and began running around.

"Found it!" Ash yelled out from the back of the room. Troy grabbed the pink Post-it from them and read it out loud. "'Up at the top of the rock, you will find the CLUE for station number TWO!'"

"Lordy," Charlie said, shaking his head. "Whoever wrote that should have their poetry license revoked."

"Rock wall?" Ash guessed, and then we all began sprinting after them to the elevators and down to the sixth floor.

We rounded the corner of the track until we arrived at the rock wall. And sure enough, right up top, we could spot something hot pink.

"I've got this," Sebastian said with a determined look on his face.

"Of course he does," Charlie muttered.

Sebastian scaled the wall in a few quick leaps. He then jumped down, landing gracefully on his feet, and read out the next clue. "'Catch a wave with me—time to find clue number three.'"

"Ah, the surfing thing!" Jules shouted. Despite how juvenile this game was, it was hard not to get caught up in the adrenaline that competitions bring out. Sebastian grabbed my hand, and I smiled widely and began sprinting for the surfing simulator. But Sebastian was moving slowly, and I adjusted my footsteps to match his.

When everyone was a few yards ahead of us, he came to a halt and wrapped his arms around my waist. He brushed his lips against my ear. "Wanna ditch?" I felt a pulse of heat rush through my veins.

"Mm-hmm," I said, lacing my fingers with his.

Sebastian pushed the door closed behind him, and we fell in a tangled heap onto his bed. As we kissed, I couldn't stop myself from thinking back to what Jules had said earlier. What if she was right, and Sebastian just thought this was a fling?

"Everything okay?" Sebastian asked, brushing a strand of hair out of my eyes.

I exhaled slowly. "I'm just . . . scared."

"Scared of what?"

"Of how much I like you," I practically whispered.

Sebastian propped himself up with one hand and looked into my eyes. "Why does that scare you?"

"I just . . . ," I croaked. "The cruise is over so soon." *And then what?* I had so many questions. I wanted to know where this was going and how he actually felt about me and if what Jules had said was true.

Sebastian's eyes were especially glassy tonight, and he was starting to slur his words together. "Let's not worry about the future. Let's make every moment we're here count."

I had been so determined to talk to him, sure I would get some clarity. But then he was kissing under my ear, and all reason disappeared. Kissing him felt good; his feelings toward me seemed undeniable.

Sebastian wrapped his arms around me and pulled me into his chest. I nuzzled my face into his neck. No matter how close our bodies got, I still wanted to remove some of the space between them.

We didn't say anything for a few minutes, and then I realized he was snoring. I lay there, listening to the steady rhythm of his heartbeat and inhaling his oaky scent. I couldn't believe how much I liked this boy. No one had ever smelled so good.

I finally understood why people made such a big deal about sleeping together. Not the euphemistic version—actual sleeping in the same bed together.

What we were doing now was so different, so intimate—falling asleep together, not wanting to be apart, even while unconscious.

I didn't know how I'd spent so many nights sleeping alone and never realized just how truly lonely I was. When I was younger, Logan and I had sleepovers all the time. I'd put a sleeping bag on the floor of his room when I couldn't fall asleep, and he'd hang up sheets and set up "camp." But that was years ago, and I'd forgotten just how comforting it was, how unnatural it felt to be alone all night long.

Sebastian tightened his arms around me, pulling me in closer. "Seb?" I whispered, but he was still asleep.

I knew I had to head back to my room soon. But I just wanted to lie there in his arms a little while longer. Because while they were around me, there was no doubt in my mind that Jules was wrong. This wasn't just some casual fling.

TWENTY-ONE
DAY SEVEN AD

When I opened my eyes, it took my brain a moment to figure out where I was. Sebastian's arms were still wrapped around me, and I was in his bed.

I had fallen asleep. In Sebastian's room.

The bed above us creaked, and as my eyes adjusted to the little light in the room, I realized that all four bunk beds were occupied. I very carefully repositioned myself so I could see the clock on the nightstand.

It was five a.m.

Shit.

I hadn't just fallen asleep—I'd fallen into a *deep* sleep. Stayed out all night. Broken curfew. My parents must have been freaking out. They had no way of reaching me, no way of knowing where I was.

I gingerly took Sebastian's arms and unhooked them from around me. Immediately I felt the drop in temperature. It had been so nice lying there all night with him.

So nice that I had completely forgotten to wake up.

I walked out of the room and closed the door softly behind me. I smoothed my hair out—not that it would make much of a difference—as I ran to the elevator. I pressed the button for the ninth floor three times, as if that would make the doors close so fast that they could rewind time.

When I turned the corner, I began tiptoeing toward my room, my breath coming out in short spurts. *Please don't see me please don't see me please don't see me.*

My heart was pounding. I had never so blatantly broken my parents' rules before. I couldn't even remember the last time I had ever broken *a* rule or lied to them.

The closest time I could think of was years ago, when my parents had scheduled an official "meeting" with me. I had no clue what was going on. I was terrified that one of my grandparents had died or that Mr. Snuggles Factory was sick. My parents took seats on either side of me on my green-and-purple comforter. And then very solemnly my dad asked, "Olivia, is any money missing from your piggy bank?"

I had almost laughed, I was so relieved. And confused as to why they would make such a big deal of it.

I counted the money in that bank religiously every week. Not that much money went in, and I never took any out. But I liked the order of it, keeping careful track of the few possessions that were truly mine.

So I emptied the bank out in front of them and counted the money. Long before I had gotten to the nickels and dimes, I knew for sure that money was missing. I'd had over eighty dollars, and now I had just under thirty.

I looked up at my parents' overly concerned faces.

"Nope, it's all here!" I told them with a smile.

Things were bad enough between them and Logan as it was. Monthly screaming matches had turned into daily occurrences. And who cared if a little money was missing? Logan was always complaining to me about how stingy my parents were. I would have lent him the money, if he'd asked.

I jolted back to the present as the door to my stateroom—and the adjoining door to my parents' room—came into sight. I breathed out a sigh of relief. No sign of my parents. I held the card in front of the door, wishing there was a way to silence the click it made when it unlocked.

The green light appeared.

Just as my parents' door opened.

"Olivia?" my mom asked, rubbing her eye.

"Oh, hi, Mom!" I plastered a smile across my face. My mind was racing with potential lies I could tell. *Jules.* My mom loved Jules. Jules was safe. *I was with Jules. And we were . . . listening to music. And then we . . . fell asleep. In her room.*

My mom wrinkled her brow. "What are you doing up so early?"

Early. I didn't even need some elaborate lie. My mom's question had saved me.

"I have so much work to do, so I just grabbed some breakfast."

"At five in the morning?"

"I mean, we have the beach trip today, and there's some event tonight Jules wants to go to, and I don't set the rules of ship time, so . . ."

My mom yawned. "Okay, well, I hope you're getting enough sleep."

Really? That was it? She was buying this story?

215

I smiled. "Yup, I am. See you later!"

I opened the door to my room and collapsed on my bed.

I thought about how many times Logan had made this early morning trek back to our house. How my mom said she never slept until he returned, that she lay awake all night in her bed, waiting for him.

I should have felt relieved she hadn't stayed up all night in a panic, wondering where I was.

But instead, I felt a giant lump in my throat.

My parents didn't know me at all.

I spent the morning working on my presentation. I desperately wanted to nap or grab some food, but I was terrified my mom would come into my room and ask why I wasn't working. So I skipped breakfast, doing my best to stick with the lie I had told. My stomach grumbled as we walked off the ship and out to the parking lot, where a group of buses waited to take cruise-goers to the beach.

My parents and Jules's parents had signed up for the same beach trip in Barbados that day. I shot Jules a small smile when I saw her, willing her with my eyes not to say anything about my disappearance the night before.

While our parents took the twins into the water, Jules and I lay back on our towels on the sand. The sun was strong, and I could already feel beads of sweat collecting on my back.

Jules was lying on her stomach, and I couldn't tell if she was asleep or not.

"Jules?" I asked, then once more a little louder. "You awake?"

"Mm-hmm," she murmured sleepily.

"Did we win last night?" I wanted to know, but I also hoped this would give Jules an easy excuse to bring up my disappearance. I still felt uneasy about our chat the night before, and I wondered why she wasn't grilling me like she usually did about what was going on with Sebastian.

"Nope," Jules said. I waited for her to say something else, but that was it.

I pulled my knees up against my chest. I was going to need to be more direct. "So, I need some . . . advice."

Jules rolled onto her back and grabbed the giant sun hat lying next to her, tossing it over her perfectly messy bun. "What's up?"

I turned back to the water to confirm that our parents weren't on their way back to us. But they were standing right where the tide was washing in, as the boys played in the wet sand. Or rather, as Justin gleefully created lumpy sandcastles and Matt anxiously smoothed out the sides and edges. "I think I'm ready to . . . take it to the next level." I cleared my throat. "With Sebastian."

Jules's eyebrows shot straight up. "Really?"

"Yeah," I said, surprised that Jules wasn't immediately on board. She was practically a spokesperson for casual sex, for using this cruise to "just have fun."

"I just feel like you're someone who makes a ten-page report before deciding what breakfast cereal to eat, so I'm surprised by this sudden change in . . . character."

I stiffened. It wasn't exactly a flattering depiction, but Jules wasn't far off. I had, just the other month, created an extensive pro/con list when I was debating whether to switch deodorant brands.

But maybe this was the whole point of the cruise—to get me to loosen up. To experience life. To be "normal."

"I just feel . . . ready," I said, trying to speak with as much confidence as possible. And oddly, even though it had only been a few days, I did feel ready. For something. I just wasn't sure what yet.

"Okayyy," Jules said, dragging out the last syllable. "As long as you're sure."

"I am!"

"And if Sebastian never speaks to you again after—"

"Why would that happen?" I felt my insides twisting. Did Jules know something I didn't?

"It's just a hypothetical. I want to make sure that even in a worst-case scenario, you won't regret doing this."

"I won't," I said firmly.

Jules's face lit up. "I'm so proud of you. It's gonna be great." Jules crossed her legs and sat up. "You have questions. I have answers. Shoot."

I felt my heart rate speed up. My parents were pretty tight-lipped when it came to anything risqué—sex, drugs, death, even money. Logan had been the one to teach me about the birds and the bees. We had been watching *Look Who's Talking*, and he had explained how when two people were in love, they had sex, and that if the two people were a guy and a girl, that one day the woman went to the bathroom and came out with a baby. For years, I had been terrified whenever I went to the bathroom that somehow I would come out with a baby. I'd never had a real understanding of how the anatomy of it all worked.

"Um . . ." I mean, I *did* have questions. I didn't want to screw things up with Sebastian or do things wrong. I wanted him to like me; I wanted him to more than like me. "What was your first time like?" I asked.

"Oh, awful. Truly, truly terrible. In the back of a Jeep with Jeff Findley. The condom broke and everything."

"Oh no! Did you get pregnant?"

Jules burst out laughing. "Of course not! I took Plan B and I was fine. But we both hadn't had sex before. Neither of us knew what we were doing, and it was just an awkward naked tango. I didn't even really like him that much; I just wanted to get it over with."

"So . . . what should I know, so that I'm not like . . . bad?" I gulped and lowered my voice. "In bed."

Jules then gave me the most extensively detailed sex ed I'd ever heard. All they taught in school was about every STD to avoid; no one ever talked about the stuff Jules was explaining to me.

"I think the hardest part of this all is—ugh, I hate to say it—but *sometimes*, not always—sex stuff does make you get attached. There are definitely chemicals released—I mean, you and all of your doctory knowledge would know this better than me—but . . . yeah."

"What's it like with Ash?" I asked.

"Well, it's definitely different from when I hooked up with cis boys. But in general, with anyone, it's just like—you've gotta talk about it beforehand, and check in during, and then I always like having a postmortem check-in after, to see what they liked and didn't. Because sometimes in the heat of the moment it can be harder to communicate all that stuff."

I had never realized sex was so . . . complicated. I wished I had a pen and paper with me. I was frantically taking mental notes, but a notebook would have really come in handy. What if I did everything wrong and Sebastian never wanted to see me again?

"Girls, what are we gabbing about? I want a lowdown on all of the cruise 'ships'!" I jumped when Cindy reappeared. She grabbed the hat off Jules's head and plopped down practically on top of Jules. "Scooch, make room for your momma!"

I raised my eyebrows at Jules, terrified she was about to tell her mom I was asking for sex advice.

"Just talking about Olivia's cute boyfriend," Jules said, shooting me a grin.

"He is *not* my boyfriend," I protested. Although there was a big part of me that was hoping he was. Or would be.

"Ooh, young love. Tell me everything," Cindy said.

"There's nothing to tell!" I said. "And please, don't—" But before I could finish my sentence—*tell my parents*—they had found their way back to us.

"Matt, Justin, want to go take a dip?" I grabbed the boys' hands and began heading toward the water. I turned around for a moment and shot Jules a look that said *Don't you dare mention anything to my parents.*

When we got back to the ship, I headed straight to the business center to work on the presentation. I wanted to finish it quickly, so I could find Sebastian and spend the little time we had left together.

I couldn't stop thinking about what would happen when our time ran out. There were only three nights left.

I pulled up a map online, tracing the distance between Missouri and New Jersey with my finger. I started scrolling through flight prices, calculating how many trips I could afford over the next year.

And if he never speaks to you again after . . .

I closed the sites, feeling a burning sense of shame. Why was I letting Jules's words get to me? I just wanted to make a plan; to make sure I could still see someone I had a lot of feelings for. Who had a lot of feelings for me. Was that so crazy?

I shook my head, trying to will away Jules's voice, and stared at the nearly blank presentation in front of me.

Focus, Olivia.

If I wanted to spend more time with Sebastian today, I had to finish this presentation.

I spent the next two hours completing slides that went through the technicalities of CPR, all told in Birdie's calm and kid-friendly tone. When I read through my work, I was pleased—it was actually pretty good.

I emailed Shruti to let her know I'd send over the presentation and paper in the morning. I knew that was cutting it close, but they needed to be in perfect shape if we wanted to win. And they were close—but I still needed a little more time to tweak them.

I opened up my binder and began scanning the journal articles I had highlighted, checking to see if I had missed any important information. "Opening Up Communication between Medical Providers and Family Members" discussed how important it was for doctors to establish a trusting and communicative relationship with a patient's family. I read over the passage I had highlighted in blue: Sometimes the most difficult cases are cracked when the family reveals a seemingly innocuous detail, such as the last thing the patient ate or a big fall they had years before. It is crucial that the doctor obtain this information as soon as possible, while there is still time to save the patient.

You should really talk with your parents, Liv.

I grabbed my things. I had come on this cruise to get more information about Logan's death, but I was just as clueless as I'd been a week ago.

We were docking at Antigua in less than twenty-four hours. It was time for me to finally get some answers.

When I got back to my room, my mom tapped her watch. "Seated dinner's in fifteen minutes. And remember, tonight's a formal night—family portraits."

"Okay," I said, holding back my desire to roll my eyes. It was one thing to go to a fancy restaurant and dress up; it was another for this floating mall to randomly decide some nights were "formal."

Which meant we had to put on dresses and button-down shirts for little reason other than to play dress-up. I took the world's fastest shower (not very hard to do, since I could barely fit in my shower and the water never got hot enough) and threw on the one formal dress I'd brought. I then helped button up the tiny buttons on Justin's and Matt's shirts and clipped on their adorable little plaid bow ties.

"Are we going to a bar mitzvah?" Justin asked.

"There are no bar mitzvahs on boats," Matt said. "That's silly."

I laughed. "Correct. We're just going to a fancy dinner, so we're wearing bar mitzvah *clothes*, but there's no bar mitzvah."

"Oh, okay," Justin said. "Can I still get a soda, though?"

"Mm-hmm, if it's okay with Mom and Dad."

"I didn't have a soda at lunch, so I get one at dinner," Matt said. "Justin had a soda at lunch, so no soda at dinner."

"But I WANT a—"

Before Justin could explode, I put my hand on his back and began rubbing in slow circles. "Hey, Justin, wanna race me to the elevator?"

"Yeah! I get a head start, though."

I picked Matt up, and we ran together after Justin to the elevator and off it to the main dining room, our parents trailing behind. There was a long line of people waiting for portraits, all dressed in formal attire—everything from clearly reused prom dresses to full-out tuxedos and gowns. A black tie–clad orchestra was set up in the corner, playing classical music.

After we took our photo—which required quite a few takes, as Matt was terrified of the flash and Justin kept blinking—the host gestured us inside the dining room.

Like the main theater, the dining room was three stories tall. Giant gaudy chandeliers hung from the ceiling, and groups of gold and silver balloons were placed around the room. We were seated at a round table in the back that was surrounded by five heavy-looking leather chairs. A giant bouquet of balloon flowers was the crowning centerpiece.

Maybe I had corrected Justin too soon—this *did* look like a bar mitzvah.

"Can I get chicken fingers?" Matt asked.

"You just had chicken fingers for lunch, bud," my dad answered. "How about a grilled cheese?"

"Okay," Matt said.

"And can I have a soda?" Justin asked.

"Justin, we already went over this," my dad said, his voice soft but stern. "One soda per day."

I glanced at the menu. The options seemed similar to the all-day buffet, just with fancier names. *Pommes frites* instead of *french fries*. *Macaroni Milanese* instead of *mac and cheese*.

"So, how's your paper going?" my mom asked as she took a bite of her salad.

I thought back to the article I had read earlier. About how the answers were often right under your nose. "Pretty good. I actually just read this really interesting article."

"Oh yeah? What was it about?" my mom asked.

"The importance of talking to family, to solve different medical mysteries." I took a deep breath. I knew my parents didn't want to talk about Logan, especially in front of the twins. But my patience had run out. "Which got me thinking, like, maybe there was a side effect from the accident, or something from Logan's medical history, that caused his heart attack?"

My parents dropped their silverware, so closely in sync with one another that it seemed like they had rehearsed the moment. They exchanged a look.

"Hmm," my mom finally said. "That's interesting." But her tone said she had zero interest in continuing the conversation.

I looked down at the roll on my plate, and the curves on the little pat of butter melting next to it. Why was I so upset? What had I expected?

I took a deep breath and gave it one more try. "Did you talk with the doctors after? Maybe I could call the hospital and ask for their notes," I said.

My mom shook her head. "I really don't remember, honey. It was so long ago. I doubt they even still have the records."

But it wasn't so long ago. It still felt like Logan had died yesterday. Why was he ancient history they were trying to erase?

As I walked back to the elevator, I hugged my arms against my chest. I speed walked past the hot dog stand and the Ferris wheel, where two little kids were shoving one another as their mom yelled at them to stop. My mind was racing, filled with images and clips from the days, weeks, months, after Logan died.

To how fucking eerie and quiet the house was without him.

To sitting shiva and being served ten thousand turkey-and-coleslaw sandwiches, all of which went untouched.

To how weird it was when my parents started working from home and were around all the time. Always asking me how I was doing. As if there were any answer to that other than "terrible."

I didn't . . . I didn't really know what to do. I went to school. I came home. I sat in my room. I watched videos of Logan, until one day my mom said maybe I should stop watching them for a little while, and all of a sudden I just felt gross and guilty and I stopped watching them.

And then, two weeks after Logan's death, and my dad was *cooking*? Like watching cooking shows on TV and serving up "coq au vin" at our awkward dinners, at a table meant for four, not three. And then my mom was going to yoga and they were just *living* their lives like they hadn't been *completely* destroyed, which they should have been. Like mine was.

And even worse were all the questions. My parents wanted to know about my friends and my schoolwork and what music I was listening to. They asked me about everything—except Logan. They wanted so much more love and attention than I could provide.

My actions became more regimented, leaving less and less room for error. I was more superstitious, starting and stopping homework on even hours, eating the same dinner every night, waking up at exactly 7:07 a.m., kissing the air and saying "Thank you God."

My parents sent me to a therapist, who had me play with toys like I was six and diagnosed me with prolonged grief disorder. I couldn't believe she had to get a PhD to come up with that one.

She convinced me that I needed to be honest with my parents, ask them to talk about Logan with me. We prepared a whole speech together.

But the night that I was supposed to give it, my parents sat me down and told me they were pregnant. And in a way, the pregnancy was a relief for all of us. The endless line of questions stopped.

I never gave the speech. I stopped seeing the therapist. My parents seemed to accept that, as if three months were enough time to "fix" whatever was wrong with me.

There was nothing that could be fixed, though. Because Logan was never coming back.

Sebastian pulled me into him as soon as he opened his door. I was relieved to find him alone. I didn't think I could stomach another awkward Charlie encounter.

"Hey," he said, interlocking his fingers with mine and leading me over to his bed.

I sat down next to him and put my head against his shoulder. Everything felt so comfortable, so natural, with him. My body relaxed, like it had been waiting seventeen years for me to find this position.

"How's it going?" Sebastian asked.

"Not great," I sighed. "I tried to talk to my parents and surprise, surprise—they didn't want to talk about Logan."

Sebastian furrowed his brow. "Do you think they realize how important this is to you? Is there another way you could bring this up?"

"I just think they want to forget him. Forget the part of their lives that they failed at."

Sebastian nodded, taking a moment to think before he spoke again. It was so easy to see how great of a therapist he would make one day. "Well . . . everyone handles grief differently. Maybe it's too painful for your parents to talk about his death. But there must be some parts of him that they like remembering."

I thought back to the brief moment my mom and I had at the twins' play. The way her face lit up when she remembered Logan's performance. "The other day my mom mentioned how he used to steal the show at his performances."

Sebastian's eyes lit up. "Okay, there's something! So what if you talked about his shows, what he was like while he was alive?"

I nodded, feeling a sudden urge for Sebastian to know Logan the way I did. "Do you want to see him sing?"

Sebastian pulled me in closer to him. "I'd love to."

I brought up the reprise of "I'll Cover You." Logan's face filled the screen as he did a silly musical exercise, mocking the way we were forced to warm up in middle school. "Mama makes me mash my M&M's, mm mm." Then he repeated the line in higher and higher pitches.

Sebastian laughed. "He's funny."

I nodded. Then the soft, sad piano keys started. Logan closed his eyes, and his voice entered a low, otherworldly register as he started to sing.

"Wow," Sebastian breathed.

The song was impossibly sad, but Logan was smiling throughout, somehow adding joy between the lyrics. He had been gone for six years, but whenever I watched this, it was like he was right in the room with me.

Sebastian and I sat there for a few minutes after the video finished, not saying anything.

"What is it about that song . . . that makes us feel that way?" I asked. "It's just such a supernatural experience."

Sebastian stroked my cheek with his palm. "I love the way you feel music with your entire soul."

I love you. As soon as the words popped into my head, I felt a strong urge to say them. But I held back, not wanting to ruin the moment.

"Will you do the shipwreck tour with me in Antigua tomorrow?" I blurted out instead. I wanted him to be there with me as I reconnected with Logan. I *needed* him to be there.

"Sure," he said, wrapping his arms around me. "And Liv— what if you sang this song tonight?"

"I can't," I immediately responded. "I was supposed to sing this song at his funeral." I told Sebastian about how I had frozen. I couldn't relive that experience.

"I know this sends you back to a really difficult time, but . . . can you reframe it in your mind? Use this song to purposefully travel back to a good time?" Sebastian's fingers traced their way up my arm, over my shoulder, and toward my collarbone. "Maybe your parents will finally see how much you want to talk about him."

I thought about how many times Logan and I had sung this song together while laughing. How he had transformed Mr. Bubbles's funeral into a celebration. How we'd sung this as we cruised through the Burger King drive-through after school, promising to cherish each and every french fry.

But then I thought about the tear-filled eyes at his funeral.

I looked down. "I'm just going to freeze again."

Sebastian squeezed my hand. "If you do, I promise to go up after and sing the most embarrassing Justin Bieber song ever."

I laughed before sinking farther into Sebastian, listening to the sound of his heart beating and feeling safer than I had in years.

My phone sat on my lap, still open to a freeze-frame of Logan's smiling face.

I needed to remind my parents of the son they had forgotten.

After all—what did I have to lose?

I headed over to Jules's room to get ready with her for karaoke. I was going to need to borrow some of her liquid courage if I was going to get up and sing in a few hours in front of a crowd. In front of my parents.

I knocked on Jules's door, but no one answered. I could hear music blasting, though, so I knocked again, louder.

"Who is it?" Jules finally shouted.

"Me!"

Jules opened the door. Half of her hair had fallen out of its ponytail, and her bikini top was on inside out. And behind her was—*Steph*?

"Jules—hey," I said, doing my best to hide my shock. Maybe this wasn't what it looked like. "Are you coming to the hot tub?"

"Yeah, in a minute," Jules said. Steph grabbed Jules's waist and Jules giggled.

This was definitely what it looked like.

"Okay, well . . . I guess I'll meet you there?"

"Yup, see you soon!" Jules practically shoved me out of the room as she closed the door behind me.

A wave of nausea passed over me. How could Jules do this to Ash? I knew how much Ash liked her. Did Jules care at all about their feelings? How could she be hooking up with two people at the same time?

I breathed in and out slowly and reminded myself that I didn't know Ash very well. Maybe they were just more "evolved" than I was, as Jules had said. Jules and Ash must have talked about this, come up with some type of arrangement. Maybe Ash was hooking up with other people too.

And anyway—just because Jules didn't take cruise flings seriously didn't mean no one did. Not everyone could have what Sebastian and I had.

"Just you tonight?" Ash asked with a small laugh as I climbed into the hot tub in between Troy and Seb, who instantly wrapped his arm around my waist. Ash looked a little concerned, but I convinced myself that I was just projecting.

"Just came from dinner with my family," I lied. "But Jules will be here soon!"

"So," Troy said, leaning forward conspiratorially, "Seb told me you're going to be competing against us tonight."

I nodded. "You have nothing to worry about. Let's see if I even make it onstage."

Troy smiled at me. "I can't wait to hear you sing."

"Thanks, Troy."

"Heyyy," Jules sang out as she ran over to us. She was in the same bikini top—but had fixed it so it was no longer inside out. Her hair was less messy, thrown up into a loose ponytail.

"What'd I miss?" Jules asked as she hopped into the tub and immediately placed herself on Ash's lap. *Really?* I couldn't believe she had such an easy time switching between people, as if she were merely switching pairs of flip-flops.

Jules met my eyes and smiled. I forced myself to smile back. After all, this was her life, not mine. "Can I borrow that flask?"

"Yup!" Jules said, handing it over.

"Nervous about tonight?" Sebastian asked as he pulled me onto his lap.

"A little." I took a long swig, enjoying the burning sensation the rum left in my stomach and the feeling of my back against Sebastian's chest.

"Don't worry," he whispered into my ear. "You're going to be great."

Karaoke was held in the main auditorium since it was on both the teen-and-adult schedules. Which meant it was the main show of the evening—and the three-story theater was packed. Michelle and Dan were there to judge, and there was an additional adult prize for the over-18 winner.

When we arrived, I waved to my parents. They were already seated with the twins toward the back of the first floor, so they had easy access to the exit. We carefully tiptoed past people, finally finding a row of empty seats right up front. I took a seat in between Jules and Sebastian.

As soon as I sat down, Jules passed me her flask. I sank down in my seat, out of view of the rows behind me, and took a long swig. If I was ever going to get myself up on that stage, I'd need the courage.

After a few lackluster performances of old boy-band songs sung by the other competitors, Troy leaped onstage. He performed a hilarious and impressive cover of "Bohemian Rhapsody," and was the clear favorite of the evening.

And then Sebastian's name was called.

As the opening piano notes to "It's All Coming Back to Me Now" resounded across the theater, I smiled. I loved this song—I mean, who didn't? But then I noticed Charlie, who was separated from me only by Sebastian's empty seat. He was shaking his head and muttering, "Here we go again."

I pursed my lips together and did my best to ignore the molasses feeling settling in my stomach. I didn't know why Charlie had such an issue with Sebastian. Or with me.

The piano intro to the song was almost a full minute long, and I could tell the crowd wasn't paying attention. People were laughing and talking so loudly that you could barely hear the chords.

It's hard to explain why songs like Celine's are so powerful, so objectively better than most others. The songs themselves are like entire operas told within a few minutes. The lyrics and the range and the pacing—it just adds up to this indescribably moving experience, that very few people are able to execute.

And when Sebastian sang the first line, "There were nights when the wind was so cold," a hush fell among the audience. I could see people readjusting in their seats, looking up at the stage, where a spotlight shone down on Sebastian.

I felt that giddy, awestruck feeling you get when you know you're bearing witness to a once-in-a-lifetime performance. That everyone around you is experiencing magic at the same time.

Sebastian slowly rose his arm up in the air as he sang the second verse, his voice growing louder. He gripped the mic and opened his mouth widely, hitting the first high note perfectly, which was met by wild cheers from the audience.

When he had sung to me at the piano, his voice was soft and clear and beautiful. But his song was quiet; the range was small. This was nothing like that. The way he commanded this room of hundreds—he was a literal rock star.

I had already fallen for him, but I felt like I was falling for him all over again.

Sebastian sang with his entire body, his chest heaving as he hit each note, his foot tapping and his hands wrapped so tightly around the mic that I could see his biceps bulging out from his T-shirt.

I hadn't ever seen anyone captivate a crowd like him—aside from Logan. Every seat would be filled at the musicals that Logan starred in. I always loved seeing the shocked expressions of his teammates and coaches, who had no idea that their basketball star was also a musical god.

Sebastian swayed and splayed his arms out as he sang the chorus. He looked like he was floating, like he had entered another universe. When he got to "nights of endless pleasure," he met my eyes and I practically melted into my seat. I felt drunk with glee. Nothing had the power to make me as happy as music did. That had been one of the hardest parts of losing Logan—the way his singing could always cheer me up, no matter what was going on in my life.

"Every single person in this room is picturing having sex with your boyfriend right now," Jules whispered, breaking me out of my trance.

I smirked at her. "He's not my boyfriend."

But she didn't seem to be wrong. Everyone's eyes were glued to Sebastian, and every time he so much as paused in between lines, people started cheering. In response, he'd flash a smile, take a deep breath, and belt out another heartbreaking line, causing the crowd to scream louder. But despite the hundreds of people he had screaming at him, he made me forget there was anyone else in the room, like he was performing only for me.

Sebastian had arrived at the quiet middle of the song. His eyes were nearly closed, and his voice was cracking so much that I half expected him to start crying. The way he sang about hurt and pain was so pure, so filled with emotion. There was a melancholy to his voice; I had never realized just how sad the song was before. I wondered what it was that he was thinking about. Or rather—whom.

Sebastian knew he had the audience wrapped around his finger. It was like the boat had stopped moving and time had frozen; everyone was sitting silently watching him.

"He's so hot," I heard someone whisper behind me.

I couldn't help grinning like an idiot, thinking—*he's mine. I'm with him.*

Sebastian took his time before starting the next line, waiting just a beat too long, really building up the tension and making people practically beg for him to start again.

And then he hit the climax. Everything came alive at once—the crowd was vibrating and cheering and shouting as his voice reverberated around the auditorium. I felt shivers run down my spine. I didn't think I'd ever heard a song so beautiful or so powerful.

Through the cheers, Sebastian said, "Three minutes left," with an impish grin. The shouting turned into raucous laughter. I nearly choked I was laughing so hard.

Charlie rolled his eyes. "He does that every time."

But there was nothing Charlie could say or do that could ruin this moment for me.

Sebastian grabbed the mic off its stand and spread his arms as he belted out the final verse. He was putting every ounce of his body and soul into the performance. Small beads of sweat had formed on his forehead, and it looked like a vein was about to burst. As he let out the last long, final note, his mouth was open wide and I could see his lungs working overtime.

The audience was on their feet and giving an earsplitting standing ovation before he had even finished the note.

"He's so good," I blurted out to Jules and Ash, purposefully angling my body away from Charlie. I knew I sounded like a fangirl, but I couldn't help it.

Ash just laughed. "Ah, Sebastian the Traveling Musician."

What did that mean?

"I'm pretty sure that boy just impregnated every person in this room," Jules said.

Sebastian shot one last, almost embarrassed-looking grin before hopping off the stage and walking back to our seats. My heart beat wildly—I knew it was silly, but I felt almost nervous, wondering if he'd say hi to me first.

He sat down next to me and squeezed my shoulder. "You're up next," he said before putting his lips on my neck. In his kiss, I could still feel all the power and emotion of the song. I felt light-headed and dizzy as I stood up and found myself approaching the stage.

The spotlight was hot, and when I turned to face the crowd, the light nearly blinded me. I blinked and found that the audience had been replaced by a bunch of blurry circles, which helped to slow the rapid beating of my heart.

Sebastian mouthed, "You've got this." Jules cupped her hands around her mouth. "GOOO, LIV!!!" she screamed as Troy stomped his feet.

I took a deep breath. How the hell was I supposed to follow Sebastian's rock-star performance? People came to karaoke for fun songs, not for girls singing supersad songs about their dead brothers.

I gazed around the auditorium and found my parents' silhouettes at the back. I had to do this. I needed them to finally talk to me about Logan.

It was now or never.

The piano chords began.

I felt every part of my body go numb. It was happening again. I couldn't do this.

But then I looked at Sebastian. He was smiling and nodding. I focused on him, forgetting about everyone else in the room. I opened my mouth and began to sing. Softly at first, but then I found my voice and it was like I'd never stopped singing, like I was biking downhill and I couldn't stop myself from going faster.

The audience faded away and I could *feel* Logan there, smiling and telling me to sing with my full heart.

I was back in the car with him as he drove us to school and blasted the *Rent* soundtrack. I could feel the wind on my face and hear people cheering as he belted out the window, making random people's mornings with his free performance.

When I stopped singing, it felt like a trance had been broken. I walked dizzily offstage. People were clapping, but I had no idea how long I'd been up there or how it had gone.

Sebastian ran up to me and pulled me into him. He ran his hands through my hair and kissed me deeply.

When we finally parted, I looked up.

And found my parents, staring at the two of us.

TWENTY-TWO

I quickly pulled away from Sebastian. *Oh. My. God.* My parents had just seen me kiss a boy. I felt my face become beet red.

"Bastian!" Justin cheered, running over and hugging Sebastian's leg.

"Mom, Dad, hey," I said, tucking my hair behind my ear and praying they hadn't seen too much.

But their faces were dark.

"Can we talk to you privately, Olivia?" my mom asked.

I felt my heart pounding as the five of us walked out of the auditorium and into the bright lights of the boardwalk.

I gulped. "So, um, thanks for coming." Maybe if I followed their tactics, steering clear of any uncomfortable topics, we could forget what they had just witnessed. I didn't want that to ruin the night, our chance of reconnecting. I was desperate to know what they thought of my song.

My mom pursed her lips. "Your performance was very nice."

Oh. That was her response. I felt my stomach drop.

"What was going on back there?" my dad asked.

"I—" My parents were both staring at me. But did I really owe them an explanation? "Am I not allowed to kiss boys? I'm not eight, you know."

My mom shook her head. "And we're supposed to believe you were *getting breakfast* at five in the morning, after seeing you with that boy?"

My dad laid a hand on my mom's arm, code for *Take a second here, Diane.* But my mom wasn't having it. "We weren't born yesterday, Olivia. We didn't give you rules on this cruise because we trusted you. But you betrayed that trust."

Betrayed that trust. I hadn't heard them speak those words since Logan was alive. That was their go-to line, whenever they were missing money, or he came home late, or they smelled liquor on his breath. Logan used to mockingly repeat them to me, like if I ate the last slice of the microwave pizza, he'd be all— "Olivia, you have *betrayed* my *trust.*"

But no one was laughing now.

My mom took a step closer and inhaled. "And is that *alcohol* I smell?"

"What? No, I—"

"Unbelievable, Olivia. We expect you to remain in your *own* room tonight and tomorrow night."

No. No no no. There were only three nights left of the cruise. Three nights left with Sebastian. How could they *do* this to me? "Are you kidding me? You were the ones who forced me onto this cruise, which I never wanted to come on in the first place. And after all this time, you decide to start playing the role of parents *now*?"

"Olivia—" my dad started.

I cut him off. "This might have been a good idea, I dunno, like seventeen years ago? Maybe you could've been actual parents for Logan and me. Maybe you could've been *home* some of the time. Maybe then he wouldn't have just died, *alone*, for me to find him—" I was full-on shouting now.

"You're being very emotional right now," my mom said. "So I don't think this is going to be a productive conversation. Especially in front of the twins."

Was she kidding me? She was going to cut me off for being *emotional* about finding my dead brother when I was ten?

"We expected better from you, Olivia," my dad added, his eyes sad. "This is not the kind of behavior we'd expect, not from you."

I was shaking, I was so angry. How *dare* he bring up Logan like that. "Who *would* you expect it from, Dad?"

"Olivia—"

"No! Say his name! It's *Logan*. It's the kind of behavior you would expect from *Logan*. Well, news flash—I am *not* Logan. You always made it seem like alcohol was the freaking end of the world, but you know what? I've tried it and I'm just *fine*. Because I'm *me*. Not him, not you, not anyone else." I spun around on my heel and began storming toward the elevators.

"Let's just say that when we get back home, your actions will have consequences," my dad shouted after me.

I turned around and scoffed. "Yeah, sure. Whatever you say. Thanks for being the world's best parents."

When I got to my room, I slammed the door behind me. What right did my parents have to start making up rules for me *now*? On this cruise they had *made* me go on, when all I wanted to do during my spring break was stay home with my cat, reading medical journals? I was a *dream* child, and yet I was being punished for enjoying myself, for once?

I grabbed the towel swan on my bed and balled it up before hurling it across the room.

Then I sat down and focused on my breathing, trying to loosen up the tightness in my chest.

I needed to figure out what to do. There were only three nights left, and no way was I giving up that time with Sebastian.

I thought about what Logan would do. He was never scared of my parents' reaction. He just did what he wanted to do and dealt with the consequences after.

A few minutes later, I listened as my parents and the twins entered their room. I lay in bed with my eyes closed and kept them closed when my mom opened up the connecting door to check on me. She stood there for a moment, not saying anything, before shutting the door behind her. I lay in bed for another thirty minutes, long after the voices in the other room had fallen silent and the light was turned off.

And then I grabbed the towel, stuck it in my door so it didn't fully close, and tiptoed toward the elevators.

But when I arrived at the hot tub, no one was there. I practically sprinted over to Katz's, breathing out a large sigh of relief when I spotted Jules and the crew.

"Sorry to disappear," I said, sliding into the end of the booth, next to Sebastian. "Did we win?"

"Yesss," Troy said, slinging an arm around Sebastian's back. "Our boy pulled through! He definitely would have won the entire karaoke contest, if the winner didn't need to be over eighteen."

"Because God forbid they let us have free drinks," Sebastian said with a smirk before unscrewing the flask—which was out on the table in plain sight—and taking a long drink.

"You did awesome, by the way," Troy added, turning to me.

"Yeah, you killed it, Liv," Ash said with a smile.

"Thanks," I said. "But I was nowhere near as good as you," I told Troy. "That was the best 'Bohemian Rhapsody' I've ever heard."

I grabbed the flask, glad to find that it was still half-full. I drank from it as the crew chatted around me about the competition. We were three and three now, which meant that the next night's challenge would determine the winner of the big steak dinner. I watched as the minute hand on the old-timey yellow-and-red clock on the wall inched closer and closer to midnight. I was wasting precious time that I could be alone with Sebastian.

I was hoping for an easy out, a change in locations, but then Troy ordered another round of fries. "Wanna go back to your room?" I whispered to Sebastian, unable to wait any longer.

"Sure," he said. We stood up and waved goodbye to the crew. I felt a bit embarrassed to be this shameless. But not embarrassed enough not to leave.

"Have fun," Jules sang out, giving me a big wink. I stuck out my tongue and glanced at her and Ash. She was sprawled across their lap, and I felt my heart fall as I saw the way Ash was staring at her.

When we got to Sebastian's room, I slammed the door behind us and ran my hands through his thick hair. I pressed my lips into his and threw us together onto his bed.

My body melted as we kissed, and the world faded around us. Only his body and mine existed. I wanted to be closer. I *needed* to be closer.

If I just lost myself in him . . . I could block out all the other noise in my head. Logan being gone. My parents' unwillingness to talk about him. How much freaking trouble I was in. How Jules was treating Ash. And what the hell was going to happen to Sebastian and me after the cruise. If I just focused all my senses . . .

"Where'd this come from?" Sebastian asked as he came up for air.

"Shh." I placed my finger against his lips and grinded my hips against his. He sighed into my neck, and I felt a thrill pass through me.

"Do you have a condom?" I asked.

As soon as I said the words, Sebastian sprung up like a jack-in-the-box and started shaking his head. "Hold on."

I pulled the covers up over my body, suddenly feeling exposed. Since when did guys hesitate about having sex?

"Have you ever . . . had sex before?" Sebastian asked carefully.

I shook my head.

"I didn't think so." Sebastian sighed. "Your first time should be . . . special."

"But this *is* special," I said.

"I know," he said, covering my hand with his. "It is. But . . . we just met."

I felt like he'd just thrown a bucket of ice water over my head. That was what he thought of me? That I was some random girl he'd just met? I had been dreaming of flying to Kansas City, of asking him to my junior prom, of showing him around NYC. I felt so stupid.

"Okay—well, I should go, then." I turned so I was facing the wall and began sitting up, so I could step off the end of the bed.

"Hey, hey," he said, rolling me over and pulling me in toward him. "Please don't be mad, Liv." He loosened my hold on the sheets and ran a hand down the side of my body. "There are so many things we can do aside from sex."

I swallowed. "It's just . . . there are only two days left, and . . ."

Sebastian tucked a strand of hair behind my ear. "You mean there are two whole cruise *years* left."

I tried to smile but couldn't. "So . . . then, that's it? We're just . . . hooking up?"

"No, of course not." He looked down, as if my words had hurt him.

Jules's words came back to me, and I blurted out, "I saw Jules hooking up with someone else. She said no one takes cruise flings seriously; that you're just going to stop talking to me after the cruise ends."

"Whoa, whoa, slow down there. Jules is . . . a different person. With different interests and attachment styles than us. Please don't let her speak for me and what I want."

"Okay, but . . . what happens after we leave?" I couldn't help but ask. I wanted to just enjoy the moment—I really did. But my mind was still racing, trying to prevent future disaster.

"Liv." He put a finger under my chin and tipped up my face so that I was staring into his eyes. "I think we just have to see where fate leads us. I've tried to make promises before and I've been burned." His voice was low, and I had never seen him look so serious. "But what we have here, right now, is amazing. I've never felt such an instant connection to anyone."

I nodded and exhaled. Sebastian was right. I needed to stop listening to Jules, stop freaking out, and stop ruining these perfect nights we had left together.

I nuzzled back into Sebastian. "I'm really excited for tomorrow." I couldn't believe that in just a few hours, I'd finally be at the shipwreck in Antigua. With Sebastian.

"Me too," Sebastian murmured.

And even though he couldn't tell me what was going to happen in three days, or three months, or three years—right now, for some reason, that felt okay.

I was awoken by the sound of footsteps, followed by the lights being flicked on and then right back off.

"Shh," Troy whispered. "They're sleeping."

"Surprise, surprise," Charlie muttered. "Look who slept together again."

It's not what it looks like, I wanted to hiss at Charlie. *I'm not that type of girl, and this isn't that type of relationship.* But I kept my eyes—and my lips—shut.

Ash let out a sigh. "That boy can't be alone for longer than an hour, can he?"

What did *that* mean?

"Hey, hey, be nice," Troy said. "Give Seb a break. He went through a lot with Claire."

Claire? Who was Claire?

As the crew shuffled around and got ready for bed, I lay there, doing my best not to move. Sebastian's arm was still wound tightly around me, and he was lightly snoring.

But I couldn't stop my brain from racing, trying to figure out what Troy and Ash were talking about. If they thought I was asleep. Or worse—if they wanted me to hear them.

I felt a sinking feeling in my chest. I didn't know Sebastian as well as I'd thought. I had no idea who he was when he wasn't on this cruise. Or who he'd be next week, after it ended.

I waited until I was sure the crew had fallen asleep before walking back to my room. My heart sped up as I slipped inside the room, leaving the towel in place so the door didn't click closed behind me.

I lay down in bed and waited to see if my parents would storm in. But their room stayed dark.

I turned over onto my stomach and put "Cigarettes and Cola" on repeat. Then I closed my eyes, running through everything that had happened in the past few hours. When I was alone with Sebastian, our bond felt unbreakable. He was the best listener I'd ever met. Being with him felt so good, so natural.

But then I thought about what I had overheard. What Jules had said about cruise flings. And I just had no idea what to think.

Sometimes it felt like I had missed out on learning how to act like a "normal" teen because I was too busy grieving Logan. Was this how love was supposed to feel? Fire and magic mixed in with nausea and pain?

If Logan were still alive, he'd tell me.

Things had been so great between him and Patrick—until the accident. In one night, everything seemed to have changed. I began seeing Patrick less and less—until he wasn't around at all. When I asked Logan about him, he just shrugged it off. "Things didn't work out," he grumbled.

I had assumed that Patrick had ended things, that he hadn't stuck things out because of everything Logan was going through.

But then, three weeks before Logan had died, Patrick texted me.

hey Olive, hows it going?

We texted back and forth for a bit.

Patrick: Hows Logan doing?

Olivia: Hes okay.

Patrick: He needs help, Olive.

I had stared at that text for a while. I knew Logan wasn't in a good place—he was still having a lot of unexplained pain after the accident. He couldn't play basketball, and he had no interest in the musical. But that didn't mean he needed *help*. Who the hell was Patrick to insinuate that? What, just because Logan hadn't wanted to date him anymore?

Patrick had sent me a few more texts after that, but I had ignored them. At the funeral, he had given me the saddest look I had ever seen. I had immediately turned away.

I turned up my music and tried to fall asleep, tried not to think about how little time Sebastian and I had left together. But I just kept picturing Patrick's sad, dark eyes.

TWENTY-THREE
DAY EIGHT AD

I gave my parents the silent treatment as we walked to Penne Station the next morning. I knew I was acting like a child, but I didn't care.

I poured myself a bowl of Frosted Flakes and was relieved to find Jules at a table by herself.

"So glad to see you," I said, sliding in across from her. "I need to get away from my parents."

Jules laughed. "Are they still mad about seeing you and Sebastian together? That's some fucked-up patriarchal parenting."

"Yeah," I said. "I know."

"So . . . how did last night go? Did you follow my advice?" Jules wiggled her eyebrows at me.

I considered explaining what had happened. How Sebastian had turned me down. But I knew Jules wouldn't get it.

"Decided to wait," I told her as I spooned a few sugary corn flakes into my mouth.

"That's probably for the best."

"Why do you say that?" I thought about the conversation I had overheard the night before. Had Ash said something to Jules? Did she know something I didn't?

Jules put down her fork and sighed. "I just don't want you to get hurt, Liv. I know this is your first big thing, and yes, you may end up running off into the sunset together and living happily ever after, but in *case* that doesn't happen . . . it might hurt less if you wait."

"It's not like that," I said. "I mean, things are serious with us."

"Okayyy," Jules said slowly. She picked up her fork and began absentmindedly circling around a piece of pancake in the puddle of syrup on her plate.

I knew Jules didn't believe me, but I didn't see why she had to be such a pain about it, why she couldn't just keep her feelings to herself. And I was tired of just going along with everything she said, when it came to my own relationship.

"Why is it so impossible for you to believe that this isn't just some fling for Sebastian and me?" My words came out sharper than intended.

"Because it's been one *week*, Liv! This isn't a fairy tale."

"Well, real people can form feelings in a week," I said. "Even if you haven't."

"I'm sorry—do you think I'm *jealous* of you? That I'm green with envy because I haven't *fallen in love* with some random guy over the last *seven* days?" Jules threw her hands in the air as she spoke, and her bracelets rose and fell down her arm, the silver bands clanging together.

I felt my chest tightening—my "defense dragon," as Shruti

called it, coming forward. "Maybe you could have formed real feelings if you weren't so busy juggling all the people you're hooking up with. Ash really likes you, you know. And you don't seem to care at all about their feelings."

Jules scoffed. "Please don't tell me how I feel, or how Ash feels. You know nothing about it."

"Well, I know what general human decency is, and I don't think scheduling your hookups on the same day falls within that realm." My voice was rising now, my defense dragon breathing fire.

"Whoa, Ms. Judgy Face. Can you not tell me who I am and am not allowed to hook up with?"

"I just don't think it's very nice."

"Well, maybe not everyone cares about being *nice* and boring."

"I'd rather be boring than a—"

"A what? Seriously? You want to call me a slut? Go for it."

I just shook my head and gritted my teeth.

"Maybe go check the fine print on your prenup with Sebastian before you go judging everyone else."

"What does that mean?" I put down my spoon and stared straight at Jules, willing her to tell me whatever it was she was hinting at.

"You avoid any obvious truths that don't suit your five-year plan, even when they're staring you right in the face."

"What, should I be more like you? Plan nothing, just go to college wherever, and have the best years of my life as a teen and then . . . grow up to be a . . . what? Do you even have any goals or ambitions?"

"Jesus, Olivia, do you hear yourself? Who the hell needs to know what they want to do when they're *seventeen*? Don't you realize that the whole point of college is figuring out what you want to do with your life? That you don't need to decide that at eight years old?"

"I thought the whole point of college was *partying* and making *connections*," I replied sarcastically.

Jules let out a loud huff of air. "Not that my future plans are any of your business, but I got a perfect score on my SAT, which I plan on using to get a full ride to Rutgers. Just because I don't constantly blabber on about college all the time like you doesn't mean I don't have plans for my future."

I was speechless for a moment. Jules bit back a smirk, clearly satisfied that her words had had their intended effect. "And you know what, Olivia? I've *tried* to be nice. I know you're still hurting because of Logan. But I've texted every single year on your birthday since he died. You never even send a simple 'thank you' back. All you ever think of is yourself and how to get what *you* want."

"*I'm* the one who only thinks of myself? Well, that's rich, coming from you, after a week of forcing me to do whatever it was *you* wanted me to do."

"Oh, please. The only time you ever even want to *talk* to me is to get advice on how to get Sebastian to, like, fall in love with you and propose. Which I hate to tell you, but it's not going to happen. And maybe if you just *lived* a little more, you'd know that you can't go around trying to control everything in your life. Unless you want to live a very, very sad and lonely existence."

"Not everyone's lives are butterflies and tequila flasks," I said through clenched teeth. "Some of us have *reasons* for sticking to plans. I live every moment of my life regretting the one moment I didn't. If it weren't for me, Logan would still be alive."

"You don't really believe it's your fault he died, do you? You know that's magical thinking, right?"

"I'm sorry, but were you there? We were *supposed* to watch a movie, and if I had just stuck to the *plan*—"

"Then he would have overdosed another night!" Jules practically shouted.

I felt every molecule in my body freeze. "What the hell did you just say?"

Jules slapped a hand over her mouth. "I'm sorry, I shouldn't have said—"

"Fuck you, Jules. You know *nothing* about Logan." I practically knocked over my chair as I jumped up and ran out of the room. I had to find Sebastian.

I rushed to the fifteenth floor. Sebastian was supposed to meet me there at ten to grab a quick breakfast, before we headed out to Antigua. It was only 9:30, though, and I had no way of texting him. I could show up at his room, but I just couldn't face another run-in with Charlie. Not while I was like this.

So I waited.

He overdosed, Olivia.

I knew Jules was angry, but that didn't give her the right to make up such a cruel lie about Logan. She *knew* how much that would hurt me.

What if she was telling the truth?

I shook my head. I needed to think about anything else. Antigua. The shipwreck. Sebastian. I couldn't wait to get out to sea with him again. I thought about the perfect afternoon we'd had together on our last excursion. Running on the beach. How amazing everything looked underwater. The sea turtles.

In only two hours, we would finally be in Antigua. I knew it wasn't a coincidence that I had met Sebastian. Together, in Antigua, I would get the answers I needed. Sebastian and I would figure things out. Maybe I'd even make up with my parents.

I checked the time on the ship's display. 9:58.

Two more minutes.

I stared at the screen as the time changed to 10:00.

"What time IS IT?"

Oh no.

"SHOWTIME!" shouted a group of kids. Everyone on this ship now knew the call-and-response.

To my left, the performers began blasting a boombox and break-dancing.

10:01.

The lead performer started flipping dangerously close to me. A large group formed, cheering loudly. I did my best not to openly groan.

10:03. 10:07. 10:13.

Where was Sebastian?

10:15. 10:18. 10:20.

Finally, at 10:30, I started walking toward his room. The excursion started at noon, and I couldn't miss it. I was sure he wouldn't want to either.

TWENTY-FOUR

When Troy opened the door, I looked past him and found Sebastian passed out on his stomach, wearing nothing but his boxer briefs.

It took a moment for Troy to shake him awake. Sebastian rubbed his eyes and groggily made his way to the door. "Liv—hey." His eyes were bloodshot and his breath was sour. He must have been a lot drunker the night before than I'd realized.

"Hey, we have that thing this morning, remember?" I could feel four pairs of eyes on me as I spoke.

Sebastian squinted. "Oh yeah, right . . ."

"Did you still want to . . ."

"Hold on," he said. He slipped on a pair of flip-flops and threw on a T-shirt and shorts. "Let's go for a walk?"

"Okay," I said wearily, not sure why he wasn't getting dressed for the excursion. But I didn't want to have that conversation in front of an audience.

We walked for a minute in silence, down a flight of stairs and to a bench that was out of earshot of any passengers. There weren't really any empty, quiet spots on this entire freaking ship—well, they had gotten that part of NYC right, at least.

"Are you still coming with me to Antigua?" I asked as I took a seat next to him on the bench. I hated how my words reeked of desperation. Because it wasn't really a question. I was begging.

Sebastian began drawing small circles on the ground with his foot. "I'm not sure if it's a good idea for me to go."

I felt the passageway from my heart to my lungs narrow, constricting my breathing. "Why?"

"This just seems like something you should do alone, for Logan," Sebastian said softly, his eyes still focused on the ground. "I don't want to intrude."

"You wouldn't be intruding." I placed a hand on his arm. I needed him to look at me, to know how much I wanted him to come with me.

"Liv," Sebastian said, finally looking me straight in the eye. "I don't want you getting the wrong impression."

"What do you mean?" My heart was pounding harder, causing my words to come out fragmented and jumbled, like I had just sprinted a mile.

"I'm just so scared of hurting you," Sebastian said.

I tried to swallow, but my mouth was completely dry. My words came out half croak, half whisper, as if they didn't want to escape my body. "Why would you be hurting me?"

Sebastian looked down again and twisted his hands. Every moment he waited to speak made it harder for me to breathe. "I know you want to know what's going to happen after the cruise. And I haven't given you a straight answer. It's just that—" He paused and raked a hand through his hair before letting out a deep breath. "I'm still so fucked up from my last relationship . . ."

"Oh." I felt my body disappear, leaving only the sensation of my heart pounding in my ears.

He pressed his lips together. "Claire and I are on a break right now, and it's not fair to anyone to make promises about the future."

Claire. The name from the night before rang over and over in my ears as my brain tried to process his words. *On a break.* Which meant Sebastian had a girlfriend. "I don't . . . I don't understand why . . ."

"I really, really like you, Liv." Sebastian took my hands in his. "I was drawn to you right away, and being on the ship . . . it really does feel like another reality. And then you kissed me and . . ."

I yanked my hands away from him. He was blaming this on *me*? For kissing him when we were alone in his room and he had his arm wrapped around me, and he had been following me around for days? When he had a *girlfriend*, who he was first mentioning to me *now*? "You didn't want me to?" Then why the hell had he kissed me back, kept kissing me?

"No, no, fuck no, of course I wanted you to. I was just trying so hard to hold back, to be good, to keep things platonic and uncomplicated . . ."

I had never felt so completely and utterly mortified. I stood up. "I—I have to go."

"Wait—no. Please. Let's talk about this."

"*What* is there to talk about exactly?" My voice was ice, and tears were running down my face. "You want to be a good guy, make sure you don't hurt me? News flash—it's too late. You've fucking hurt me, Sebastian. You've hurt me a lot."

"Fuck. I'm sorry. I really—that wasn't my intention. It felt really nice being around you. I thought we were having a good time."

"That's not exactly how I roll. I *never* would have kissed you if I knew you had a girlfriend."

"You're twisting my words. We're on a break. And do you really regret the time we spent together? After everything."

His eyes were searching mine. I looked away. "Yes," I said. "I do."

"I'm really sorry, Liv. I thought we were having fun."

"*Fun?* I poured my heart out to you about my dead brother. I don't *talk* to people about Logan. Especially people who plan on ghosting me after a week."

"Jesus, I'm not ghosting you." Sebastian reeled back, as if I had slapped him. Then he lowered his voice. "But maybe you should talk about him. I really think it would help."

I narrowed my eyes at him. "Please don't tell me what I *should* be doing; I don't really feel like taking advice from you right now."

"Fair."

"And who would I talk about him to, anyway? My parents? *Jules?* Who just told me she thinks Logan fucking *overdosed*?"

The air hung heavy and silent and suffocating as Sebastian continued sitting there, not saying anything.

"She thinks he *overdosed*. On *drugs*," I repeated, as if Sebastian hadn't understood me the first time.

Sebastian nodded. "I'm sorry."

"No, no." I was looking for indignation, not sympathy. "I mean—that's crazy, right?"

He stared at me with such pity in his eyes that I had to look away.

"Well . . . with everything you've told me, it sounds like it might have been a possibility?" He gulped. "I mean—his sudden change in mood, and all the trips to the doctors for painkillers, and how your parents never want to talk about his death . . ." He looked down. "I talked to Jules about it, a little."

"*Jules* told you he overdosed?"

"No, that's not what— I just brought up what I thought, and she didn't exactly tell me I was wrong—"

Jules and Sebastian and EVERYONE thought they knew how Logan had died, and I was the only one too stupid to see it? No. That couldn't be true.

"Jules doesn't know *any*thing about Logan. And neither do you. He wasn't a freaking *drug addict*," I spit out.

"Overdosing doesn't reduce someone's identity to a—"

"I don't really need your pseudo-therapy bullshit right now."

"You're right. I'm sorry."

I breathed in and out, but I couldn't get enough air. I felt the walls closing in on me. I stood up and began walking toward the elevator. I needed to get off this fucking ship and away from the endless street performers and gross fake hot dogs and people who couldn't stop *smiling*.

This time, Sebastian didn't try to stop me.

I ran down three flights of stairs to the boardwalk. And then I froze.

The boardwalk was filled with wall-to-wall people. I could barely see more than a few feet in front of me, but I finally realized what was causing the traffic jam: we were stuck behind a barricade.

As I pushed my way to the front of the crowd, I saw what was causing all the commotion—a stream of performers, clad in neon wigs and dark green skirts.

The Mermaid Parade.

My mind flashed back to the first day of the cruise when Shari had advertised this as the big event of the week. I glanced desperately from side to side, but couldn't find any way out of the barricades, toward the exit.

Trombones blared and maracas shook as dozens and dozens of crew members floated by, dressed in bikinis and sparkling face paint. And then, as a section of the crew walked past in kilts, the bagpipes began blaring.

The bagpipes were so loud I couldn't hear the sound of my own thoughts, just someone screaming, *Out out out!*

Until I realized that someone was me.

I took a few deep breaths and scanned around, trying to figure out how to exit this hellish maze. But all I could see were people crammed together, filled with sparkles and jiggling flesh and acrylic green legs.

I found myself locking eyes with the giant clown painted on the archway. The clown was all red lips and devilish eyes. I was stuck in a ghoulish fun-house mirror, a nightmare I couldn't wake up from. I needed to get out.

A new group of performers streamed in and broke into a dance, followed by a marching band, striking their drums with all their might. Cheers filled the boardwalk as the male leads twirled the females high above them.

I glanced behind me at the windows overlooking the Caribbean waves, wondering if that was my only way out.

Then—finally—the dance came to an end. *Screw it.* I made a run for it, ducking under a barrier, across the floor to the other side, not caring who was looking at me, my hair flying everywhere as tears streamed down my face.

When I flung myself under the barrier on the other side of the boardwalk, my heart was hammering in my ears. But I had made it out. The exit sign was in sight.

The ship blurred past me as I sprinted through the gangway and across the pier, where a group of men was playing an upbeat melody on steel drums.

I didn't stop running until I was on the bus to the beach, and I began running again as soon as the bus pulled into the parking lot.

I was sweating and out of breath, but I made it just in time for the excursion. I was the last one to arrive. Two surfer-looking guys in their thirties or forties smiled at me as I ran up, but I turned away, letting them know I was not in the mood for conversation.

The baby-faced instructor handed me my gear. I haphazardly threw on the wetsuit before following the woman and the surfer bros onto the boat. I sat and nodded as we sailed out to the shipwreck and the instructor babbled on about the ship's history, how to properly use the snorkeling gear, and what hand signals to use if we needed help.

But there were no hand signals to give me the help I needed now.

Finally, we arrived. I let out a small gasp as I laid eyes on the sight in front of me. The ship was entirely rusted over and covered in coral. Schools of tropical fish bobbed around it.

It really was a moment frozen in time. Logan would be in full-on Cap'n Plank mode, seeing this. The dive instructor would have to tell him to keep it down because he wouldn't be able to stop flipping out.

I slipped on my flippers and secured the scuba mask to my face. When the instructor gave the signal, I practically threw myself off the boat and into the water. My brain was too foggy to be scared. All I could focus on was getting underwater as quickly as possible, away from my racing thoughts about Sebastian and Jules.

I just needed to fulfill this final promise to Logan. I didn't hesitate before inhaling deeply and kicking my flippers behind me with all my might, shooting at full speed underwater and into the entrance of the shipwreck. Where I would find peace and clarity. And Logan.

When I got to the floor of the shipwreck, I saw a sharp, spiky piece of metal sticking straight into the air.

I shut my eyes, fighting against the memory that was threatening to resurface. But it just became clearer.

I could see Logan lying on the ground, his hand limp by his side.

A needle to his left.

The image I had tried so hard to erase.

And then I was screaming underwater.

Screaming and screaming and no one could hear me.

Why hadn't I stuck to our plans?

Why hadn't I checked on him earlier?

Why hadn't I saved him?

Why was he stuck trapped in this shipwreck forever? Always seventeen? Never anyone's husband or father? Why was death so permanent?

"I AM SO MAD AT YOU!" I screamed into the endless blue waters.

Water began filling my lungs. I shot straight up, choking so hard that I nearly puked.

But the pain felt warranted. Because it wasn't Logan that I was mad at.

It was myself. For not noticing. For not helping.

This could have been prevented.

I had come to Antigua to feel closer to Logan. But I had never felt farther away.

TWENTY-FIVE

I tore off my scuba gear and stormed out of the water. I needed to find my parents. I knew they were here, somewhere, with the twins. And sure enough, they were seated on a group of towels, a few feet away from the lifeguard stand.

"Why did you lie to me?"

My mom put a bookmark in the book she was reading.

My dad put a hand over his eyes, shielding himself from the sun, and looked up at me. "What are you proposing that we lied about?"

"About Logan. I know the truth. He didn't have a heart attack. Jules said that he *overdosed*, like he was some fucking drug addict."

I was confronting them, telling them I knew the truth. But I needed with every fiber of my being for them to tell me that I was wrong, that Jules had made this up, how dare I say something so nasty about my brother.

But then my mom's face contorted, and in that moment everything inside of me collapsed. And then I was sobbing and shaking. She reached for me, but I pulled back.

"So it's true?"

My mom just nodded. "Your brother—" She swallowed. "He was sick. Very, very sick."

"I don't think this is the best time for—" my dad started.

My mom laid a hand on his arm. "Paul," she said, "I don't think it's ever the best time for this." And then she began to cry. *I* had made her cry. Why was I such a monster? "This needs to stop being a secret. We need to stop being ashamed."

"I—I have to go." All I had wanted was for them to finally tell me the truth about Logan. But I was never prepared for this to be the truth.

"Olivia, can we talk about this?" my mom asked.

"I can't." I shook my head. "Not now."

I took off, my bare feet kicking up a wake of hot sand behind me. I ran out much harder than I usually started. I ran until my lungs felt like they were going to burst. I was probably setting a new record, but I didn't care. I just wanted to escape my body, to detach from my mind, to run so hard that I couldn't think about everything else going on around me. How stupid I had been. How much I hurt.

Because while running made my throat constrict and turned my legs to lead, nothing—*nothing*—had ever felt as bad as this.

How could I have been so fucking *stupid*?

I thought I knew Logan so well.

But I had been lying to myself, remembering a fictional person. The Logan before the accident. The all-state athlete. The musical-theater star. The caring older brother.

Not the moody, agitated boy who had become a stranger to me. Who snapped if I went into his room without asking. Who was always getting into fights with my parents. Who answered questions after long pauses. Who stole money. Who never seemed to be telling the truth.

Nothing would ever fix this, not becoming a doctor or saving lives or falling in love.

Because the brother I wanted to remember would *never* be back. He had disappeared long before Logan died.

I kept running, hoping the aching in my lungs could erase everything I felt.

But it just made the pain worse.

I finally collapsed on the sand, my heart pounding wildly.

I had been wrong about everything.

When I got back to my room, I opened the desk drawer and grabbed my journal, my vision blurring as I scanned the first page. I read the last note Logan had left me, but I could no longer hear Logan's cheerful, familiar voice. Instead it came out garbled and distant. Was he high when he wrote those words to me? I slammed the journal shut.

I put on my headphones, but every song I tried to listen to only made me feel sadder, so I threw my phone across the room and buried my head in my pillow and screamed.

The connecting door to my room opened, and my mom stuck her head in. "Do you want to talk, honey?"

"I'm not ready," I said into my pillow.

"Okay." She closed the door softly behind her.

Why hadn't I just stuck to my plans? I never should have followed Jules's stupid advice to live in the moment. Because what had that gotten me? Disappointment. Disappointment that could have been prevented if I had simply done my research and planned in advance. I had purposefully ignored all the red flags—never even bothering to ask if Sebastian had a girlfriend. Or why Charlie gave him so many weird looks. Or why he drank so much. Or why Jules kept warning me about him.

Jules was completely right. I avoided any obvious truths that didn't suit my vision.

Just like I had with Logan.

I should have known something was wrong—really wrong. I should have *done* something. Instead, I was just hurt and upset that he wasn't paying more attention to me. So I punished him, rather than asking him if he needed help.

And because of that, he was gone.

When I opened my eyes, everything came rushing back.

Sebastian had a girlfriend.

Logan had overdosed.

I breathed in and out and reached for my phone. The screen was lit up with an alert.

SCIENCE RESEARCH FAIR in 1 hour

Oh no. *The conference.*

I had been so upset that I had forgotten all about it. I had never sent Shruti the notes or PowerPoint I had promised her. She must have thought I was dead. Or wanted to kill me. Or both.

I ran to the business center and opened my email to find four new messages from Shruti.

are you sending the presentation?

the research fair is tomorrow!! where is the presentation?!

Did the boat sink?? Crash into an iceberg??? Are you okay???

Really can't believe you're doing this, Olivia

Instead of responding, I found myself typing in Sebastian's name. Something I could have so easily done earlier.

And sure enough—there he was. Standing on the roof of what must have been his high school, a crowd watching him from the parking lot.

My heart dropped.

He was performing the exact same version of "It's All Coming Back to Me Now" as he had the night before at karaoke. The same hand gestures. The same "three minutes left" joke. The same sad, longing stares.

Except these were directed at someone else.

Sebastian bent over and removed something from his bag. And then I realized it was the teddy bear, the one I had found in his room during the scavenger hunt. The one he hadn't wanted me to touch.

Sebastian squeezed the bear and held it out to the mic. "I love you Clairebear," a prerecorded voice inside the bear said. The sound of Claire's name was like a knife to my gut.

Sebastian put the mic back up to his mouth. His voice was soft and pleading, like it had been with me the morning before. "Please forgive me, Claire?"

I scrolled down to the video details.

It had been uploaded two weeks before the cruise.

I felt like I was going to puke.

This had been right in front of my face, the entire time. I was sure Jules had seen this. And obviously the crew had witnessed it firsthand. That was what Sebastian had been talking about in the hot tub during Two Truths and a Lie—singing on the roof of his school. And that's why the crew had given him weird looks for bringing it up.

Everyone knew.

Everyone, except for me.

How could I have been so stupid, when it had been so obvious to everyone else what Sebastian was doing? They all must have pitied me, this poor naive little girl who was obsessed with someone who was clearly just using her as a rebound.

My feelings were so strong they seemed like fact, and so I had let myself believe a lie. But Sebastian had never had any real feelings for me. He was in love with someone else. I didn't know him at all.

Just like I never knew Logan. I had no idea that he was suffering, even though the signs were clear as day.

My internal compass was broken. How was I ever supposed to plan for anything when my instincts were so far off base? And how the hell was I ever supposed to provide medical care to people, when I couldn't see what was right in front of my face?

I opened up my email chain with Dr. Klober and began to type.

Dr. Klober,

I just wanted to apologize for missing the conference. My brother Logan died at seventeen from a heart attack, and it was my life goal to become a cardiologist and figure out why, and make sure no other families had to go through what mine did.

But then yesterday, I learned that it wasn't a heart attack—Logan overdosed. His death wasn't some medical mystery to be solved.

So what is even the point of studying cardiology? No amount of science or medical care could have prevented this. And nothing will bring him back.

So I'm a mess. I don't know what I want anymore in life. I'm sorry for wasting your time.

—Olivia Schwartz

I hit send without even rereading what I wrote.

"Liv?"

I turned around to find Troy walking up to me. He took a seat next to me. "Thought I'd find you here."

I nodded. I wanted to say something, but I knew I'd just start crying.

"We missed you last night. Everything okay?"

I shook my head, feeling a giant lump forming in my throat. "I saw the video of Sebastian. I feel so stupid."

Troy slung one of his giant arms behind me, pulling my chair closer to his. "You're not stupid. You're *human*. You fell for a literal dreamboat of a man."

"Who was clearly just using me."

"Hey—no, no, not at all. Seb's not a bad guy; he just . . . throws himself into relationships at light speed, without thinking through the consequences, or who he hurts in his wake. I love the guy, but we've all been pretty fucking pissed at him for how he's handled things with you."

I stared down at the keyboard in front of me. "I just can't believe he didn't tell me he had a *girlfriend*."

"I know. He should have been up-front with you from the get-go. I almost said something, but—you just seemed so happy. I didn't want to ruin it for you."

I looked back up at Troy. "Is it worth it, to have a few days of happiness, just to feel like complete shit after?"

"I don't know," he said with a small shrug. "Maybe not? But maybe. I fell for a Sebastian once."

"You did?"

"Yup. Dustin Jones. Sophomore year. Loved that fucker so fucking much," he said, shaking his head.

"How long were you together?"

"Two weeks. Which some people would call instalove. But it's been over a year, and I've never doubted those feelings. Because it doesn't matter how long you know someone—you can't measure love in days. Love and feelings just exist on a different dimension. They hit maxes and peaks regardless of time. In one instant, your heart binds to someone, and there's no turning back."

I nodded, knowing exactly what he meant. I felt a little better, like I wasn't some sucker who had been bamboozled.

"Like, think about when a parent meets their kid for the first time. That's instalove! No one denies that. Babies would die without instalove. So fuck anyone who says it doesn't exist."

I laughed. "I just wish I had taken things slower. Not gotten so attached."

"See to me, instalove is not a weakness. It's a superpower. And it's partly why you're going to be such a good doctor."

I thought about the email I had just sent, effectively ending my medical career before it had even begun. "I don't think I even want to be a doctor anymore."

"What? No! You're so driven and smart and empathetic. It would really be a loss to the world not to have you in it as a doctor."

I smiled. "I guess. Thanks."

We sat there for a moment. I wondered if I should press him for the information I really wanted. And then, before I could change my mind, I asked, "What happened with Claire?" I had spent too long in the dark. I wanted it all out there.

Troy nodded, as if he had been expecting my question. "They dated for two years. They were having some problems, and he wasn't being a great boyfriend. She got drunk one night and kissed someone else."

"Oh," I croaked out. My throat had completely dried up; my eyes were stinging.

"Sebastian freaked out and broke up with her . . . and then regretted it and tried to win her back. Hence the song on the roof. And then when that didn't work—he booked this cruise and convinced Charlie, Ash, and me to come. Said he wanted some time away from chicks, to heal. Charlie had this whole romantic trip planned with his girlfriend, but he canceled it to be here for Seb."

So that was why Charlie had been so pissed about Sebastian missing out on crew time. Sebastian had made it seem like Charlie was just being needy, when really, Charlie had every right to be furious.

"Why would Seb get involved with me if he cares so much about someone else?"

Troy shrugged. "I can't speak for the boy. All I know is that love is complicated. But you—you are *amazing*. You're going to break a lot of guys' hearts. Seb's just the first."

I sighed.

"Someday he'll be a not-so-terrible memory from your past."

"I hope so," I mumbled.

Troy stood up and put a hand on my shoulder. "Almost forgot—we won!"

I stared up at him blankly.

"The competition! Our celebration dinner is at the Empire Steak Building tonight. You're coming, right? Team Pineapple Pizza won't be the same without you there."

I bit the inside of my lip. "I . . . I don't think so."

"No—you have to come. And I promise if Sebastian acts weird, we'll throw him overboard."

Even though he was joking, I hated the way my stomach contracted at the idea of Sebastian getting hurt. Because as much as I wanted to hate him, I couldn't. Not even close. And if we only had one night left . . . there was still a part of me that wanted to see him.

"I'll consider it."

"Yes!" Troy cheered, so loudly that I laughed in surprise. I was so grateful for his kindness that I worried I was going to start crying all over again.

Troy wrapped me up in a hug. He felt so safe, like hugging

a giant teddy bear. I really hoped we'd stay in touch after the cruise ended.

"And seriously, Liv—this happens to the best of us. I mean, with Seb's voice? How could you *not* fall in love with that silly boy?"

I sighed. "I know."

TWENTY-SEVEN

I put a sad-looking turkey sandwich on my plate and began looking for a table for one. Which is when I spotted a familiar silky black ponytail. Before I could stop myself, I began walking over toward Jules's table. I felt awful about everything I'd said to her. She had clearly just been trying to protect me from Sebastian.

Jules looked up when she saw me and raised an eyebrow.

"I'm so sorry," I said. "Can we talk?"

Jules didn't say anything for a moment. Finally, she shrugged. I took that as the best opening I was going to get and put my plate down next to hers.

"I'm sorry," I said again. "I was awful. And you were right—about everything. Sebastian never wanted to be with me. I was just too stupid to notice."

Jules bit her lip. "What happened?"

"He said he didn't want to give me the wrong *impression* and then decided now was the right time to mention he had a secret girlfriend back home. He said he didn't want to *hurt* me and then basically blamed me for starting everything by kissing him."

Jules let out a low whistle. "Holy shit. That is some fucking ninja gaslighting on his part. Bravo."

I groaned. "I assume you knew this whole time?"

Jules winced. "Not this *whole* time. But you seemed so happy, and I didn't know what to do . . ."

"It's not your fault."

"Yeah, but I encouraged the whole thing . . ."

"Before you knew. I just can't believe he didn't tell me sooner. I feel so stupid."

She shrugged. "He set his sights on you. It would have been metaphysically impossible to avoid that boy's advances."

I looked down at my untouched sandwich. Even if this wasn't my fault, that didn't stop it from hurting so much. "When does it feel better?"

". . . Never?" Jules said with a sad laugh. "My mom says she still thinks about the first guy she fell for when she was our age, and she's *old* now."

I laughed. "Ugh. I don't want to think about Sebastian when I'm like *thirty*."

"I don't think it's the same, though. Like, you'll remember him, but . . . you'll be a different person by then."

In a small voice I said, "I just didn't know it would hurt this much."

Jules wrapped her arms around me, and I inhaled her familiar grapefruit scent. "I know," she said. "I act all blasé, but the truth is . . . I've had my heart ripped to pieces too. That's why

I don't like being monogamous—I don't want to get burned again."

"I'm so sorry about what I said yesterday, Jules. I have no right to judge who you hook up with."

Jules began lining up the carrots on her plate. "You weren't wrong, though. It wasn't fair to Ash, or to Steph. I came clean to both of them. And it's not like kissing Steph helped at all. I still like Ash a lot."

"I'm sorry. I really hope everything works out between you two. Ash clearly likes you too."

Jules sighed. "I guess I'll see tonight. You're coming to dinner, right?"

"I'm not sure." I really, really didn't want to go. I couldn't imagine facing Sebastian again, after what had happened. But I also didn't want everyone to think I was some broken little girl, destroyed by a weeklong relationship.

Jules put a hand on my knee. "I really hope you decide to come."

When I got back to my room, I hesitated at the door. And then I turned and knocked on my parents' door.

My mom answered, but no one else was behind her.

"Where's everyone?" I asked.

"Your dad took the boys to the pool."

I debated waiting until my dad was back. But maybe it would be easier, one-on-one. I walked over to my mom's bed and sat down.

"I think I'm ready to talk."

My mom took a seat next to me. "Ask me anything. I'll tell you whatever you want to know."

"Why did you lie to me for so long?" The words came out sharper than I'd intended. But I was still so angry that I was the last to know. That Jules and even freaking Sebastian knew about what happened to Logan before I did.

My mom took a deep breath and let it out. "We had always planned on telling you. I just kept saying, Paul, wait until she's older. And then you'd get older, and I'd say that again."

"How long was he . . . ?" My voice cracked before I could finish the question.

My mom looked down. "He was drinking since he started high school."

"Was that why he got in the accident?"

My mom nodded. "Partially. He had been drinking that night. But that's not what led to—his illness. He got prescribed pain medication after the accident. And your father and I—we didn't know how strong the pills were. We didn't know to ask questions. We just trusted the doctors. A month before he died, we found out that when Logan couldn't get a doctor to refill his prescription, he started using whatever he could get his hands on."

"Like what?" I asked.

"At the end, Fentanyl."

At the word, I inhaled sharply. I had heard of the drug before. I knew it was deadly.

"We just—we had no idea about any of this. Until it was too late. The day he died . . . we weren't at a work meeting. Your father and I were in Albany, visiting a rehabilitation facility that we were planning to send Logan to."

Sadness filled my chest, heavy as concrete. I had been angry for so long that they had left me alone with him that night. I'd had no idea they were trying to save him.

"I wish you had told me this sooner."

"I'm so, so sorry that we didn't. We didn't want to tarnish your image of your brother. You looked up to him so much. And you still should—he was a wonderful person. That was the Logan we wanted you to remember." My mom pressed her lips together. "We just figured it was better if you hated us than him."

I stared into the blanket, blinking back tears. "I thought you didn't care. That you'd forgotten him."

My mom wrapped an arm around my back. "Oh, honey, there isn't a day that I don't wake up and immediately think about Logan. But then I go downstairs and make breakfast and do my best to take care of my children who are here with me now. I have never regretted anything more than I regret that day. That I couldn't save him, and worse—I left you alone with him. Only the worst mom in the world could be so naive." My mom gulped back tears. "Nobody knew about your brother's struggle. I just . . . couldn't think of any other way."

I swiped away a few tears and put my head on my mom's shoulder. "You couldn't have known."

My mom sighed again and rubbed her brow. "I always thought moms were like—born knowing what to do. But we're just people, making things up as we go along. No one prepares you for any of this," she said, her voice cracking. "Not for being parents, and definitely not for losing a child. Never in a million years did we think this would happen to us."

I looked at my mom. She looked so fragile. She was just a person, going through the hardest thing a person could ever go through.

My mom took out her phone. She scrolled for a moment and then turned up the volume. A series of soft guitar chords was followed by a melancholic, folksy voice. "This came on the radio after I got the worst phone call of my life. I played it over and over as your father drove home that night. Nothing felt real."

I had never heard the song before, but it was beautiful. "What's it called?"

"'Fire and Rain,'" my mom told me. "I've played this song every day since your brother died."

I was shocked. I'd had no idea my mom connected to music like I did. Or thought about Logan so much.

As we listened, my mom began humming along with the song. Tears fell down her face, and then I couldn't hold back any longer and I was full-on sobbing. I was so used to blinking away my tears, hiding my pain from my mom. I'd just felt so embarrassed, so alienated in my sadness.

It felt good to finally let it all out, to no longer hide how I felt.

My mom grabbed a few tissues and handed two to me. She blew her nose before speaking again. "After Logan died, I didn't want to grieve in front of you. I just wanted to protect you, because I didn't protect you when it mattered most. And so the one promise I made to myself was to not make that worse, to try to figure out how to make things easier for you. That became the only thing I focused on; I needed that tunnel vision. And I—I wanted you to still have a sibling."

"I thought you had the twins to try to replace him," I admitted softly. It had never occurred to me that she had been thinking of *me* when she got pregnant. I felt my heart squeeze painfully.

We sat there for a few minutes. And then I asked my mom the question I had been thinking about, since my first conversation with Troy. "Do you wish you waited until finishing law school before having kids?"

My mom didn't hesitate before answering. "Nope, not one bit." Her face was still red and puffy, but she was smiling. "Often, the best things in life are the ones you don't plan for. When you have kids, you'll understand . . . but if I'd done things any differently, I never would have ended up with Logan, and you, and Matt and Justin. My four favorite people in the whole entire world. And even though Logan left us way too soon . . . I wouldn't trade those seventeen years for anything."

I nodded. I wouldn't either.

"Can you put that song on again?" I asked.

My mom pressed play and then put her arms around me. She held me like that until the song was over.

When she finally let go, she turned to face me. "He would be so, so proud of the person you've grown up to be, Olivia. Just like your father and I are."

I lay in my bed thinking of everything my mom had told me. I couldn't believe how wrong I'd been about what she and my dad had been going through. I wished I had known. But at least I did now.

It was almost eight, but my body felt impossibly heavy with all the new information I was carrying. I didn't want to disappoint Troy and Jules, but I couldn't imagine somehow getting it together enough to make it out of my room. I knew I'd fall apart if I had to face Sebastian.

When I heard the knock on my door, my heart sped up, and I wondered if it was Sebastian.

But it was probably just Jules, trying to convince me to come to dinner.

I slowly walked over to the door.

When I opened it, I found—Charlie? He was standing there with a slight frown, his hands in his pockets.

"Hey," he said. "Can we talk?"

I swallowed. Was he just here to make me feel worse? To tell me I should have left Sebastian alone, that I ruined his cruise? But I couldn't exactly close the door in his face, so I let him in.

Charlie took a seat at my desk and started twisting his hands together. "I heard about everything that happened with Sebastian," he finally said. "I'm really sorry."

I looked down at my feet. "Yeah, I'm sorry for ruining your crew cruise."

"No—that wasn't your fault at all. I'm sorry for being such a jerk. That energy was supposed to be directed at Sebastian."

"I can't believe he made you cancel your plans to come here."

Charlie narrowed his eyes. "That's classic Sebastian. Can talk you into anything."

"Yup," I said, knowing all too well what he meant.

"And it just infuriates me because everything he did to you—he did this to Claire too. I got close with her when they were dating, and she came to me whenever he did something that hurt her. But then, somehow, Sebastian had me convinced that it was all *her* fault, that *he* was the one who was hurting, that I needed to take this cruise with him to help him *heal*. And I believed him! Only to come here and watch him pull the exact same bullshit with you. I felt like such a traitor. Claire's a really nice girl—she didn't deserve this. And neither do you."

Wow. Never in a million years had I expected this from Charlie. I had just thought he hated me—not that he was mad at Sebastian, for how he was treating me. "Why are you still friends with him, then?"

"Great question." Charlie let out a bitter laugh. "Somehow, I still don't think he's a bad guy, or that he does any of this intentionally. It's just always the Sebastian Show. He can't breathe without attention."

I shook my head. "It would be so much easier if he were just an asshole who had used me for sex."

Charlie's eyebrows shot up.

"We didn't have sex," I quickly clarified. "I just meant, hypothetically."

"Oh, okay—phew. And I know he wasn't using you. He really does like you. He talked my ear off this entire cruise about how incredible you are. And he's right! You're cute and smart and way, *way* too good for him. Just sometimes . . . you meet people who aren't ready for things at the same time you are."

I felt myself blushing. "Thanks, Charlie."

His words lifted such a giant weight, made me feel a little less stupid for falling for Sebastian. I had always thought that guys either liked you or used you. That there were assholes and there were "good" guys. Heroes and villains. No one warned you about the guys who told you they'd never felt such an instant connection with anyone before, but also sort of had a girlfriend back home. There weren't songs about those in-between types of guys.

When Charlie spoke again, his voice was softer. "And I was extra pissed when Seb told me about your brother."

I looked up. "He told you?"

Charlie didn't answer me. Instead, he brought up a website on his phone and then expanded the video.

"Happy birthday to you," a large group of adults and kids sang out. An adorable older woman stared with huge, excited eyes at the giant chocolate cake in front of her.

"Happy birthday to meeee," she joined in with a broad smile, revealing a mouth full of gold teeth.

"That's my grandma," Charlie told me. "She died last year."

"I'm sorry," I said.

"From an overdose."

"Wait—what?" I looked back at the white-haired lady on the screen. I could never even imagine her littering, much less doing drugs.

"Yeah." Charlie ran a hand through his hair. "Everyone pictures drug addicts as like, homeless people or rock stars, but the majority are just normal people. My grandma died at seventy, but she was otherwise perfectly healthy, and everyone else on her side of the family lived until well into their nineties."

I had thought you could visibly recognize someone who used drugs, like the people I saw singing to themselves on the subway in NYC. It had never occurred to me that the person I loved most could be using them. Or someone's grandma.

"She was living alone," Charlie said, "when she fell and broke her hip. The doctors prescribed her opioids and . . . the rest is history. The way they change your brain chemistry—*any*one can become addicted. I don't care how smart or how rich or how 'in control' you are. But then, when you—surprise, surprise—get addicted to these insanely addictive substances, you're treated like a leper, like a *criminal*. And the pharmaceutical industry just continues prescribing opioids like M&M's; they don't care whose lives they're ruining. They *especially* don't care about old people, as if they were going to die anyway. That's why you never hear about grandmas dying from overdoses. They don't fit the *narrative*. But it happens all the time."

"My brother," I told him. "Same thing."

Charlie shook his head sadly. He clicked out of the video and showed me the rest of the web page. "This is the page we made for her, on this website that helps to destigmatize the opioid crisis. It shows that the lives that were taken were people's grandmas and brothers and children and wives. Lawyers and doctors and artists. Real fucking *people* with families who loved them. Not *drug addicts* or people defined by their illnesses."

He told me all about his grandma. The famous chocolate chip cookies she made and the storybook home she lived in, in Michigan. How she had been with his grandpa for over fifty years, before his grandpa died of cancer.

"She sounds amazing."

Charlie smiled. "She was." He slid his phone back into his pocket. "Please come to dinner? It won't be the same without you."

I stood up, feeling better than I had all day. "Let's go."

When Charlie and I entered the Empire Steak Building, we found the rest of the crew waiting for us. My breath caught in my throat as I sat down at the round table, where every seat was either next to or across from Sebastian. He was dressed up in suspenders and a bow tie. It was the first time I'd ever seen him in nice clothes, a stark reminder of just how short our time together had actually been. I hated how good he looked.

When he noticed me, Sebastian's eyes widened for a brief moment. I realized it was the first time he'd seen me dressed up as well. Jules had lent me a slinky, silky black dress, and had done my hair in a top bun, with a few curled pieces hanging in front of my face. But Sebastian quickly readjusted, smiling back at me as if everything was totally fine between us.

"Welcome to the Empire Steak Building, ladies and gentle-men," our waiter said. I looked up at him, glad for somewhere else to direct my attention.

"And esteemed guests," Troy added with a smile, kindly correcting the gendered greeting.

"Yes, and esteemed guests," the waiter said without missing a beat. He passed out heavy leather-bound menus and explained how dinner that night would work. His speech went on and on as he went through the details of each and every course. Because we hadn't just won a free meal. We'd won an elaborate, over-the-top *six-course* feast.

As the endless dinner continued, I used every ounce of energy I had to keep myself upright, to keep my face level, not hurt or sad, just—blank. Devoid of all emotion. I needed to keep it together. Not just for Sebastian, but to prove to Troy and Charlie that I was okay. They kept checking in on me, shooting me sympathetic looks. I knew they just wanted me to feel better.

Meanwhile, Sebastian laughed and joked along with his crew, as if he didn't have a care in the world. Every time I heard the sound of his voice, it felt like I was being incinerated. Every bone in my body turning to ash, sitting across from him. It hurt *so much*. To be in the same room as him. For the last time.

There was a part of me that hoped if we were in the same room, the pain would be too much for him. That he'd apologize and beg for me back, tell me that his feelings were just too strong to ignore. I wish I could say I was smarter than that, after everything I'd been told. But my heart still hadn't caught up to my brain.

When our steak came out, Troy began tapping a fork against his glass. "I'd like to make a toast to Team Pineapple Pizza."

We all clinked our glasses together. Sebastian held eye contact with me until I finally looked away, grabbing a condiment jar and absentmindedly holding it over my steak, desperate for something to focus my attention on.

When I took a bite of the steak, my throat seized up. I realized I had just doused my steak in *hot* sauce. I began to cough, one of those uncomfortably loud fits that makes everyone feel obligated to ask if you're okay. I knew I would be, but I couldn't answer, couldn't get myself to stop choking. To make matters worse, tears were streaming down my face from the heat.

When I emptied my water glass, Sebastian pushed his glass toward me. I downed that one as well.

When I finally, mercifully, stopped coughing, Sebastian drew his brows together. "Are you okay?" He reached across the table and put a hand on my arm.

I inhaled sharply at the touch. *No*, I thought. *You have no idea how not okay I am.* But I just nodded. His hand was still there. Touching the same arm he had kissed up and down. The contact made me burn up from head to toe. I wanted to scream.

I had never wanted something so badly, matched only by the feeling of how badly I didn't want it. How was it possible that just two days before, our bodies had been pressed against one another? That I had felt so safe, closer to him than I'd ever felt to anyone else? And now, all of that was over. We'd be nothing to one another. The change felt dizzying, impossible to comprehend.

"Liv, I'm—" Sebastian started.

But he was cut off by a group of waiters who had come out singing loudly, carrying six flaming dishes. "The final course of the evening is our special Baked Alaska Flambé."

Troy led a round of applause for the waiters when we had finished dessert. The food actually *had* been markedly better than whatever mystery meat they served at Penne Station. (But is it *sixty dollars* better? *Probably not*, I couldn't stop myself from thinking, my dad's upcharge skepticism firmly woven into my DNA.)

Troy hung back as the crew filed out of the restaurant. He put an arm around my shoulders and walked out with me, a few steps behind everyone else. "Thanks for coming tonight. I'm sorry if that was horrible. Are you okay?"

"Yeah," I said. "I am." I was shocked to find my heart beating slower, that my words were half-true. Maybe not fully true now. But they would be, one day.

I tossed and turned in my bed that night. Things were really over with Sebastian. I knew that the sadness I felt wasn't really just about Sebastian, though. It was loss in general. The way someone could be in your life one moment and gone the next.

What hurt the most was that Sebastian had reminded me of my favorite parts of Logan. He was funny, spontaneous, talented . . .

Ending things with Sebastian felt like twisting a knife into an open wound, a painful reminder that there was a gaping hole in my heart that would never fully heal or go away.

I finally gave up on trying to fall asleep and walked over to my desk. I pulled the journal out of the drawer and ran my fingers over the embossed cover, feeling the curves of the ocean waves.

And then I began to sing, the opening verse of the "I'll Cover You" reprise flowing out of me.

When I shut my eyes, I saw Logan running after me. I was screaming and then he was tapping my shoulder, shouting, "Tag, you're it!"

I saw him wiping tomato sauce off my face and wrapping a sheet around my shoulders so I could have a cape.

Lifting me up in his arms and flying me around as the queen of Antigua.

I kept singing, a little louder, each verse bringing back more memories.

Skipping through the streets of NYC, singing *Rent* at the top of our lungs, high off another show. Waiting after for signatures from the cast. Logan smiling at me and saying without a doubt that that would be him one day.

Logan scoring the winning point in the championship game and then doing a victory lap of the court and running up to me and swinging me around, before handing me the trophy and putting me on his shoulders.

And then the connecting door was swinging open and my parents were standing there.

"You have such a beautiful voice, Olivia," my mom said, walking over to me. "Just like Logan."

The memories started flooding out.

"And do you remember that time he absolutely *refused* to wear a suit to your cousin's bar mitzvah and showed up in his superhero costume?" my dad was saying with a laugh.

My mom shook her head. "That boy always did need to be the center of attention."

I had forgotten all about that moment. I felt warm inside, knowing I had another piece of Logan to hold on to. I was so scared that with each passing day, I was losing him, little by little. But the more we talked about him, the more memories I had to hold on to, the more alive he felt.

The boys had been asleep, but now they were wandering in. They sat down on my parents' laps.

"What's going on?" Matt asked, rubbing his eye.

My parents looked at one another and then at me.

"I think it's time," my mom said. My dad nodded.

And then I had an idea. "Can I?" I asked. "And is it okay if I buy a one-time-use internet pass?"

"Sure, hon," my mom said.

I took out my phone and brought up Birdie's channel. The boys leaned into me, and I could smell their graham-cracker breath and lavender shampoo.

I was not surprised to learn that Birdie somehow had come up with a perfect way to explain death to children. His speech was truly beautiful—all about how our souls become part of the wind and the leaves and the sun. That the whole world is powered by the spirits of those who came before us. I found myself crying again as I watched the video.

For so long, I had been so careful about keeping everything I'd done with Logan—our songs and dances and secret rituals—separate from what I did with the twins. I felt guilty about loving Matt and Justin, as if by loving them, I was replacing Logan.

But I wasn't replacing him—I was expanding his memory by making him a part of the twins too.

"Matt, Justin," I said when the video ended. "I want to tell you about our older brother, Logan."

When my parents and the twins went to sleep, I walked over to the business center. I couldn't stop thinking about what Charlie had told me about his grandma. And I knew at some point I was going to have to face Shruti and explain to her what had happened.

When I opened my email, I found a new message—from Dr. Klober.

Dear Olivia,

Thank you so much for your email. I'm so sorry to hear about everything you've been going through. One thing I really wish someone had told me when I was your age was the importance of being an active participant in life outside of school and work. Because so many of the skills you need to be a great doctor—empathy, experience dealing with the unknown, a bedside manner—come from taking an active role in real life. So in a way, while I'm not happy that you had to go through all of these heartbreaking experiences, I do think they will make you a better doctor. And if you find that is still an occupation you are interested in—whether that is this summer or in a few years—there will be an open internship position waiting for you.

And even if you find that you are not interested in studying cardiology, do remember that there are so many other important medical fields that could use someone like you—including learning how to more empathetically treat and prevent substance abuse. Unfortunately, doctors are overprescribing opiates, which has led to devastating situations like what your family had to go through. I am attaching a few different websites, in case they may be of any avail to you. I think it's so important to have doctors who truly understand these issues, to best help patients and their families.

Wishing you the best of luck, with whatever path you choose.

Sincerely,

Dr. Klober

I spent the next few hours clicking through the links that Dr. Klober had sent. I came across so many tragic stories about families who had suffered losses like mine.

The final link was the same website Charlie had shown me, the one with different memorial pages. I read through page after page—different people who were brothers and sisters and sons and daughters and mothers and fathers and grandparents. I wanted to take the time to get to know each and every person's story. Because they were real people, not drug addicts or statistics.

And then I was creating a new page and entering:

Logan Schwartz, 17

Logan is so many things: an amazing older brother. A beautiful singer. A star basketball player. A loving, kind, hilarious person.

I had wanted for so long to believe that Logan had died from a mysterious illness. But there was a part of me that always knew something had been wrong, that his death wasn't some freak accident. I had kept Logan to myself, because if I never talked about him, I'd get to remember him as I wanted to: Special. Perfect. But doing so had kept me so alienated and alone.

I posted a link to the page I had created on my Facebook. I tagged my parents and a few family members. And then I added Patrick. A few minutes later, a new message appeared in my inbox from him.

Great to hear from you, Olive. Thanks for putting this together. It's beautiful.

Then I took a deep breath and pulled up a blank email. I didn't know if Shruti would ever forgive me after how royally I had screwed up. But it was worth a shot. I explained everything that had happened that week.

I finished the email and added in a link to Logan's page.

I have an older brother I never told you about, I wrote. And he's the freaking best.

TWENTY-EIGHT
DAY TEN: D DAY (DEPARTURE DAY)

I had only been asleep for a few hours when I heard a pounding on my door.

I opened the door to find Jules. "One final dip in the hot tub?" Jules asked, holding out her flask.

"Sure," I said. "But I am not drinking at eight in the morning."

"Suit yourself!" Jules said, but she was smiling.

I changed into my bathing suit and walked out of the room with Jules. When we got to the elevator, Jules turned to me. "Thanks for inviting me to Logan's page."

I nodded. "Course. Sorry it took me so long."

Jules shook her head. "No need to apologize. I'm just glad there's still a way to talk about him." Jules's eyes had gotten glassy. "I really miss him."

For a moment, I was surprised by Jules's words. But then I realized—of course she felt that way. She had seen Logan every summer at camp; the three of us were inseparable. I had been so focused on what I was going through that it had never occurred to me that Jules had been reaching out for all those years because she was grieving too.

"I just felt selfish even bringing him up," Jules continued, "because he wasn't my brother, and I know nothing I'm feeling is anything in the same universe as what you've gone through, but—"

I put a hand on Jules's arm. "That still doesn't make it any easier for you. And it's really nice to hear that you miss him." That I wasn't the only one carrying around his memories.

"He was so fucking funny," Jules said. "Remember that time he stole all the counselors' bras and strung them up the flagpole?"

I laughed. I had forgotten all about that. As Jules and I chatted, I felt the same rush as when I talked to Sebastian about Logan. But it felt even better now, because Jules had actually known what an amazing person Logan was. And she wasn't going anywhere.

Jules and I stepped out of the elevator and began walking across the pool deck to our usual spot. The Naked Cowboy was swaying with Elmo as the cruise-ship Frank Sinatra crooned out "New York, New York." I couldn't believe that in a few hours, this would no longer be our spot. Somehow, I had become very attached to this crazy floating mall.

When we got to the hot tub, we found Troy, Ash, and Charlie—but no Sebastian. I couldn't help feeling deflated. He clearly wanted to avoid an awkward goodbye.

"Our flight's in three hours, so hop in quickly, ladies," Charlie said.

I exhaled as I sunk into the hot water. "I'm going to miss it here," I admitted. "Which I never thought I'd say."

"Me too," Jules said. "I can't believe we have to go back to school in two days."

Charlie groaned. "Don't remind me."

"At least you're not headed back to New Jersey," I said.

"True," Charlie said. "That would be much worse."

We sat in silence for a few moments, listening to the gurgle of the bubbles around us. Time had flown by so quickly—and so slowly—at once.

"Okay, time's up!" Charlie announced. We all got out of the tub and began drying off and getting dressed.

Troy reached into his shorts and handed me a slip of paper. "Here's my phone number, Instagram, Facebook, Snapchat handle, and address. I expect daily updates."

I threw my arms around him. "Of course. Thank you for everything."

Then I turned and hugged Charlie. "Thanks so much for telling me about that website," I said.

"Thanks for inviting me to Logan's page. And if you ever want to chat more, about anything . . ."

"I will." I took his phone and put my number in. "It's really helpful to know someone else who's gone through this."

I had to practically pull Jules off Ash so that I could hug them both goodbye. I gave up and just wrapped my arms around both of them in a group hug. "So what's going on with you two?"

A guilty smile filled Jules's face. "I think we're actually going to . . . try long-distance."

"Jules, that's amazing!"

Jules smiled. "Yeah. But more important—can *we* hang when we get back? Since we don't live one thousand miles away?"

"For sure," I said, and I meant it. I had a lot of catching up to do. I'd had so much fun this week; I couldn't return to the same life I'd left. And I knew Jules would be the perfect shepherd. My SATs and Common Application essay were complete, and I still had over a year left—to take part in real high school life.

"So we made Seb hang back in the room," Troy said. "We didn't know if you wanted to see him."

Oh. So that's why he wasn't there.

"But also if you want to say goodbye . . . ," Troy added.

"We won't judge," Jules said. "Closure is never a bad idea."

"Hey," Sebastian said when he opened the door. "I didn't think you wanted to see me."

I shrugged. "Thought it would be weird to leave without saying goodbye."

"I'm glad you came."

We stood in the doorway for a moment before Sebastian took a hesitant step toward his bed. I followed him and sat down a few inches away.

"I fucked things up this week," Sebastian finally said. "I'm really sorry."

I bit the inside of my cheek and nodded.

"Charlie gave me a real piece of his mind earlier," he told me. "I think he hates me."

"He doesn't hate you."

Sebastian sighed. "Maybe not, but he's pretty fucking pissed, and he should be. He was there for me with all of the stuff that went down with Claire, and . . ."

I felt a sharp pain in my heart, hearing him say her name out loud. I wondered what she was like, what she looked like, if she'd hurt as much as I did. Or more. If this week would break her heart all over again.

"I know I ruined things, but . . . I hope that doesn't take away from what we had this week."

"I don't think it will," I told him.

"Really?"

I nodded. "Yeah, I mean . . . I know telling you about Logan was a lot of emotional baggage to put on one person. But you made me realize that I need to talk about him more. That I *can* talk about him more."

Sebastian's eyes crinkled as he smiled. "I'm so glad to hear that."

"And when I get back home—I'm going to try out for the musical. Have some fun. And figure out the rest when I get to college."

"Yes! That's awesome, Liv." Then Sebastian held up a finger. "One second, don't go anywhere."

As Sebastian stood up, he pulled up his shorts, which were a size too big on him. It was just a small action, but it reminded me that he was human. I had idealized him, imbued him with some kind of aura.

The mirage around him was chipping, though. He was not some perfect Adonis or some heartless asshole. He was just a boy. A charming, messy, and imperfect boy who I had told a lot of things to and thought I'd loved.

Sebastian returned with an unmarked white envelope, which he handed to me. Then he lowered his voice and brought his face closer to mine. "I just want you to know—even though things didn't work out—that you are fucking *incredible*, okay?" I felt a chill shoot straight down my spine. Sebastian leaned over, as if he was about to give me a hug. I stood up and defensively stuck out my hand, knowing I wouldn't be able to take the feeling of his arms wrapped around me for the last time.

Sebastian smiled and stepped back before shaking my hand. "It was a true honor getting to know you, Olivia Schwartz. Stay safe."

I nodded and swallowed. "You too."

I took one final look back at the ship as we disembarked, at the floors and floors of staterooms, the giant flashing Regal Islands sign, the 130-foot waterslide crowning the top of the ship. It didn't look as big as it had when we had first embarked.

"We have a few hours until our flight," my mom said. "Do you want to find somewhere so you can catch up on schoolwork?"

I shook my head. "Any chance we can spend the remaining time at the beach?"

My parents looked surprised, but they nodded. "Course. I think there's a hotel nearby that holds luggage for Regal Islands passengers."

After we dropped off our suitcases, we rented a few towels and chairs. My dad and the twins walked out to where the tide was washing in. I spread out my towel, lay down, and closed my eyes. My mom took a seat next to me.

"How are you feeling?" she asked.

"Okay," I said. "I've been thinking a lot about Logan."

She nodded. "Me too. He would have really loved this trip."

"Yeah," I said. "He would have." I began tracing lines in the sand with my toe.

My mom took a deep breath. "You don't have to answer this if you don't want to, but—did something happen with you and that boy?"

I nodded.

"I knew since the second day at lunch when I saw your starry eyes," my mom said, smiling. "I did my best to hide what was going on from your father."

"You knew the whole time?" I couldn't believe she hadn't said anything. "And you just let me run around without a curfew?"

"I was so happy to see you enjoying yourself. I've been worried about how closed off you've been since . . ." She trailed off.

"Mom, you can say his name," I reminded her.

". . . since Logan died. I didn't want you to be too scared of loss to open up to anyone new."

I swallowed. "It didn't work out."

My mom put a hand on my back. "I'm sorry. Did I ever tell you about the first boy I fell in love with?"

I shook my head. I didn't know anything about my mom's love life, except that she'd married my dad.

"Billy—but I knew he liked Cindy. Which I didn't realize until I was in too deep. I cried over him for weeks—no, months."

"How long did you and Billy date?"

"That's the craziest part—we never even dated. I think we kissed, maybe two or three times? But that was enough to break my heart completely."

I laughed, knowing exactly how she felt.

"Hurt is going to happen," my mom continued. "You can't prevent that or shut everyone out in advance to avoid that. But you are *so* much stronger and more resilient than you realize, sweetie. And the pain you feel now—that's cracks and fissures in your heart that will fill and eventually make your heart stronger. You'll love more fully, and more deeply the next time around."

"Thanks, Mom," I said.

"I'm sorry that I'm no good at this. I know I'm no Cindy."

"I'm so glad you're not Cindy." We both laughed. "I'm not super interested in discussing my sex life with my mom."

Just then, Justin ran up and grabbed my mom's hand. "I want to show you the turtles!"

"Okay, sweetie, one second." My mom turned back to me. "I'm always here if there's anything you want to talk about."

I lay down again and closed my eyes, thinking about what my mom had told me.

Sebastian had gotten me to open up. About Logan. About life. To love. And for that, I couldn't hate him. Not even close.

I reached into my bag and pulled out the envelope he had given me.

But when I opened the letter, I found it wasn't addressed to me.

Dear Logan,

I know we never technically met, but I feel like I got to know you this week. From what your sister has told me, you seem like one amazing, loving, and awesome person. I really wish I could have met you.

I know for sure that I would have liked you, because I can see so much of you in Olivia. When her eyes light up, and she chooses to take a new risk and ignore her fear—I know that's your voice she's listening to. You opened her up to so much love and life and joy. So, thank you for that.

She's one ridiculously amazing girl. You did a really great job as an older brother. That said, you made it pretty freaking hard for any future boyfriends to live up to your image. But you gave us a really great standard to shoot for.

Enjoy your time up in the clouds. I hope it's just one endless performance of Rent, and that you're the star.

Love,
Sebastian

I smiled. That boy. Always needing to be the center of attention.

When my parents came back with the twins, I walked out to the water. I waded out until I couldn't stand and then I lay on my back, the calm waters slowly rocking me.

Logan would have loved this trip so much.

And then I could hear his voice in my ear.

Stop being so sad, Olive.

Look at that supercool rainbow fish!

Look how blue the sky is!

Doesn't Dad look so geeky in his glasses?

And I started laughing like a maniac.

Because I knew for certain—I'd never been so sure of anything else—what he'd say, how his voice would sound, how he'd make me feel. And I knew then that he was still with me, that he always would be.

He'd be belting out *The Little Mermaid* songs and throwing on a bikini top to make me laugh.

He'd be parading around on the beach, to the shock and delight of unassuming midwestern tourists.

And he would have been so, so good with Matt and Justin.

He would have loved them.

They would have loved *him*.

I lay on my back and just floated and stared at the deep blue sky. I thought about how rare it was that I just *lay* anywhere; I was always thinking and worrying about what was coming next.

But now the sun was shining on my face, and the water was supporting me, and I was just—existing. And it felt pretty nice.

ACKNOWLEDGMENTS

Sabrina, you have been the absolute best agent and life mentor I could ask for. I am so grateful I met you at the WME conference, even if initially you said I couldn't sit next to you. I knew right away that you were someone I wanted in my life, and I have never been so right. Thank you for always believing in me and this story.

Kristen—what a dream come true it was to get to work with you on this book. Thank you so much to everyone at Harper-Teen. Tara, I was so lucky to have your guidance. Clare, I'm so thrilled I got to work with you. And thank you to Catherine for the most amazing cover.

To Jennifer: Thank you for teaching me how to write and for putting up with my ten thousand emo emails.

To Annie: Wow, those days of editing during peak covid. You were my lifeline during that time. Without you, *We Ship It* would not exist.

To my friends and critique partners—Val: you read this book chapter by chapter, and I can never thank you enough for your support and love of this book. Rachel—one time you told me Sebastian reminded you of a Taylor Swift song and that made me feel like this book was a Real Book. Jennie, Kalie, and Emily— thank you for being such amazing beta readers and friends. To Casey—your edit letters were maybe the nicest letters I have ever gotten. They inspired me to finish this book.

To Ali, for that time you asked me how writing was going. It hadn't been going, but because of that question, I started going again.

I wrote this book for every family who has had to lose a loved one too soon to this terrible disease. Whether nineteen or ninety, it is still an untimely death. This is a disease that needs to be spoken about, not silenced.

This book is also a tribute to my brother, Jon. So often, we only celebrate those who have passed. I want to celebrate Jon for putting in nearly two decades of hard work to stay healthy and for always being such an amazing big brother to me.

To my parents—thank you for raising me to be a reader and a writer, for making me believe from day one that I could write a book. And for dragging me on that cruise that one time.

To Eric, may you ALWAYS get that second soda. To Daniel, for reminding me to take risks.

Sneezy—you sat on my back and purred and comforted me during the hardest days of writing. I promise no one in this book is in any way, shape, or form based on any real-life people, but Mr. Snuggles Factory is 100 percent based on you.

Lila—you hadn't yet entered this world when I wrote this book, but to me, you were always here. You are my everything, and I cannot wait for you to grow up and read a [very heavily censored] version of this book one day.

And finally—Craig—you are what people in the publishing industry would probably deem the exact opposite of the target market for this book and YET. You read every half-finished chapter as I wrote it, supporting me through years of tears and trying and flailing. Thank you for everything.